PLAGUED

Marie Keates

On his return to Southampton, a wounded Great War soldier is plagued by memories as he faces a changed world, dangerous secrets and a mysterious illness that threatens everything he has been fighting for.

In the summer of 1918, a sniper's bullet ends Thomas's war and brings him home to Mary, but it is not quite the reprieve either of them imagined. Mary's happy, joking husband has become a sullen, uncommunicative stranger and she is afraid the man she remembers is gone forever. The world Thomas dreamed of and fought for has moved on without him and, as he struggles with the horrific memories that plague his dreams, he focuses his anger on their annoying widowed neighbour.

Thomas wasn't the only thing to come back to Southampton on the hospital ship. An invisible enemy stalks the wards of Netley Hospital, a strange flu that soon escapes into the town.

Will Thomas and Mary ever come to terms with the changes the war has brought? Moreover, will the secrets he unearths tear them apart, or will the mysterious plague snatch away their future before they can be revealed?

For Freda Haley

1 - Thursday 27 June 1918

If Mary could see him now, stirring his underwear in a bubbling dixie of petrol-tainted water, she'd laugh her head off. It was a far cry from any kind of laundry she knew, with no soap or mangle and a metal tin precariously perched over four stubby candles in the dark instead of the copper boiler she used at home. That he was attempting the task at all would have amused her, but it wasn't something he could add to the letter he was trying to write. For a start, he wouldn't want to mention the bayonet he was using to stir the pot, or the lice he was trying to kill. She didn't need to be worrying about that kind of thing. The trouble was it was difficult to find anything to write about that wouldn't make her worry. One way or another, even the most innocuous things tended to end up running to horror, and every letter he wrote could so easily be his last.

This letter had started off well enough, with the glorious day, all bright sun and patches of blue sky, and the green shoots poking their heads up here and there in No Man's Land. He'd written about the ragged clumps of poppies, cornflowers and white daisies bravely sprouting along the chalky rubble of the parapets, adding splashes of colour to the endless sea of dusty brown and khaki, and he'd been quite poetic about the butterfly he'd seen flitting from one to another. She'd probably laugh about him being called Joe all the time, because of the chalky dust that made them all look the same. It came up in choking clouds whenever they moved and fell again in a gritty layer that coated everything. He and Joe were both short, dark-haired and lean, but Joe fancied himself a handsome devil and acted all offended whenever he was mistakenly called Corporal Brodrick, or Thomas. The letter was all going well until he got to the magpie. He'd heard the rasping call and seen it swoop down somewhere amongst all those green shoots after something shiny, but he daren't mention the dead man the trinket had once belonged to, or the shot that rang out. She didn't need to be thinking about a bored German sniper getting his eye in, even if the magpie had flown off unharmed, a flash of black and white against the periwinkle blue. Seeing it escape had pleased him, but, if Mary knew about it, she'd only worry about who the sniper was going to aim at next. He never wrote about that kind of stuff. She didn't need to know how the snipers picked off anything that moved, or how they'd all learned to keep their heads down or risk losing them. It was easier for short arses like him and Joe, but poor old Lofty said he was developing a dowager's hump from all the crouching. She'd have laughed at that, too, but he couldn't write it.

'Anyone want to have a whip round to get Corporal Brodrick a washboard and an apron?'

Joe interrupted his thoughts. His grin was a flash of white teeth in the gloom as he drained the last drop of tea from his tin mug.

'No, but I've got some smalls he could wash while he's at it.' Wally slouched against the earthen wall of the dugout, a Woodbine glued to his lip and his notebook open on his knee. He imagined he was a poet, but the likes of Graves, Owen and Sassoon had little to worry about on that score.

'If they're yours they'll hardly be smalls and, if I hang them out, Jerry's likely to think it's a white flag and we're surrendering.' Thomas laughed along with them. The mickey taking was just a bit of banter to break the monotony.

'Oh, I thought it was soup,' Lofty chuckled and ran the flame of a candle along the seams of his jacket. Like the boiling underwear, this was meant to kill the lice and their eggs, although it was like pissing in the wind. 'It smells just like the stuff we had yesterday.'

'Louse soup, the speciality of the house.' Joe smiled and looked down affectionately at the rat nestled on his lap. Thomas had got a few letters out of Joe's attempts to tame the creature, despite Wally's objections. Boredom created strange bedfellows and Ruby the rat, with her beady red eyes, was the closest thing to a pet any of them had. Joe said she was their mascot.

Wally disagreed. 'I swear that filthy bloody animal is just waiting for you to cop it so it can eat you.'

'There's more meat on your bones,' Joe said, 'so she's probably got her eye on you.'

Thomas blew out the candles, lit a cigarette and thought about what else to write. He tried to send a letter every few days, but they'd been in this forward trench for four days now and he hadn't sent one. Nothing much was happening other than a little gentle strafing and the distant rumble of artillery. He couldn't tell her that and he was running out of material. Last time they were here he'd told her about the dugout, a cave-like place the size of a box room, with a tarpaulin across the doorway to keep the dim light of the Tilley lamp inside. He'd waxed lyrical about the earthy, musty smell of damp that permeated everything but he hadn't mentioned the stink of unwashed, flatulent men, Wally being the prime example of the latter. For now, this was home and his real home, the terraced house by the river, was like a beautiful, barely remembered dream. He squeezed his eyes shut and thought of Mary's fine-boned face, her chestnut curls and her eyes the blue of a summer sky. Six years they'd been married, and he still couldn't quite believe his luck. Of course, he'd only been at home for two of them, which might explain why she hadn't thrown him out on the street yet.

'Just four more days of this, if we're lucky.' Wally dragged him back to the present. 'Then we can go back to the support line.'

They'd settled into a kind of torpid routine. There'd been no action for weeks and the only hospital cases they'd had were all the chaps who'd caught the flu. Though all they'd needed was a few days rest and they were as right as rain.

'It's the billets after that I'm looking forward to. There's a little mademoiselle waiting for me in that village,' Joe said with something between a leer and a wink.

'This quiet can't last.' Wally licked the end of his pencil, squinted and wrote a few words. 'They're building up the ammo. There's a big storm brewing, mark my words.'

'Perhaps it'll turn around and this next push will be the last?' Even as he said it, Thomas knew it was rubbish.

'How many times have we said that?' Joe snorted.

He was right. When the Yanks and the tanks came, they said it would all be over soon, but they'd had tanks since the summer of '16 and Yanks since last spring, yet here they were still, barely fifty miles from where they'd been at the start. When it did kick off again there was no guarantee any of them would make it through to see the end. All they could hope was that death would be quick and relatively painless, something like a bullet through the head would do nicely.

'It could be worse,' Joe said. 'It could be raining like it was when we were here by the Somme in '16.'

'I'm glad I missed that,' Lofty said. 'The snow was bad enough.'

'I'm not sure what I hate the most, the mud or this chalky bloody dust.' Thomas stubbed out his cigarette and began to fish his underwear from the pot with the bayonet.

Joe laughed at his attempts to wring out the clothes without burning his hands. The underwear was still hot and stank of petrol from the cans all their water came in. They drank the stuff, cleaned their teeth in it, cooked in it and even shaved with it. He must have consumed so much petrol by now he ought to have a starting handle fitted to his chest to make him run. Still, between the heat, the water and the petrol, his underwear should be louse free for a little while. As he moved about, the Tilley lamp flickered and cast towering shadows on the drab walls. Sometimes it felt as if all the men they'd lost lingered in the gloom watching them. Like thoughts of home, they were never far from his mind.

He took the dripping washing out into the darkness of the trench. If Mary could see him now, she'd probably wonder why he was hanging his clothes out in the dark when it had been such a perfect drying day. There was so much about this place she would never understand, especially how they'd all become more or less nocturnal, as it wasn't safe to move about much in the daylight. The silvery blue glow of the moon gave him just enough light to fumble his way towards the makeshift washing line they'd rigged up between two dugouts. He reached up into the shadows and felt around for the line. He got the undershirt over and managed to skewer it in a couple of places with the dolly pegs Mary had sent him. As he lifted his left arm to hang his underpants, he caught sight of the hands of his watch glowing in the darkness, five and twenty to midnight. A second later, a blow from behind, like a cricket bat to the back, sent him to his knees gasping. What had happened? Why couldn't he get his breath? A sickening panic knotted his stomach. He struggled to inhale. Blood pounded in his ears. Then the edges of the world turned black.

2 – Monday 1 July 1918

Mary rolled up her sleeves, began to sort the laundry and smiled at Freda singing her version of a nursery rhyme to her beloved rag doll, Tilly.

'Mary, Mary little fairy, cows in the garden go, with silver bells and cockerel smells and pretty maids, ho, ho, ho . . .'

She sat on the flagstone floor cradling the doll in her arms like a baby. A sunbeam slanted through the open door and turned her short blonde hair into a halo around her head. Mary tried to memorise the words of the song so she could write them in her next letter to Thomas. He liked to hear about the children; he'd missed so much of their lives, especially Freda's. He was already in France when she was born, and he'd only had one lot of leave since.

By the time Alice appeared at the door, the battered old copper boiler had started to bubble. At the sight of her, Freda danced out into the garden in search of Alice's son Harold. The two of them would keep each other amused while she and Alice got on with washing the clothes.

'Is Hetty not back yet?' Alice tutted. 'I don't know why she takes so long or why either of you bother, come to that. Eric and George could walk to school with Gordon. He's quite sensible enough to make sure they use the railway bridge rather than crossing the track.'

She plonked her washing basket on the kitchen table. Her clothes were already neatly sorted into separate piles. Everything about Alice was neat and tidy, right down to her auburn hair, wrapped in a green-spotted scarf made from the same fabric as her apron.

'Then Hetty would have to do her share of the work,' Mary sniggered, as she began to put the whites into the copper.

'Remind me again why we asked her to join our little laundry club?'

Alice began to pile the coloured clothes into the tin bath. She was always smiling. Thomas's brother Harry said it was her dimples, her green eyes and her red hair that had attracted him to her, in that exact order.

'Many hands make light work. Besides, it'd be rude for us not to include her, especially when we walk through her back garden to get to each other's sculleries.'

Irritating as Hetty could be, Mary felt sorry for her. Being a Titanic widow was a hard life. Thomas had had a notion to give up his baker's round and join the Titanic as a steward. He'd always had a hankering to travel, and the White Star money was good – at least the tips were. If the coal strike hadn't put so many men out of work, he might have got the job and she might have been a Titanic widow too. Barely a street in the town was untouched by the disaster. There were three other widows in this road alone. Of course, they didn't harp on about it as much as Hetty.

Even with the back door open, laundry was a moist, hot job, especially on this sultry summer morning. The vapour settled on everything; it fogged the glass doors of the dresser and little rivulets of soap-scented condensation ran down the walls. By the time Hetty finally deigned to make an appearance, Mary had transferred hot soapy water into the tin bath and begun to pound all the coloured clothes with the wooden dolly. Alice was busy filling buckets with cold rinsing water. Hetty's job was to run the clothes through the mangle. It didn't much matter that she'd taken so long to get back, but the way she faffed about as she pinned her long dark plait up onto her head and fussed tying her apron over her broad hips annoyed Mary. She couldn't just get on with the task at hand, either; she had to pass comment on everything.

'Look at the size of these.' Hetty held up a pair of Zillah's old-fashioned bloomers. 'I don't know why we do her stuff. It's not as if any of us is behind with the rent, or beholden to her. You're not behind with the rent are you, Mary?'

'Of course not. She's your landlady, not mine, and the poor old thing has no one else to help her. Besides, there's never much of it.'

'What about that son of hers, the bank manager?' Hetty turned the mangle handle furiously.

'Well, he's hardly going to do her laundry, is he?' Alice

straightened up and rubbed the small of her back. 'For a start, imagine if he saw those bloomers. He'd probably have heart failure.'

'He's got enough money to pay someone, though,' Hetty said. 'In fact, by rights, he should pay us. He's too much of a tight arse.'

'Have you heard anything from Thomas?' Alice changed the subject before Hetty really got on her high horse. She had a bee in her bonnet about Zillah's son for some reason, and once she got going there was no stopping her.

'His last letter was all about their billets in a village somewhere. I'm not sure if he's still there now. It sounds like a very strange place, even without the war. He says the French women paint their faces but, when they smile, most have terrible black teeth. Apparently, they drink coffee instead of tea, too, and eat cakes for breakfast. Can you imagine?'

As always, Mary and Alice did the bulk of the work, but every bit of help made it go faster, so they couldn't complain. Unlike Hetty, who seemed to thrive on grumbles.

'So much for rationing putting paid to shortages and queues, that was just a load of bunkum,' Hetty muttered as she turned the mangle handle. 'There's no cheese to be had for love nor money. Hours and hours I queued on Friday, and me with my feet, too. You know how I suffer. All that time standing out in the open in pain and terrified of the Zeppelins or the Gothas coming. I could have been killed.'

'Zeppelins and Gothas?' Mary couldn't suppress her laughter. 'There have never been any air raids here.'

'I don't think they can get this far, lovely.' Alice poured another bucket of water into the tin bath. 'Besides, if they could you'd probably be safer outside in the open.'

'They've bombed London and Kent and goodness knows where else.' Hetty folded her arms across her chest and stuck out her pointy chin haughtily. 'They even tried to get Portsmouth Docks. Who's to say they won't bomb us? Anyhow, whether they can or they can't, I was afraid, and my feet were hurting. Then, after all that, there was no cheese. When they sent all the farmers off to war, they never gave a thought to us. Don't even get me started on the stuff they call bread these days. We'll all be starved before this stupid war is over, if the Zeppelins don't get us first. Then there's the U-boats to worry about.'

'U-boats? Why are *you* worried about U-boats?' Alice raised an eyebrow.

'Well, they keep sinking ships, obviously.'

'But you're not going on a ship, Hetty.'

Mary swore she liked to complain about things so much she looked around for extra things to worry over.

'No, but the food we eat comes here on ships, doesn't it? Stuff like sugar and tea. If they keep sinking ships, we'll have even less to eat.' She pushed back a damp strand of hair impatiently. 'Don't forget the Lusitania. She was full of women and children, but did they care? No, they sank her. They even sink the hospital ships. Remember Asturias last spring? Young Bobby across the road died when she went down. Only last week a U-boat torpedoed another one. I forget its name, but nearly all the wounded soldiers and the nurses were killed, not to mention the crew. Imagine surviving getting wounded and thinking you were going to be fine because you were being sent home, only to have that happen. Poor buggers. It doesn't bear thinking about.'

'My Harry is in the navy and so is his brother, Hariph.' Alice straightened up and put her hands on her hips. 'I'd rather not think about ships being torpedoed thank you very much.'

'Have you heard anything from him?' Mary tried to change the subject.

'Nothing lately, his letters have likely got caught up in the post. I'll probably get lots all at once. You know how it is. You wait and wait for a letter, half afraid it's going to be from the War Office. Then when one does come, it's only really proof they were alive at the time they wrote it.'

For once, Alice had no smile. Hetty and her talk about U-boats had rattled her. She didn't mean anything by it, she just didn't think before she opened her mouth.

'It's awful not knowing what's happening to them, isn't it? The other night, I dreamed I got a letter from the War Office . . .'

Mary shuddered at the memory. It had been in her head ever since. Unable to drift off again, she'd crept out of bed, leaving Freda peacefully asleep in her cot, her thumb in her mouth, the other hand rhythmically stroking the blanket. The moon had cast an eerie light through the bedroom window and turned her into a ghost child, with blue-white skin and silver hair. It made the dream seem more of an omen.

'You worry too much. I'm sure Thomas will be fine, and so will my Harry.'

'If I were you, I'd be more concerned about those French women with their red lips and black teeth,' Hetty said.

'Thomas would never . . .' Mary gasped.

'It was only a joke,' Hetty replied, as if it should have been obvious.

There was a knock at the door and Mary went to answer it, still fuming at Hetty's comment. Her heart froze when she saw the post boy on the step. She shouldn't have said anything about that dream because now she'd made it come true. Even before the thin envelope was in her hands, she could see the official stamp and the words 'On His Majesty's Service.' Reluctantly, she took it from the poor boy. He couldn't even look her in the eye and didn't hang around to see what happened next. In a daze, Mary staggered back to the scullery. She fumbled with the envelope. Her hands shook so much she had trouble opening the seal. After a couple of deep breaths, she looked at the flimsy sheet of paper.

'I regret to inform you that a report has been received from the War Office that Corporal Thomas Brodrick . . .'

Mary's hands flew to her mouth. The letter fluttered to the floor and Alice and Hetty stopped work and stared at her.

3 - Monday 1 July 1918

A parade of strange, disjointed snippets swirled sluggishly across Thomas's consciousness. It was like dying in slow motion. The hands of his watch glowing in the darkness, a thwack as someone hit him on the back with a cricket bat, dusty duckboards, a tight band around his chest, Lofty's voice, 'still alive', and Joe's, 'stretcher bearers'. He was colder than he'd ever been in his life and every shallow, metallic breath bubbled, as if he were drowning in his own blood. Was he dead, or had he tumbled down a rabbit hole to another world, like Alice in Wonderland? He opened his eyes and saw the folds of a dimly lit tent. It certainly didn't look like heaven. It didn't sound like heaven, either. There were cries, coughs and groans all around. It could have been the battlefield, except there were no explosions and he could feel the rough wool of a blanket under his fingers and smell a hint of paraffin and carbolic soap rather than wet earth, decay and cordite. He tried to lift his arm to look at his watch. It was as if he was being ripped apart inside.

He'd been looking at his watch when the cricket bat hit him. He was sure of that much. Though the Western Front was hardly awash with men in white trousers setting up stumps and bails and carrying cricket bats around. At least not any part of it he'd seen. It made no sense, or did it? He remembered the magpie and the sniper. Had he been hit by a sniper's bullet? Somehow, he'd expected being shot to feel different; a sharp, pointed pain, maybe a burning. This was more like being winded, as if all the air had been knocked out of him. He'd felt all the warmth and life ebbing away. When the black edges of the world closed in, he knew he was dying. There'd been no fear, except what would become of Mary, Eric and Freda? He closed his eyes again and let it all go.

*

The River Windrush slid gently through the long grass; deep green, almost black, with ripples of reflected blue sky. Beside him, Hariph laughed and dropped a little wooden boat with a paper sail into the water.

'Look, Tom, mine's faster, it's catching yours.' He turned to the field behind them. 'See, Harry, I told you mine would be faster . . . Harry? Where has he gone?'

They'd told him he was too little to sail a boat, but if he was very quiet, he could stand and watch. Now he'd run off somewhere.

'Mother's going to be furious,' Thomas said, feeling his panic rise. 'She told us to look after him.'

'He can't have gone far,' Hariph replied. 'We only turned our backs for a minute.'

Up and down the field they ran, becoming more frantic with

every second. They called out, 'Harry, where are you?' and, 'If you come out you can sail a boat.'

They searched every patch of long grass, every corner of the field. They were desperate to find him – all dimpled knees, dark tousled hair and cheeky grin – hiding somewhere. Eventually, they set off towards home, heads down, feet dragging, defeated. Cold fingers of fear clutched at Thomas's innards. What if he'd fallen in the river?

When they skulked into the house, Mother was at the spinning wheel. Her foot rhythmically moved the treadle, and her hands stretched the fluffy wool out into yarn. Harry was at her feet. He was watching the wheel spin round and round as he bit into an apple, as bold as brass. He gave them a crafty smile. The rush of relief at the sight of him was soon driven away by Mother's angry voice.

'I told you two to look after him. You're lucky I'm doing this, or I'd give you both a good hiding.'

*

When Thomas opened his eyes again, a young man was leaning across him. He wore a white gown of some kind, spattered with blood like a butcher's apron. Was any of it *his* blood? The poor man looked half dead. Beneath receding black hair, his face had a greyish pallor.

'He looks a better colour at least.'

Was he talking about him? If he looked a worse colour than the man stood over him, he was in big trouble.

A raven-haired angel with a halo of white hovered above him. 'He'll do now, I hope.'

It was an English woman's voice. He could hardly believe it after all this time of shouting, swearing men and chirruping French villagers with their 'parlez-vous.' Perhaps this was heaven.

'He will or he won't, but I've done my best. With morphia his chances are as good as any. He can go down on the next train.'

The angel took his pulse and temperature. When she looked at her watch, he half expected her to mention her ears and whiskers and say she was late. He smiled at the scent of freshly laundered cotton and soap.

'We'll get you cleaned up and your dressing changed. Then you'll be ready to go,' she said cheerfully.

Were they sending him back to the front already? He didn't feel too bad apart from his foggy head and the elephant sitting on his chest. Perhaps it was one of the Flanders elephants that he, Dougie, Wally and Joe had joked about in Passchendaele, the ones they should have used instead of horses. The thought made him smile again.

'I'll just give you another little shot of morphia to make you more comfortable. You'll be back in England before you know it.'

England? Had he got himself a Blighty wound? Hadn't most of them secretly hoped for something, not too bad but bad enough to be sent home? Well, everyone except poor Percy. He'd been more upset at going home than he had over having his leg smashed to pieces. He felt the prick of the needle and closed his eyes again.

*

Powdery snow fell as Lofty dropped down into the trench with Percy half on his back. They'd been out in No Man's Land retrieving the dead for burial, while he and Joe searched each body they brought back for the little oilcloth packages of pay books, photographs, and the like. Some of them had been out there since the first day of the battle more than four months ago. They were not a pretty sight. All they could do for them now was bring them in, bury them, and send word to their families. Percy had been hit by shrapnel in the leg, face and arm. The arm wound looked clean and, although a flap of skin hung from his face, the shell fragment had merely dented his helmet and grazed him, doing no mortal harm. The leg was another matter. It was a mess. He'd been hit halfway between his knee and hip. Part of his broken thighbone protruded from the bloody wound. Somehow, Lofty had escaped with nothing more than cuts and grazes.

'Will I get three wound stripes or just one?' Percy shivered. He was deathly pale, perhaps from shock.

'Just the one I think,' Joe said.

'How long before I'm back in action, do you think?'

'It'll be Blighty for you, mate,' Joe told him. 'I'd say your war is probably over.'

Percy's tears reminded Thomas that he was just twenty years old, with the slight chubbiness and smooth skin of youth and barely enough hair on his face to shave. All he'd ever wanted was to join the army, and now he was distraught at the thought of being sent home.

*

A scraping, sliding noise woke him. It took a moment to work out that he was on a train, an old wooden '40 hommes 8 chevaux' truck, like the one that had taken them to Le Cateau back in 1914. The noise must have been the door sliding shut. It was dark, apart from a few slanted shafts of sun that had found their way through gaps in the wooden carriage walls. Beneath the smell of wood, coal and straw, the stench of sweaty bodies, blood and decay was unpleasantly pungent, and all around there were groans and whimpers. It looked like his war was going to end just as it had begun, rumbling across France in a goods wagon. He shut his eyes.

Back in 1914, they'd been singing 'Pack up your troubles in your old kit bag and smile, smile, smile . . .' The carriage had been jam-packed with hordes of excited men in pristine uniforms proudly heading off to fight for king and country. Then the smell had been mostly sweat, tobacco and Joe Wilson's cologne. He'd been a tram driver in civilian life. By the smell of him, he thought he was off to romance all the French mademoiselles.

'I wish they'd get a move on. At this rate, it'll be over before we get there.'

That was Ronnie, the great hairy bear. His brass buttons strained against his belly, and he grinned like a Cheshire cat.

'There's plenty of Hun for everyone,' Joe snorted.

Then the train began to move, and they were jostled together.

'What's the use of worrying? It never was worthwhile . . .'

Laughing, they joined in with the song. The laughter and singing made it feel as if they were off on holiday.

*

When he opened his eyes again, it was still dark, but he could see he was on a station platform. A row of blanket-covered wrecks stretched off in each direction. With a sense of abandonment, he watched the long goods train slowly move away. Then he noticed the station sign: Amiens. They'd barely moved from the trench where he'd been shot. Home receded into the distance, a cruel trick, a promise snatched away. Would he ever see it again? Nurses' skirts and aprons swished past as they checked on the men. Did the poor things ever get the chance to sleep or rest? Occasionally, stretcher-bearers were summoned to take someone away. The selection appeared random. Were they dead, dying or being taken to some other place? At any moment, he expected to die or to be carted off, too. He was tired of the struggle to breathe, tired of this war. Desolate, he closed his eyes and waited to die.

*

'Buck up. It can't go on forever.'

Ronnie sat cross-legged on the fire step. Little rivulets of water poured off his tin helmet and ran down his big round face.

'The war or the rain?'

It was teeming down. He couldn't see more than a few feet in any direction, but there was nothing to see anyway, save for mud, sandbags and the hunched khaki shapes of soldiers huddled under their cape-like groundsheets. The rubber coating kept the worst of the wet out, but it seeped its way from the ground upwards anyway. They were cold and their teeth chattered, but there was nowhere to shelter. Even the dugouts sloshed with water or had crumbled under the weight of it.

'I meant the waiting, but I suppose it all has to stop in the end.'

'It's torture.' Joe reached into his pocket for his cigarettes, but it was too wet to light one.

'Imagine if it was all over but they forgot about us and left us here in this bloody trench in the mud,' Ronnie said.

*

Thomas opened his eyes and saw a blur of green fields through a train window. He'd forgotten fields could be green. There was a babble of voices, English of every class, gabbling French and, he swore, German, but that couldn't be right, could it? This must be a real hospital train, with windows and red crosses on the sides. He heard the hiss of steam and the engine noise, a soothing de-dah-de-dah of wheels on rails, and saw white walls and tiers of clean bunks. A nurse moved up and down the carriage in the shadowy glow of overhead lights and checked on her charges. He had a label pinned to his pyjama jacket, as if he were a parcel being posted. She glanced at it and gave him another injection of morphia.

'We're nearly at Havre. This should make you more comfortable when they move you onto the boat.'

The needle pricked, the cold liquid crept up his arm and he spiralled down the rabbit hole again . . .

4 - Wednesday 3 July 1918

Alice was on her hands and knees scrubbing the red tiles of her front step. Her face broke into a bright smile at the sight of Freda. She wiped her wet hands on her apron, picked up her brush and bucket and ushered Freda and Mary inside and into the kitchen.

'You're early,' Alice said, putting the kettle on the range and waving Freda out into the back garden.

'I couldn't stop brooding over Thomas, or settle to any work.' Mary sank onto a chair at the kitchen table and put her head in her hands. She'd hardly slept and knitting socks for soldiers with Alice, Vera and Effie seemed like torture when her mind so was full of Thomas. Alice had insisted she came, though. She said it would do her good.

'You've had no more news then?'

'Nothing. I hardly know what to do with myself for worrying. It's all very well sending me a letter saying he's been wounded in the lung, but what exactly does that mean? What if it's gas? They say lots have died from the gas. What if he dies, Alice . . . ?'

Her eyes filled with tears. She brushed them away impatiently.

'Oh, my lovely, I know how worried you must be but look on the bright side. If they thought he was going to die they wouldn't have sent you a letter until they knew for sure.'

'I suppose not.'

She'd like to believe it, but the army had hardly been paragons of compassion or thoughtfulness. They hadn't even given Thomas any leave when Freda was born.

'I'm sure they wouldn't. Back in 1916, there was an officer, a poet I believe, and they sent his family a letter to say he was dead when he wasn't. Imagine that! It was announced in *The Times*. They're a bit more careful now because of that, and a good job too.'

'Do you really think he'll be all right? I'd have thought he'd have written to me by now if he was.'

'I'm sure he will soon.'

'I should probably write to Esther, but . . .'

'It's better to wait until you know something more and then send her a telegram. Best not to worry her until you have good news to tell, and I'm certain it will be good news. It's hard for her too, with all her sons so far away. She told me once she'd never expected any of her children to leave Witney. She thought the boys would all follow in the family footsteps and become blanket weavers. Of course, they all had other ideas. Still, I suppose life never does turn out quite like we plan, does it? Which of us ever imagined we'd end up where we are today? I'm sure you never expected to leave Burghfield, any more than I expected to leave Witney, or Hariph to end up in Plymouth with an actress, two children and no wedding ring. We certainly didn't expect to watch all our men going off to war. All any of us can do really is hope the fates are kind to us and deal with whatever they bring. Now, go and sit yourself down in the parlour while I make the tea. Effie and Vera will be here in a minute, and I know you don't want them to get wind of anything.'

*

Alice's house was an exact copy of Mary's, but tidier. The back parlour was dominated by a large dining table and smelled of beeswax and lavender polish. She should really have polished her parlour before she came out, but she couldn't seem to get herself going. Instead, she'd sat and stared at Thomas's wingback chair, wishing he was sitting in it and worrying if he ever would again. Then she'd closed her eyes and tried to remember him. She could see his dark hair, which was always perfectly combed, oiled and parted to the side, and his clothes; the starched white collar and tie with his waistcoat buttoned and his jacket open. What frightened her was how hard she had to concentrate to see his face. It came to her in pieces; his kind eyes, his strong nose, the wide mischievous smile that could fill the room, but it was so long since she'd seen it that she couldn't quite imagine it as a whole. She had a photograph of him in his uniform taken just before he left for France, and there was a studio photograph of the brothers arranged in order of age, Thomas, Hariph then Harry, hanging on the wall above Alice's fireplace. It had been taken years ago, in Witney. They were all just like their father. Now, she paused in front of the fireplace and stared at Thomas's face. An image in black and white wasn't the same as the real thing, though. Would she ever see it again for real? She sat on one of the mismatched dining chairs near the window and watched Freda chase Harold around the tiny back garden. He was the image of Harry, dark-haired and brown as a berry. Thomas must have looked like that as a boy.

When Alice came in with the tray of refreshments, she had Vera and Effie with her. While everyone settled themselves and their knitting around the table, Alice poured the tea and handed out slices of cake. 'It's made with carrots and beetroot to replace the sugar,' she said apologetically. 'I know it sounds horrible but it's actually not bad.'

'Who'd have thought we could manage so well without sugar?' Vera said with a suspicious look at the plate of odd-looking pinkish-brown cake.

Vera was the one who organised all the wool and sent the socks they made off to France. She was a gruff, opinionated woman and Mary was half scared of her. She was a good decade older than the rest of them, with a careworn face and grey hair that she wore in a long plait wrapped around her crown. Mary was fascinated by the way the plait was darker at the ends and how Vera kept it pinned so precisely, but she never quite had the nerve to ask her about it.

'Hetty offered to get me a bag of sugar the other day,' Effie said. The youngest of the group, at twenty-six, she was snub nosed, with laughing eyes and dark blonde hair that never stayed up no matter what she did with it. 'She wouldn't say where from, but it must be the black market. She's going to get herself into a whole bloody world of trouble like that.'

'Where has she got the money for black market stuff? She can't make much from a few cleaning jobs and the Mansion House fund.' Alice took a bite of cake.

'I don't know, but when I was cleaning my step earlier, I saw her meeting a chap on the corner of Union Road.' Vera raised her eyebrows suggestively. 'A real shifty looking character he was, dark, like a gypsy, and very scruffy, with a flat cap pulled down over his face, like he was trying to hide it, and a limp when they walked off together. I thought she might have been selling something other than black market goods, if you know what I mean. Very secretive they looked. Mind you, I'm not sure she'd make much money if *that* was what she was selling.'

There was no love lost between Vera and Hetty, but there was no need for that kind of talk at all. Mary looked across at Alice and could tell from her face she felt the same. Neither of them said anything. Passing comment would only draw more attention to the suggestion that Hetty would sell her body.

'That sounds like one of the men from the Milbank Street wharves,' Effie said. 'Half of them are gypsies, or from the Ferry Village. There are plenty of whores down there, so I hear, and a lot of smuggling goes on, too; stuff out of the docks and such. They say the houses are damp all the time because the river floods them, and TB is rife.'

'I've always said little George looks consumptive.' Alice looked worried. 'You don't think he is, do you?'

'No, he's just small for his age.' Mary nibbled her cake. It was surprisingly good. 'Hetty says her George wasn't a large man, even though he shovelled coal for a living, and little George takes after him.'

'Well, I suppose it's better than taking after his mother,' Vera sneered. 'She's always running off at the mouth and upsetting people.'

'She doesn't mean anything by it. She just doesn't think.' Mary was annoyed that she always had to defend Hetty.

'She rubs people up the wrong way, though,' Vera said, 'and one of these days it's going to get her in trouble, if the black market thing doesn't first. That one has skeletons in her closet, you mark my words. Her gossip and chatter are just ways of covering them up.'

'This cake really is very good.' Effie licked her fingers and picked up her teacup. Samuel, the smallest of her boys, had sneaked into the room. He climbed onto her knee, reached into her blouse and began to suck at her breast. She barely paid him any more notice than the other two, who were out in the garden with Harold and Freda. 'You'll have to give me the recipe, Alice, my Charlie has quite a sweet tooth, he'd love it. He's working all hours down at the docks loading cargo onto the ships to go to France. He deserves a treat.'

'Better my Arthur and your Charlie are working at the docks than over in France or out at sea like Mary and Alice's husbands,' Vera said. 'I'm sure I'd worry myself sick.'

'At least none of you have to worry about them coming home covered in tattoos like some fairground attraction.' Alice winked at Mary. She wasn't going to let the conversation turn to the war. 'Harry says he's going to get one, and I'm sure his brother Hariph is egging him on. He's wanted one ever since they saw the sailors with them on a Charabanc trip to the seaside years and years ago. He still talks about how they decided to do their own when they got home. Mary's Thomas got a bottle of India ink and a needle—'

'Then his mother came in and caught him.' Mary smiled at the memory of Thomas telling her the story. 'She took Thomas by the ear and rubbed at his arm with a scrubbing brush and carbolic. It didn't work, though. To this day, he has T-H-O on the inside of his left arm.'

*

By the time Mary left Alice's house, she felt better than she had when she'd arrived. They hadn't made much progress on their socks, and she didn't much like some of the gossip, especially when Vera got herself all worked up about Hetty, but thinking about what Hetty might be up to had taken her mind off worrying about Thomas for a while. She didn't believe all the rubbish about skeletons in closets, but, if it was true about the strange man, it sounded like Hetty was heading for a fall.

5 - Wednesday 3 July 1918

Dawn was breaking. A pinkish glow tinted the face of the Quartermaster as he went along the line with the rum ration. It burned the back of Thomas's throat, but he tossed it back. The warmth in his belly was more than welcome. For a whole week the bombardment had been more intense than anything any of them had ever heard. Heavy artillery flew over their heads towards the Hun Line at such a rate he couldn't tell where one explosion ended and the next began. When it stopped, it was like going suddenly deaf. At this rate, they'd be able to stroll to the Munich trench without a shot being fired. How could there be any Hun left after such a show?

Twenty minutes to go. The whistle blew for the first wave, the East Lancashires. His ears were still ringing from the gigantic mine detonated under Hawthorn Ridge. No sooner had the poor buggers climbed over the sandbags than they began to fall. Some didn't even make it out of the trench. They fell straight back mid-climb, as if they'd changed their minds and decided not to go after all. Where was all the gunfire coming from? Had some of the Hun survived, and, if so, how?

He checked his watch. Seven thirty. Just ten minutes to go. His heart was pounding. He looked at the makeshift ladders; old bits of wood nailed together any which way, leaning against the side of the trench here and there. Some of the men couldn't take their eyes

off them. Others couldn't look at them. The weight of his pack cut
into his shoulders. Would those flimsy ladders stand up to the job?
Should he just scramble up the sandbags and earth as best he could?
The call came, 'Ten seconds . . . get ready!' He smiled at Ronnie. One
foot on the first rung. A hand on the sandbags. Heart beating so loud
everyone must be able to hear it. Then the whistle blew.

*

The familiar strains of reveille drifted through the hut. Thomas
opened his eyes and for a moment couldn't work out where he was.
The clean, comfortable, safe world of Netley Hospital, with its white-
painted walls and metal-framed beds, still didn't seem real. Beams of
sunlight streamed through the windows and gave it a light, airy feel.
Several windows were open, and the air carried a hint of the sea,
which mixed pleasantly with the long wooden hut's faint pine scent.
If only they didn't play the bloody bugle all the time; reveille every
morning to wake them, the retreat at sunset, the last post at night,
and every time another train came in with more wounded, even if it
was in the middle of the night. Geoffrey, the chap in the next bed,
had warned him about it yesterday. He was a chatty type, about
Harry's age, with a long, thin face, a soft mouth and ears that stuck
out like jug handles. He'd been shot in the guts at Wipers three
months ago and was now well on the way to recovery, or so he said.

'The first morning I was here I woke up thinking I was back in sodding training. Almost did myself a mischief trying to jump out of bed and stand to attention,' he'd said.

This was his second morning, and he hadn't had the urge to jump out of bed so far, but the blasted bugle got on his nerves. At least now they'd stopped giving him the morphia he had his wits about him. He still had to keep pinching himself to be sure he really was back in Blighty, in a real bed with crisp white sheets and soft blankets, alive and with a future to look forward to.

Future.

The very word seemed as unreal as having a roof over his head. In France, death had lurked around every corner, and the difference between his warm, breathing body and all the bloated corpses in No Man's Land was but a moment away. Now he was at Netley and life was all buglers, nurses and Geoffrey trying to play tricks on him. Yesterday he'd tried to persuade him to ask Nurse Macklin for a bed bath.

'She's quite a good sport, if you know what I mean,' he'd said with an exaggerated wink.

Even if it had been true, he wouldn't have been interested, but John in the opposite bed, had come to his rescue.

'Leave off,' he'd said. 'The poor bugger has only just got here and you're trying to get him in trouble with Sister.'

He was a chubby lad with dark hair and very straight white teeth. By the look of him, he was only just out of his teens, and he had earned himself a shattered knee, 'Trying to hold Jerry back at the Aisne in late May.'

Nurse Macklin hadn't struck him as the 'good sport' kind anyway. She had a round, childlike face, small, wire-rimmed spectacles and a cheerful, no-nonsense manner. She was the one who'd explained to him about his lung.

'It was a terrific mess. The surgeon at the Casualty Clearing Station had to remove it to save your heart. You should be fine, God willing. They've had a lot of practice dealing with lungs lately. They're really very good at it now. You were extremely lucky. They'd probably have kept you over there a little longer, if so many flu cases weren't coming in. The Medical Officer says you'd have been done for if you caught that.'

He didn't bother to tell her he'd already had it back in the spring, mainly because getting enough breath to talk was still a chore and wore him out. She'd also brought him a shaving kit. Without the morphia it hurt to move his arm, but she told him he needed to get used to it if he wanted to recover enough to go home to his wife.

'Getting spruced up a bit will make you feel much better,' she'd said.

As it happened, it made him feel worse. When he looked in the mirror the face of an old man looked back at him. It was more like his father's than his own. There were deep bags under haunted eyes, furrows across his forehead and a sickly, grey tinge under his tan. The most shocking thing was his hair. The last time he'd looked in a mirror it had been dark, with just a touch of grey at the temples. Now there was barely a dark hair left. He'd never believed the tales of people's hair turning white overnight. Although he was almost used to it now, he dreaded to think what Mary would make of it when she came at the weekend. When he'd written to her to set her mind at rest, he hadn't known about his hair.

Nurse Macklin had been so matter-of-fact about his lung being taken away, as if it were an everyday thing. It wasn't to him, though, even if it did explain why breathing was so difficult. He'd imagined he would be bedbound for a while, but he'd been wrong about that. Nurse Macklin positively pestered him.

'You need to get up and walk around every day, Doctor's orders. You'll feel very tired at first but walking and getting lots of fresh air will soon build up your strength.'

Once she'd helped him into the clothes she'd brought for him, a white shirt, red tie and the light-blue woollen suit they called hospital blues, she'd taken him out to a kind of veranda at the front of the hut. It was a slow, painful walk. Being upright made him lightheaded, and he had to lean on her for support. Luckily, she was stronger than she looked. It was also lucky there was a bench for him to flop down onto. She was right about being tired. The few dozen steps made him so breathless his head spun, and he could hardly keep his eyes open.

Today, he'd managed a walk around the outside of the hut under his own steam. It wasn't much, but as far as he was concerned, every bit of progress was a step towards home and a step further from the bloody bugle. The sun on his face felt good. The sky was deep blue with barely a cloud to be seen. He closed his eyes and inhaled slowly. He could smell the sea and the mouth-watering aroma of baking bread. The combination reminded him of his days in Southsea. He could almost see the delicate rose pink of the morning sky reflected on the tips of the waves, like rose petals sprinkled on the sea, and hear the gentle swoosh of tide lapping at shingle. Getting shot and losing a lung hadn't sounded in the least bit lucky when Nurse Macklin explained it to him, but now he saw he'd led a charmed life. By chance he'd ended up in Southsea, lodging with Arthur, another of the baker's men, and his wife, Lib. Lady luck had brought him Lib's sister, Mary. Now, some guardian angel had pulled him through four years of war and brought him back to her alive. He could hardly wait for the weekend.

6 - Thursday 4 July 1918

'Is that you, Mary? Come in, come in,' Zillah called through her French window.

Mary stepped out of the sunshine and into the cool room. It was stuffed to the gills with expensive-looking furniture: dark wood cabinets, gilt-framed paintings and photographs, side tables, Chesterfield armchairs and opulent rugs. Every surface groaned under the weight of countless knickknacks. There was even a telephone, although the fancy contraption of ebony and brass must surely be more of a whimsical decoration than a thing of use. It was as if Zillah had squashed the furniture from a much larger house into this modest terrace. Perhaps she'd once lived in a fancy place like her son, William, but if she had, why on earth would she choose to move here? It would make no sense at all.

As always, Freda ran straight to the large dolls' house crammed into the corner. It was filled with miniature furniture and tiny wooden dolls with painted faces. Their clothes, old fashioned crinoline dresses and frock coats, were made from scraps of ancient fabric. Zillah said she'd had it since she was a child.

'Be careful.' Mary gave her the usual warning. 'Don't break anything.'

'Leave her be,' Zillah said. 'It's nice to see it played with after all these years.'

'I've brought you some vegetables from the garden: tomatoes, lettuce and some new potatoes.'

'That's lovely. Why don't you put them in the kitchen and make a pot of tea? There's some cake in the larder. Make sure you cut yourself a slice.'

Mary went to the kitchen with a smile on her face. For the first time in as long as she could remember, the knot of fear inside her had loosened. Yesterday, when she'd found Thomas's letter on the mat, she couldn't describe her joy. He was alive. He was in England. Nothing else mattered. She could hardly believe he was safe and so very close. She breezed through her housework with a smile on her face and a song on her lips. In a burst of energy, she'd even weeded the vegetable garden and gathered a few bits and pieces for Zillah. Most of the houses in the street grew vegetables or, like Alice and Zillah, had fruit trees, and the residents got together in groups to share the bounty. Poor Zillah was as old as the hills. She reminded Mary of Queen Victoria, with her white hair and voluminous black gowns. She even wore a veiled hat to church. Mary worried about her living all on her own next door, and she popped in to check on her often.

She put the vegetables away and carefully took Zillah's delicate bone china tea set out of the cabinet. As she waited for the kettle to boil, she thought about her garden. It was strange the way the weeds grew so much quicker than the vegetables. Dandelions mostly, because Freda was fond of making wishes and blowing the fluffy seed heads when she found them. Mary didn't have the heart to spoil her fun. She found the cake; a rich, dark fruit loaf. There was always cake in Zillah's larder, despite the rationing and the shortages.

*

'How are you getting on with *Mr. Polly*?' Zillah asked. She often lent her books and H. G. Wells was a special favourite.

'I'm really enjoying it. He does seem to get himself into some scrapes. I just wish I had more time to read about them,' Mary said, between nibbles of cake that tasted like it was made with real flour, butter and sugar. Where on earth did she get it? Did William buy it for her? For all his faults, he looked after his mother well. He had the money to buy things on the black market, unlike Hetty. She hoped Vera and Effie were wrong about that, because the penalty for getting caught selling black market goods was likely to be harsh. If Hetty went to prison what would become of little George? He was the clingiest child she'd ever seen.

'That's the problem when you have children, my dear. They keep you busy. Mind you, they keep you on your toes even when they've grown up. William has got an idea that I'm too old and feeble to live on my own. It's ridiculous of course, but once he has an idea in his head, he's impossible. He's read all about the epidemic of influenza in Spain and has convinced himself it will come here. He says I'll get it if I keep going outside. I told him, "The fresh air is good for me. There's influenza every year. I'm old and when my time comes it comes, but if I can't go out on my promenades then I might as well be dead." He worries too much.' She took a sip of tea. 'Talking of worrying, have you heard any more about that husband of yours?'

'Yes. I had a letter yesterday. He's at the big hospital at Netley. I'm going to see him on Saturday.'

7 - Saturday 6 July 1918

Howitzer shells whined overhead, heading for the Hun Line. Explosions shook the ground. Bright flashes lit up the snow. If they stuck to the plan, they'd keep behind their own barrage. The snow crunched under his feet. It stung as it swirled around his cheeks. Who'd have thought there'd be a snowstorm on Easter Monday? Not the bloody generals, that's for sure. The flakes were small and fell thickly. The smoke swirled. The flashes were blinding. He couldn't see anything. At least it was blowing at his back. The Hun would have it in their faces. Joe, Wally, Dougie, Lofty, Fred, Davie – the lot of them – had disappeared into the blizzard. Was he the only one left alive in the whole world? He kept blindly running forward. Bullets buzzed around him like wasps in an autumn orchard. How had he not been hit yet?

More by luck than judgment, he reached the scattered remains of the German wire. Bodies were caught on it; dark, snow-dusted shapes in impossible poses. He looked away, afraid he'd recognise what was left of their faces. The snowflakes spun, eddied and parted. There was a gap in the wire. A trio of Hun heads poked up from their trench. Unthinking, he put his rifle to his shoulder and fired. Their eyes turned from surprise to horror. One by one, they fell. He kept firing long after they were dead. When his heartrate had slowed, he cautiously jumped down into the trench, Mills bombs at the ready. It was empty apart from the corpses of the men he'd killed.

He stared at them. He'd never killed a man face-to-face before, with them looking into his eyes. Around him the guns crackled, the shells burst and the snow and smoke swirled, but he couldn't look away. This tangle of bodies with pale faces and grey uniforms spattered with mud and blood were men just like him. They had homes and families: mothers, brothers and perhaps children – people who loved them. What if they all stopped fighting, like they had that first Christmas? Then the generals and the kings would all have to sort it out amongst themselves.

*

'It's just a thunderstorm.' The young nurse had hair the colour of ripe barley, freckles and wide, grey eyes. Flashes of white light lit the dark hut and there was a distant rumble of thunder. 'It's upset quite a few of the men. Reminded them of the fighting, I expect. Would you like some cocoa? I've just made some.'

She said her name was Amelia. She sat with him while he drank the cocoa and chased away the horror of the dream with talk of normal, everyday things. She asked about his family and he told her all about Mary and her bright blue eyes, Eric and his strawberry blonde curls and Freda, the little girl he only knew from his wife's letters.

*

By the morning, when the Medical Officer began his rounds, the storm had blown itself out and the sun was shining through the windows. With his waxed moustache, stethoscope and the long white coat over his uniform, the doctor cut a dashing figure. The sister, a rather dour, middle-aged woman with a sharp, pointed face and a beaky nose, shadowed his every step as if he were God, or at least the King. Perhaps she was a little in love with him, although she was almost old enough to be his mother. They had to stand to attention by their beds while he inspected them, but this morning Geoffrey stayed in bed. At first, Thomas thought it must be one of his jokes, except he was strangely quiet. Usually, he barely stopped talking to draw breath. The doctor frowned over his thermometer and whispered something urgently to the sister. He spoke quietly, but not so quietly that Thomas didn't catch '. . . it may be influenza. We should get him to the isolation ward at once.'

'Of course, Captain Holder.' Such was the sister's eagerness to please she all but curtsied. 'I'll call the orderlies right away.'

In a flash, poor Geoffrey was carted off on a stretcher with a weak smile and a half-hearted wave. His face was pale with a deep red spot on each cheek, like badly applied rouge on a French whore. Amelia was just about to finish her shift when the sister ordered her to change Geoffrey's bed right away. 'Be sure to disinfect everything thoroughly, too,' she ordered.

The air was clearer after the storm. The world glistened and the distant green dome of the chapel sparkled like a jewel. Where the sun shone, wisps of steam rose from the damp earth. Thomas walked twice around the hut, although it was closer to a shuffle than a march. Still, it was progress of a kind. After that he was glad of the bench on the veranda. Birds sang. He looked around for them but all he saw was a magpie watching him from the roof of the hut next door. It reminded him of the bird he'd seen stealing treasure in No Man's Land a lifetime ago. He saluted it, then closed his eyes and dozed in the sun. He'd slept so much since he'd been shot, so why was he tired all the time? Perhaps his body was trying to catch up on all the hours of sleep he'd lost since 1914. In France, he'd longed for time to sleep, especially when he was in the trenches snatching just a few hours here and there. Now that he had all the time in the world he'd rather have stayed awake. With sleep came dreams, like the one he'd had last night. In the middle of a war, a man had little time to think about the things he'd seen and done. Now everything he wanted to forget kept popping into his head.

Still, Mary would be here soon. Waiting for her reminded him of his wedding day. He'd felt like the luckiest man on earth, although he was full of nerves. Standing at the altar with Hariph by his side, he'd looked anxiously up at the wooden beams. His brand-new suit was stiff, the starched shirt collar rubbed his neck, and he was sure his tie was crooked. He'd been worried she'd change her mind. He wouldn't have blamed her. He was hardly a catch. When Hariph noticed him fiddling nervously with his tie he'd poked him in the ribs and said, 'It'll be fine. I'm not even going to pretend I've forgotten the ring.'

Then Mary walked in on the arm of her father and everyone else in the church disappeared. She was a vision in her white dress and long veil, carrying a posy of dog roses and wearing a circle of silk flowers on her head. Thomas had never seen anything so beautiful in his whole life. He thought his heart would burst with pride. Now he felt the same nervousness. What was she going to make of his white hair and his weakened state?

8 - Saturday 6 July 1918

They left for the hospital straight after breakfast. Mary had hardly slept because of the storm and her nerves about the day ahead. The need to see Thomas was a physical ache, but she was frightened what she might find when she did. What did a lost lung look like? Would he be swathed in bloody bandages that frightened the children? She could have left them with Alice, but Eric would never have forgiven her if she went to see his pappy without him. He was beside himself at the idea of catching a train and ran ahead all the way to the station.

Mary was nervous. She sometimes caught the train to Reading to visit her family, or to Witney with Thomas, but she didn't know how to get to the hospital once she got to Netley Station. Soon enough, though, they were on the train and steaming along. Freda curled up on her lap while Eric pressed his face to the window and gave a running commentary. 'We're going across the river; I can see swans . . . there's a station and lots of houses like ours.'

His chatter did nothing to calm Mary's nerves. She was glad to get off the train and find the stationmaster, a young, smiling woman with dark bobbed hair. She confirmed that the hospital gates were more or less straight down the road.

'You can't miss them, just turn left when you reach the shore.'

Mary breathed a sigh of relief when she saw the sea. Gulls squabbled in the hazy blue sky and bobbed on the grey-green waves. They stopped to watch one soar from the shingle and drop something, probably a cockle, from a great height. The tiny dark speck fell, and the gull shot down behind it to gather up the spoils. What eyes the gulls must have to pick out one little broken cockleshell amongst a million pebbles.

The two soldiers at the hospital gates directed her further. 'Just follow the path. The huts are behind the main hospital.'

Mary had been afraid they wouldn't let her pass, but they barely gave her a second look. Filled with a mixture of fear and excitement, she did as they said. When the hospital finally came into view her worries turned to despair. The building was gigantic, far bigger than anything she'd ever seen. It stretched endlessly into the distance, an edifice of red brick and pale stone with towers, domes and row upon row of arched windows. The wide lawns were dotted with figures in pale blue. They moved about singly or in small groups, like the gulls they'd watched bobbing on the waves. As she got closer and the details of the men became clearer, her worst fears were realised. Nurses in red capes and white aprons wheeled men with empty trouser legs in contraptions resembling giant baby carriages. Others had missing arms or limped crookedly on crutches. Some, with eyes swathed in bandages, were being guided. They looked like broken wrecks of men. Like her brother Charlie, they smiled but with a dead look in their eyes. Poor Charlie would never be the same after the sap caved in on him and crushed his arm. Mum must be out of her mind knowing her other son was still underground and digging those tunnels with the shells going off all the time. To be buried alive must be the worst fate in the world.

The scale and horror of this place was beyond anything Mary could have imagined. Freda began to cry and clutch at her skirt, so Mary picked her up. She wrapped her arms around Mary's neck and hid her face in her hair. Eric moved closer to her side. His eyes grew wider by the second and his face became more and more serious. Mary realised it had been a mistake to bring the children. She couldn't see how she was ever going to find Thomas. She'd need eyes as keen as the gull searching for his broken cockleshell amongst the millions of pebbles.

The village of large wooden huts reminded her of giant versions of Thomas's garden shed. By the time she reached them she was close to tears and feeling hopeless. She looked about for someone to ask where she might find her husband. There were a few men in blue wandering about or sitting outside in the sun. They all looked far fitter than the men she'd seen earlier on the lawn. If this was a place for the less severe cases, then didn't it follow that Thomas wasn't too badly hurt? An old man sitting on a bench on a sort of rustic veranda caught her eye. His own eyes had a haunted look, and his clenched fists were resting on his knees. There was something familiar in the way he sat. When he noticed her, his face broke into a wide smile. Perhaps she'd ask him if he knew where

Thomas was. She smiled back and walked towards him. When he called out her name, she stared at him confused. Then she realised the old man was Thomas.

Her eyes filled with tears. How could she not have recognised her own husband? With Freda still clinging to her neck, she ran to him, knelt at his feet and took his hands in hers.

Thomas leaned slowly forward and kissed her gently on the lips. 'You will never know how much I've dreamed about this moment,' he whispered. He couldn't seem to catch his breath. Was it the emotion of the moment or his lost lung?

'Freda, do you have a kiss for your pappy?'

Mary tried to peel the little arms from around her neck, but Freda clung all the tighter. She probably didn't even remember the last time she saw her father, or understand who he was.

'Let her be, she's bound to be feeling a little shy,' Thomas said, although she could see how it pained him.

'Eric, I'm sure *you* have a kiss for Pappy, don't you?'

She forced brightness into her voice. Eric stood behind her with a very solemn look on his face. Reluctantly, he stepped forward with his hands clasped behind his back. He looked at Thomas suspiciously, as if he couldn't quite believe this really was his pappy.

'He's too big a boy for kissing now,' Thomas said. 'He's been the man of the house while I've been away . . . and men shake hands.'

He held out his hand and, after a long pause, Eric shook it.

'Did you get shot?' he asked.

'I did.'

'Did it hurt?'

'A little.'

'Can I see?'

'It's all bandaged up now but maybe when it's better.'

Thomas dismissed Mary's concerns about his breathlessness. His breathing was getting easier by the day, he said, and the doctors believed he would make a full recovery.

'When I looked in the mirror to shave, I thought I was looking at my father.'

He made light of his changed appearance, although his eyes told a different story.

'I think you look very distinguished with your white hair,' Mary said.

What did the colour of his hair matter as long as she had him back? The haunted look in his eyes was more of a concern. She knew from her mother's letters how poor Charlie still struggled to accept his disability, and how the war had changed him. Would Thomas be the same?

9 - Saturday 6 July 1918

Mary's visit was the best tonic he could have had, but at the same time it caused the biggest heartbreak. She hadn't recognised him at first. She'd tried to disguise the horror and shock, but he'd seen it in her face. Then there were the children. Until now they'd been shadowy ideals of children pieced together from Mary's letters. The reality was nothing like his imagination. He wasn't surprised Freda was so shy of him, even though it was like a knife in his heart. She didn't know him any more than he knew her. She was more like Mary than he'd expected. She had the same big blue eyes, and, with that blonde hair, she was going to break hearts when she grew up. At least she'd thawed a little before they left. She'd even sat on his lap and fallen asleep sucking her thumb while rubbing the lapel of his jacket.

Eric had been half afraid of him at first too, although he'd done his best not to show it. When Thomas went off to France he'd left behind a toddler. Now he'd come back to a schoolboy with Mary's curls and the chubby robustness of her loveable rogue brother Charlie. The lad was full of questions about the war, but it was almost as difficult to find things to tell him as it had been to find things to put in his letters home. Eric thought war was like a game of tin soldiers; lining them up in the dirt and rolling marbles at them, just as he, Hariph and Harry had done as boys. If he dug in his mother's garden, there'd probably still be a few rusting away. Thank God the boy wouldn't have to see the reality of rotting bodies half buried in

No Man's Land. The war surely couldn't go on that long, could it?

Watching his wife and children walk away was such a wrench it brought tears to his eyes. The emotion of the visit wore him out and soon he was asleep.

*

'All the way to bloody Germany!'

Ronnie screamed at the top of his lungs and ran, rifle poised, bayonet fixed. Ahead was all smoke and noise. The boom, boom, boom of the big guns, the deafening crash of shells and the crackle of rifle fire vibrated through Thomas's body. It was like a November fog shot through with flashes of fire. It smelled of Guy Fawkes Night. His heart felt fit to burst as he tried to keep pace with his big lance corporal. It was heavy going. They clambered through shell holes and leapt over the bodies of the first wave, those poor East Lancashires. It was supposed to be easy. They'd seen the mine explode under Hawthorn Ridge. The Hun were all meant to be dead. Dead men don't shoot machine guns, though. They went forwards, as if protected by an invisible shield. All around them shadowy men fell. The fog churned. They saw the thick tangle of wire ahead. How the hell was it still there? Suddenly, they were flying through the air in a plume of black smoke, raining mud and jagged metal.

When he came round, he was on his back in a deep, wet shell hole, with the sky above him. He tried to move but something soft and heavy pinned him down. He tried to push it off. It groaned. It was Ronnie. Warm blood trickled onto his hands. Machine guns fired, shells burst, men screamed in agony and called out for their mothers, but all he could think about was saving his friend. Somehow, he managed to dig himself out and find the field dressing in the inside pocket of Ronnie's jacket, but it was useless. There was so much blood coming from so many places that all the dressings in the world would have been no good.

'Are we in Germany yet?' Ronnie whispered.

'We are,' he said through his tears. If he'd run faster, he'd have been the one dying, and Ronnie would have been the one trying to save him.

*

The men woke him when they came back from their gardening.

'I've never known a man so fond of sleeping as you,' John said.

Usually, they all trooped off to the mess hut for dinner straight away, but tonight they gathered in a knot on the veranda. He knew something was wrong by the looks on their worried faces. Had there been bad news from France while he'd been sleeping?

'What's happened?' He rubbed his eyes and slowly stood up.

'Old Geoffrey's bought it,' John said solemnly.

'How? He was joking and larking about last night.'

He'd almost recovered from his wounds and had even talked about getting discharged and going home to his family. Surely a wound couldn't just un-heal itself, could it? He swore he'd heard the M.O. say it was flu, but a man couldn't die of that in a matter of hours.

'The sister said it was an infection,' John shrugged.

Stanley, the sandy haired lad with the shattered shoulder, said, 'It was the flu, I heard the sister talking to the M.O. about it.'

'That makes no sense.' John leaned on the rustic fence for support. 'Nearly all of us had the flu in our section. It knocked us for six for a few days, but we were back digging trenches and shooting the Hun in no time. It was just a fever and a few days' rest. To tell the truth, the ones that didn't get it were quite miffed to be left out. It wouldn't kill a man.'

'And so quick,' said Stanley.

Thomas's legs suddenly felt wobbly, so he lowered himself back onto the bench. What a cruel twist of fate to live through four years of war, suffer a horrible injury and more or less recover from it, only to be killed by something as silly as the flu. He'd heard the M.O. this morning too, so he wasn't as sceptical as John, but it still seemed very strange.

'There's been others like Geoffrey.' Stanley pulled a packet of Woodbines out of his breast pocket and tapped the bottom. 'The sister was yapping about it. Something about a more violent strain of flu taking advantage of us sick men.'

'Sister told us all it was an infection. Flu doesn't kill a man just like that.' John clicked his fingers to illustrate the speed with which Geoffrey had gone from perfectly healthy to dead.

'She would say that, wouldn't she?' Stanley lit his cigarette and shook out the match. 'Not good for morale, is it, if we all start worrying about being killed by flu. Anyhow, I heard her talking to the M.O., so I know it was flu, and her telling lies about it makes me wonder what she's got to hide. What I really want to know is where it came from?'

Then Donald, the chubby Black Watch chap with half his thigh blown away, chipped in. 'My mother heard it was in the schools in Glasgow. Some bairns in an orphanage died. Mighty bad flu, she said it was. And I heard hundreds of girls in a leather factory in Bermondsey got sick in June. I don't think any of them died, though.'

'If it was flu, it was probably just the same old Spanish flu, and most people get better from that pretty quick.' John shook his head. 'You know what Geoffrey was like. He was everybody's mate, always wandering off talking to people and making friends with the new chaps. If it was flu, one of the men just off the boat from France probably brought it back with him. Stands to reason, really.'

'It still seems odd for it to be so sudden.' Thomas accepted a Woodbine from Stanley and lit it. It hurt to inhale the smoke and made him dizzy, but Nurse Macklin said it was good exercise for his lung, so he persevered. 'One minute he was right as rain, the next he was dead.'

'Probably because he was weakened by his wounds.' John said.

'Do you think we could catch it, then?' Stanley exhaled a plume of smoke with a worried frown. 'From Geoffrey like?'

'Perhaps if you haven't had it already,' John said. For most people, though, it's likely to be something and nothing. Flu only takes the old, the very young or the sick.'

'But we're all sick here.' Stanley pulled nervously on his cigarette.

'Maybe it's from the Hun,' Donald suggested. 'Some kind of germ spread about to kill us all off. There's nothing I'd put past those devils. Maybe the gas was just a test to see how well they could spread it round, or maybe it was in the gas? I read in the paper that a whole camp of Jerry prisoners went down with it at the end of June.

That was in Hampshire – Bramley, I think.'

'They're only Hun, they don't matter.' John laughed bitterly. 'In fact, the less of them the better.'

'Even some of the guards got sick, though,' Donald said. '*The Times* reckoned it was a German bug, spread about by German spies. Devious bastards the Jerry's, I wouldn't put anything past them. Trying to win the bloody war by fair means or foul.'

'A bit pointless if they're the ones catching it, though, isn't it?' John was dismissive.

'Not if they've got an antidote.' Donald raised an eyebrow. 'The prisoners were probably infected then got captured on purpose to spread it around. You mark my words, the truth will come out one of these days.'

'Maybe it came from the French brothels,' John laughed. 'I'm pretty sure old Geoffrey saw the inside of them more than once.'

'Along with half the British Army,' Thomas snorted.

'Seriously, though, how do we avoid getting it, if it's so bad?' Stanley threw the stub of his cigarette down and ground it out with his foot.

10 - Wednesday 10 July 1918

Mary opened the front door, took Freda's hand and wrinkled her nose at the pungent waft of low tide. A long-tailed flash of black and white flew low across her path. She raised her hand to salute it, muttering, 'Good morning, Mr Magpie, how are you today?' Then she looked around for another bird to bring good luck. There had been enough bad luck already. There were no other magpies, but a figure on the corner of Union Road looked very much like Hetty. It was hard to mistake those hips, or the dark grey coat with the astrakhan collar. Only Hetty would wear such a thing on a warm day like this. She loved that coat, even if it was moth-eaten and out of fashion. Why was she hanging around on the corner, though?

The question was answered almost as soon as Mary had thought it, when a man limped into view and stopped in front of Hetty. With his cap pulled down over his eyes and his shirt sleeves rolled up, he seemed rough and decidedly shady. They both looked furtive. Was this the man Vera had seen? Perhaps he really was a black marketeer? It would explain the sugar Hetty had offered to Effie the other day, but it didn't explain where she'd got the money for it. The black market was expensive. Was Hetty getting herself into something that could land her in prison, and right on her own doorstep, too? Maybe Vera had got it all wrong and Hetty was secretly courting this man? After all, her husband had been dead for more than six years. But it was unlikely. She'd never shown any interest in finding a new man before, and this chap didn't look like husband material. Still, it was a better explanation than the alternative.

There was no time to think about it. The sound of hooves on the dusty road announced the funeral cortege as it came out of Parsonage Road. She glanced towards Alice's house and saw her at her door with Harold. One door down, Effie stood with her three boys gathered around her feet. With a bowed head and a tight hold of Freda's hand, Mary waited for the two black horses to slowly pull the hearse past. Once the carriage behind it had gone by, she made her way sadly to Alice's gate. Effie had already gone inside and shut her door. Alice gave her a tight smile, stood back and waved her into the cool darkness of the narrow hallway. The children ran ahead, through the scullery and out of the back door into the garden.

There would be no knitting today. The coffin in the hearse belonged to Vera's husband, Arthur, and, although she hadn't looked up, she knew Vera had been in the carriage with her son, Timmy. Was it really only last week that Vera had said how lucky it was that her Arthur and Effie's Charlie were working at the docks and didn't have to go to war? Had it been an accident, it would have been more understandable, but Vera said it was flu. She said he'd come home from work feeling fine. After dinner he went to bed with a headache and a bit of a fever, and she'd woken in the morning to find him dead beside her. It seemed impossible that the big, one-eyed docker, who'd been so proud of helping with the war effort, could die of something like flu.

She sat with Alice in the back parlour sipping tea, eating cake and half watching Freda and Harold as they circled the fruit trees in the little garden and danced from one spot of shade to the next. The flower border had burst into a riot of colour: blue and purple delphiniums, spikes of deep pink foxgloves and nodding white daisies spilled over onto the path.

'I've never heard of someone dropping dead like that of flu,' Alice said. 'Especially not a fit, healthy man like him, and in the summer, too.'

'Poor Vera. Perhaps he had something else wrong. His heart, maybe, and he didn't know about it.' It made Mary realise how lucky she was to have got Thomas back more or less in one piece.

'That's what I thought, but he seemed as strong as an ox. Vera said he hadn't had a day sick in his life. I suppose you never know, though, do you? Just because someone looks strong . . . He was working night and day helping to take the wounded men off the boats. Maybe he was just worn out. Anyway, enough morbid talk, tell me properly about Thomas. We were so busy with the washing on Monday, and then with the news about Arthur, I hardly had time to take it all in.'

Mary told Alice about the giant hospital at Netley, the wounded men she'd seen and the huts that Thomas said were much better than the main hospital.

'It looks nice enough from the outside, but he says it's stuffy, smelly and dark inside. The poor nurses have to walk miles every day up and down endless corridors, and the windows of the wards don't even look out over the sea.'

'I still can't believe you didn't recognise him at first.'

'Neither can I. Thank goodness he didn't notice. He looked shrunken somehow, all hunched up on a bench like an old man, with his hair completely white. I suppose it's from the shock of being shot. He looks dreadfully sick, and he struggles to breathe or get about, but they say he *will* recover.'

'I doubt any of our men will come back to us quite how they were when they left.' Alice licked her finger and picked up a crumb from the tablecloth. 'Come to that, none of us is quite the same, either. We've got so used to being without them and managing on our own. I imagine Thomas looks quite striking with white hair, though.'

'He does, but I wouldn't have cared if he had no hair at all, as long as I got him back.'

'Have you let Esther know?'

'Yes, I sent a telegram. They're so busy making blankets for the war she probably doesn't have a moment to herself. They aren't going to send him back to France, so that will please her. I should probably write to Martha so she can let Hariph know.'

'She might welcome a letter.' Alice laid the back of her hand against the teapot to check the temperature. Finding it satisfactory, she then topped up their cups. 'I don't think Hariph writes much, he's too busy mending the guns, or whatever it is he does. He's always been more interested in machines than people. Poor Martha only really has her mother, and I think she has to look after her as much as she does Terrence, Kathleen and little Leonard.'

'I wish she didn't live so far away. She makes me laugh with all her funny songs and stories.' Mary waved away another slice of beetroot and carrot cake. 'At least we have each other to visit and share our worries with. Martha seems to be quite cut off down in Plymouth.'

'In lots of ways, it's harder for her than it is for us. If something happens to Hariph, I doubt she'll get any help from the Navy.'

'Or from Esther.'

Thomas's mother saw everything as black or white, good or bad. Martha and Hariph weren't married, so that made Martha bad. The reason for it didn't matter. She didn't blame Hariph, of course. Her boys could do no wrong. Martha was eight years older than him, so she had obviously led him astray. If Esther spoke of her at all, she called her 'The Actress'. It was better than whore, but only just.

'Especially not from Esther. Even if they married now, it wouldn't get Martha into Esther's good books. Look at the fuss she made over Gordon. Harry and I were married by the time he was born, but she still looks at me as if I'm a fallen woman. You're the only good daughter-in-law, Mary.'

11 - Sunday 14 July 1918

Two uniformed men were standing at the gate beside a little house of red and yellow brick with arched windows like the main hospital. Were they guards stopping the wounded men from escaping?

'Sneaking off to the pub?' one of them laughed.

'Is there a pub?' Thomas looked along the dusty road. He couldn't see a pub, just sea, a stretch of shingly shore, a slipway and something that looked like a wooden watchhouse, probably for the coastguards.

'Yes. Just up yonder a little way. It's called the Prince Consort because Prince Albert popped in there when he and the Queen were visiting the hospital. It's not open yet, though, wartime hours and all that, so you'll have a bit of a wait.'

'So, I'm not a prisoner here, then? I could go to the pub if I wanted? Only seeing you two, I thought I might be.'

He laughed as if it was a joke.

'Of course you can, unless you're one of them German prisoners in disguise. We had one a while back, kept getting out. Where did the silly bugger think he was going to go, back to the Hun Line?'

When he'd promised to meet Mary at the gate, he hadn't

known what an ambitious journey it would be. Had he really been able to march for miles just a few weeks ago without giving it a second thought? Now he could barely make it a few hundred yards without stopping to gasp for air, as if he'd run across No Man's Land, through bullets, shells and smoke with a pack on his back and a rifle in his hand. Mary deserved so much more than a broken, white-haired old man with a head full of nightmares. The walk to the chapel for the morning service had worn him out. The enormous hospital building was a marvel. He'd been sure Amelia was exaggerating when she said it was the largest building in England. Now he'd seen it with his own eyes he believed it might be the biggest in the whole world. He'd dozed through most of the service and scarcely noticed more than the ceiling of the chapel, which was the colour of a November sky, and the stunning stained-glass window behind the altar. When they began to sing *Onward Christian Soldiers,* he'd jolted awake, but he had no breath for singing even if he'd wanted to, and anyway, a song about war and battles was not one he wanted to waste it on.

While the guards chatted and joked, he shielded his eyes from the sun and watched for Mary and the children. He had the same tingle of anticipation he used to feel when they were courting. Eric appeared first. Behind him came Mary, with Freda holding her hand. As soon as Eric saw him, he broke into the brightest of smiles and spread his arms wide. 'Pappy, Pappy, look how fast I can run.'

Thomas crouched down and welcomed his boy into his arms.

Out of the corner of his eye, he saw the guards smiling. He and Eric had a lot of catching up to do, but his chubby face, full of joy, and his little legs pumping as he ran said they were going in the right direction. Moments later, Mary and Freda caught up and he was surrounded by arms and smothered with kisses. In that moment, all the nightmares of the war were forgotten, all the ghosts banished.

Hand in hand they walked across the grass towards the tall, wind sculpted pines and the sea. It was a slow, dawdling walk. Eric and Freda ran ahead. Freda was still a little shy and suspicious of him, but Eric wanted his approval.

'See how I can march like a soldier, Pappy.' He swung his arms and stamped his feet.

They sat on the scrubby grass under the shade of the pines, their feet dangling down onto the shingle, while Eric and Freda ran around combing the shore for pretty shells and hag stones. The salty wind ruffled their hair and billowed Mary's skirt. Thomas gazed into her eyes while she made small talk about writing to his mother, Lib, and Martha. Occasionally, he picked up her hand and kissed her fingers, just to see her smile.

'Alice says Hariph barely writes to Martha.'

Mary looked at the tiny Turk's cap shell Freda had dropped into her lap. She turned it over and over and watched the rainbow colours as the light caught it. Her forehead and nose were tinged slightly pink by the wind and sun.

'He was never one for writing,' Thomas explained. 'It doesn't mean he doesn't think about her. I've never seen him so smitten by something without wheels or cogs before. The first time he set eyes on her he lost his heart.'

'She was in a play, wasn't she?'

'Yes, with a troupe of actors and actresses from Plymouth, who'd come to entertain the people of Oxford. He only went because he'd seen her face on the poster, or so he said. He followed her all the way to Plymouth on his motorcycle and made quite a fool of himself. She wouldn't even give him the time of day.'

Freda stumbled across the shingle to shyly put a cockleshell in Thomas's hand. 'With silver bells and cockerel smells,' she sang coyly.

'And pretty maids all in a row,' Thomas finished, pleased she was warming to him at last.

Then Eric dashed over filled with excitement. 'Look, look.' He dropped a pebble into Thomas's hand. At first it seemed the same as any of the million other pebbles on the beach: round, greenish-brown and unremarkable. Then he looked a little closer and noticed the star-shaped outline of a sea urchin. 'It's a fossil. We learned about them at school. I knew I'd find one if I looked hard enough. I wish it were a fossil bird, though.'

When they'd run off again in search of more shells and fossils, Mary told him how William Wells was trying to persuade

Zillah to sell her house and move in with him, and how upset Hetty was about it.

'She acted as if he was doing it just to spite her. She started going on about him looking down his nose at her. I told her I was sure he was only worried about his mother, but she wouldn't have it.'

'I'm surprised Zillah hasn't bitten his hand off at the chance. I used to deliver to his house, it's like a little palace.'

It was the sort of house he and Mary would never be able to afford: a big, double-fronted villa with a curved gravel driveway and ornate wrought iron gates. He knew it was William's house, although he'd never seen him there, or even met his wife. He remembered their maid, a haughty young woman who looked with contempt at a lowly tradesmen like him.

'It's Hetty I'm worried about.' Even when she frowned and wrinkled her nose like that, Mary was as pretty as a picture. 'She said there was an awful lot she could tell me about William that he wouldn't want anyone to know. It was probably nothing but hot air. She likes to gossip, but it's unlikely she knows anything important about him. She's not above making up some scandal, though. If she does, it could land her in trouble. Zillah's her landlady after all.'

'From what you've told me about her I have a feeling she's very good at looking after herself. Perhaps it's nothing at all, and if Hetty has uncovered some dishonesty or a scandal somehow, he'll be the one with the most to lose. Either way, it's none of our business.'

Thomas wasn't sure what Hetty might or might not know, but he was aware William wasn't beyond reproach. Back when he drove the baker's van, he'd had plenty of gossip thrust upon him by customers. What he'd heard about William was a bit racy for Mary's ears, but it had a ring of truth about it.

12 - Monday 15 July 1918

The washing fluttered on the line and the smell of clean, damp laundry mingled with the sweet, earthy scent lingering after the earlier shower. Mary wanted to keep a weather eye out while they drank their tea, so she, Alice and Hetty sat in the kitchen at the old oak table, where there was a clear view of the garden. Hetty had commandeered the rickety rocking chair and had her back to the door, while Alice sat on a wobbly dining chair. This left Mary to perch on the folding stool she ordinarily used to reach things from the top of the dresser. She didn't much mind because it meant she could see through the open door and keep watch on the bank of dark cloud slowly creeping in from the west.

When Alice took Harold home for his nap, Mary expected Hetty to go off to her cleaning job. Instead, she lingered over a second cup of tea.

'Wouldn't it be wonderful if we could just wander down to the bakery and pick out a fancy cake, like we used to before the war?' She sat back in the chair and cradled her teacup as if she had all day. 'What I wouldn't give for a slab of bread pudding with thick sugar on the top like toffee, or maybe a slice of lardy cake, all moist and sticky.'

'Alice made some cake with carrots and beetroot instead of sugar the other day. It was quite good. Maybe I'll ask her for the recipe?'

'Sounds lovely,' Hetty sneered, pulling a face that said she wouldn't want to try it.

'I wonder if it will ever go back to the way it was? You know, with sugar and cakes and sweets in the shops and no rationing.' Those days and that life were like a dream now.

'It's bound to. Besides, I know where to get some bags of sugar if you want them.' Hetty tapped the side of her nose. 'Ask me no questions and I'll tell you no lies.'

'I'd rather do without, thanks,' Mary sniffed. So, it was true – she had got involved with the black market. Mary wanted nothing to do with it. She looked pointedly at the clock above the range. 'Anyway, aren't you supposed to be doing Mrs Drummond's place this afternoon?'

'Not today,' Hetty shrugged. 'I'm cutting back on that kind of thing. All the soap and hot water is playing havoc with my hands. You know how I suffer with my hands.'

'What about the money, though?' The question had been playing on Mary's mind ever since Effie mentioned the sugar. Now Hetty was missing her regular cleaning jobs. To make up the money by selling black market sugar she'd have to sell tons of the stuff. It would only be a matter of time before it all crashed down around her ears.

'Now, that's for me to know and you to find out.' Hetty tapped the side of her nose once again.

'I just hope whatever it is isn't going to land you in trouble, that's all.' The strange limping man and the furtive conversation came to mind. The black market was a dangerous game and he looked like a dangerous man. 'At least cleaning is honest work.'

'Cleaning and skivvying's not all I'm good for, you know. I'm sick of people looking down their noses at me, like I'm a piece of dirt on their shoe.'

'No one looks at you like that, Hetty.' Mary reached out to comfort her, but Hetty shook her hand away.

'Don't they? The trouble with you, Mary, is that you're too nice. You only see the good in people and think the best of them. Vera looks down her nose at me. She thinks she's so much better than me, just because she has a husband . . . well, she did have a husband. So does Effie, and probably half the people in the street. Maybe you think it too, but you're too nice to admit it? All this interest about where my money comes from and telling me I'm going to get myself in trouble. Next, you'll be saying I'm a thief, pocketing some of Zillah's forgotten trinkets while I'm dusting them?'

'Of course not.'

Mary felt terrible, because she had been thinking the worst. Whatever Hetty said, she wasn't nice at all. She was a hypocrite, and now Hetty's eyes were shining brightly, as if she were about to cry.

'But you do think cleaning's all I'm good for. The poor Titanic widow, living on scraps, a charity case with no prospects and no chance of anything better. Why shouldn't I have something better, though? Before George came along, I had a good, respectable job as a typist. Now, because I have a child, I can't even get work in the factories. Why should that mean all that's left for me is scrubbing floors?'

'I know it doesn't seem fair, but I suppose that's why Vera and Effie have been so set on the Votes for Women campaign, and the suffragettes.'

'Perhaps people like Vera and Effie would do better to worry about a woman's right to work and earn decent money, rather than her right to vote. What good does that do any of us? How does putting a cross on a piece of paper and choosing between one man and another make any difference? Not a single one of them knows, or even cares, about women's lives and struggles. We're nothing more than slaves to them, there to be used and abused.' She bit her lip, as if biting back what she was going to say next. 'Some of us don't have husbands to bring the money in, and by the time this war is over, there's going to be a lot more women in that boat.'

13 - Tuesday 16 July 1918

Thomas could hardly think for the noise of the rain on the hut roof. Yesterday morning, he'd been in the orchard leaning his back against an apple tree with the sun on his face while the other men worked in the vegetable garden. There was no chance of that today. They'd all gone off somewhere for a game of darts, but he wasn't up to throwing darts just yet. Instead, he'd borrowed a Sherlock Holmes book from the reading room. He'd read the same page three times now and still had no idea what it was about. The rain was so heavy outside the window that the world was nothing but dull, colourless shapes, and he could hear the occasional rumble of distant thunder. If it kept up there'd be no walk today and no progress. The thought was depressing.

He'd felt downcast since yesterday's afternoon walk. He'd managed to get as far as the pier, where he'd rested for a while and looked over the lead-grey sea. The sky was a mass of grizzled cloud, as if billows of smoke swirled over everything. It hinted at the storm coming. The dull light drained the colour out of the world and left nothing but shades of grey, like a photograph. Even the line of trees across the water and the little fishing boats had been lifeless monotone. He'd watched two ships pass each other; one, a hospital ship heading into the docks, no doubt filled with broken men like him, the other going the other way, probably taking more men out to France. The passing of those ships, the endless stream of men going to slaughter like cattle and coming home again ruined, underscored the futility of everything.

There was talk of discharging him in a week or two, as long as he kept making progress. The M.O. said his wound was healing nicely. He'd been lucky that it hadn't got infected. He didn't feel lucky. He'd lost a lung. It wasn't going to grow back. He was thirty but he looked fifty. He'd given up the best years of his life to fight a war, and for what? They were still killing each other over a few feet of muddy soil in Belgium and France. It was a relief to be in Blighty and know he didn't have to go back to France, but it wasn't the same as being at home. He'd had enough of being a soldier constantly ordered around. The regimented routine, the bugle calls and standing to attention for the M.O. was wearing thin. The pointlessness of it all made him angry. There were too many reminders here, too much time to think.

The rain continued to pound on the roof of the hut. Was it raining in France too? The dusty duckboards would be soaking up the water. Then the mud would begin to puddle and pool as the sides of the trenches began to slide, maybe revealing bits of the men who'd been buried there years before. Soldiers would be huddled together miserably, getting wetter and wetter while trying to hold back the slippage. His men were probably behind the line now and might have some shelter, but it was no consolation. There would be men in the trenches getting soaked with the rats and the lice. There were always men in the trenches. That he wasn't one of them didn't seem like much cause for celebration. He tried once again to read the page of his book. The effort made his eyes heavy.

*

'What we need are hippos.' Dougie nodded towards a horse with only its head stuck above the mud. Its dead, staring eyes swarmed with flies. 'Or maybe an elephant or two. They like mud, don't they?'

The wheel of the limber the horse had once pulled stuck out at an angle a little way behind, but the gun was gone. It had probably been carried off, or sunk like so much else. Machine guns chattered in the distance like a forest of mad woodpeckers. Thomas was so sleep deprived it felt as if they were walking through a dream, or maybe a nightmare. They looked around nervously but kept going, in single file, along the narrow, slippery, duckboard road. It jinked and wound between muddy hillocks and a swampy mass of water-filled shell holes. Despite the falling rain, each of them was so caked in mud they could only be told apart by their size and shape. Wally, the widest, was in the lead; behind him Lofty resembled a long, muddy pole with a tin hat on top of it. Then there was tall, stocky Dougie, wiry little Joe and, finally, Thomas. The trees they'd seen on the map were supposed to give them cover, but they were nothing but smouldering, splintered stumps on jagged islands of mud. They, along with the hazy, smoke-laden sky, were reflected in lakes of dirty brown.

'Of course, the famous hippos of Passchendaele,' Wally sniggered. 'Why on earth didn't the army think of using them instead of horses? Maybe we could capture a few and tame them?'

'I don't think there are many Flanders hippos left.' Joe acted as if this conversation was completely normal. Perhaps they were all losing their minds? 'The Hun have eaten so many they're almost extinct, and any still alive have probably got more sense than to be in this godforsaken hole waiting to be shot or blown to smithereens.'

'Mind you, I imagine it'd make the Hun think they'd gone mad if they saw a whole load of hippos and elephants coming towards them pulling guns.' Thomas chuckled at the idea.

Dougie turned to Joe and opened his mouth to say something, but he lost his footing on the slimy boards and skidded off the makeshift road, across the mud and straight into a huge water filled shell hole the size of a lake. 'Shit,' he said, as he struggled to clamber out of the sucking mud and crawl back to the relative safety of the boards.

For a moment or two, Joe kept laughing. Then he understood the danger and the smile froze on his face. The sides of the hole were too slippery. The more Dougie struggled and scrabbled, the further he sank into the stinking, soupy mud. It was like quicksand. His eyes were now wide and desperate.

'Don't just stand there, help me,' he screamed.

Joe knelt and tried to reach out to him, but he'd slid too far from the boards. If he leaned any further, he'd end up in the shell hole too. Lofty knelt and reached out his rifle. Joe, Wally and Thomas clasped him around the waist and legs to stop him sliding too. They could barely see for the rain running down their faces. Dougie grasped the rifle tip. For a split second it looked as if they'd be able to drag him out and would be laughing again in a minute or two. But Dougie's hands were so thick with the slimy mud he couldn't hold on. As the rifle slipped from his grip he sank deeper still.

If only there were more of them, or they had a rope. They'd split into smaller groups to make them less of a target for the shells on this open terrain. Now the others were far ahead. In desperation, Lofty stretched flat and, with Thomas, Wally and Joe anchoring his feet to the boards, shimmied, lizard like, across the mud. Finally, he reached out and managed to grasp Dougie's hand. Despite already beginning to sink himself, he pulled with all his might. Dougie tried to hold onto Lofty's arms, but both of them were so coated in mud there was no purchase and he slipped away. Now only his face was above the muddy water. His eyes were wild with fear.

'Shoot me,' he pleaded. 'Just fucking shoot me. I don't want to drown.'

Thomas let go of Lofty's leg, knelt and raised his rifle. He stared into Dougie's terrified eyes. He knew firing was all he could do to help him now, but he couldn't bring himself to pull the trigger. They watched in horror as Dougie finally sank. The muddy liquid gurgled and writhed for a moment, and then there was nothing but the circular ripples of rain hitting the water. Without a sign Dougie had ever been there, the whole thing felt like a mass hallucination.

*

The book thudded to the floor and Thomas woke with a start. He could still see Dougie's pleading eyes. Would he have felt any better if he'd pulled the trigger?

'Corporal Brodrick, sleeping on the job, as always.'

It was Joe's voice. He must still be dreaming. When he turned towards the sound, there was Joe sitting beside his bed as if he'd stepped right out of the dream. Only he was completely free of mud, wearing hospital blues and had his left arm in a sling. Thomas rubbed his eyes, but Joe was still there. He looked a little pale and even thinner than he had the last time he'd seen him.

'What the hell are you doing here?'

He rubbed his eyes again then swung his legs over the side of the bed and vigorously shook Joe's hand.

'Well, you didn't send so much as a postcard, so we thought one of us had better get ourselves a Blighty wound and come to check up on you. I drew the short straw, obviously. Typical to find you soundo and snoring like ten men sawing wood. I swear the windows were rattling.'

'So, what happened to you?' He still couldn't quite believe Joe was really there.

'Took some shrapnel in the shoulder and arm,' Joe said, as if it was nothing much. 'The arm's broken but the shoulder wasn't too bad, until it got infected. It's a bit of a mess now. They think it was shrapnel from a gas shell, although I didn't see any gas or smell it, thank God. Whatever it was, it got into the wound, and it keeps going bad. They open it up and clean it out every time, but I'm not sure if they'll be able to patch it up and send me back eventually or not. Frankly, I'm rather hoping not, although they wouldn't let me bring Ruby with me.'

'I should bloody well think not. If I never see another rat again . . .'

'What, you mean there aren't any here? That's it, I demand to be sent back right now.' Joe laughed briefly, then winced as his shoulder began to hurt.

'How are all the lads?'

'We blasted the hell out of the Hun after you got hit. It

seemed only right to get a bit of revenge. Hopefully, that bastard sniper bought it. They made Wally up to corporal, and a right pain in the rear he is too. The lads were going to get a petition together to get you back, wounded or not. We were just about to go back to the reserve trench when I got hit. The hospital had more cases of flu than real injuries. Apparently, even the Kaiser has caught it. Let's hope he spreads it about a bit amongst his men, eh?'

'Is it still quiet?'

'There was nothing much doing really, just the odd shell coming over. It was my bad luck to get on the wrong end of it. Well, mine and that little mademoiselle's, she's probably still waiting for me in the village.' Joe gave Thomas a cheeky wink. 'Lots of extra ammo is being brought in, though, more and more every day. There's something big coming, probably in the next couple of weeks I'd say. It really feels like it might be the final push.'

'How many times have we said that?'

'I know, but this really does feel different. Jerry's been so quiet, at least in our section. It's almost like they've given up already. The bastards had us on the run in spring, but even though they gained a lot of ground they couldn't break us. I think they've lost the stomach for it now.'

14 - Thursday 18 July 1918

It was a wrench to leave the big electric fan in the shoe shop and step back into the heat of the street. The air was so thick Mary could have cut it with a bread knife. Freda trotted along happily staring at her new red shoes with their shiny silver buckles, but Mary found every step an effort. The thunder in the night had done little to clear the air and the huge hailstones pounding against the bedroom window had kept her awake. There were a few moments when she'd worried the glass would break. This morning, the sky was the pale blue of a starling's egg, but it pressed down heavily with a suffocating humidity. Now she was tired and had little patience when Freda wanted to stop and stare at the statue on the Titanic Engineers' Memorial. She was convinced it was a giant fairy and could only be persuaded to move when Mary gave her a farthing to put through the bars of the bird aviary. A magpie perched on the wire of the roof and watched jealously, as if it wished it could be inside to collect the shiny coins.

Mary waited while Freda chattered away to all the birds. There was a little shade here and she wasn't exactly keen to get back into the sun. Idly, she wondered how much a giant fan would cost. Then she saw Hetty a little way off near the back of the bank. She was talking to a stout man in an expensive-looking suit and bowler hat. Was he one of the people she cleaned for? They seemed to be having an animated conversation. When the man turned his head, she recognised William

Wells's ruddy cheeks and the dark moustache, waxed to upturned points. What was Hetty doing arguing with Zillah's son? From this distance, she couldn't hear what they were saying, but William was obviously extremely angry. He grabbed Hetty's arm roughly and pulled her along the path towards the sundial. He worked in the bank they'd been behind. Maybe he didn't want to be seen with her. Hetty pulled her arm away and Mary swore she saw William put something in her hand. It looked like an envelope, but Hetty shoved it into her pocket before she could tell for sure. What on earth was going on? Moments later, Hetty marched off towards the street. William watched her angrily for a minute then disappeared through the back door of the bank.

By now, Freda was bored with the birds. She pulled at Mary's sleeve and sang, 'Two ickle dickie birds sitting on the wall.' Mary couldn't get what she'd seen out of her head. Was it something to do with the sugar and the cakes Zillah always had in her larder, or had Hetty told the truth when she said she knew something about William? Was she threatening him in some way, and what was in the envelope he'd given her? She'd thought getting involved with the black market and the strange gypsy man was dangerous, but this was much worse. William was a powerful bank manager and not very pleasant at the best of times. His mother was Hetty's landlady. She could end up out on the street.

It seemed hotter than ever once they left the cool green park with its avenue of trees. What she'd seen went round and round in her head and made her dizzy. Freda soon began to grizzle. Because of the storm she'd been awake half the night too. Mary picked her up and carried her. The sticky little body against hers made her even hotter, but they didn't have far to go now. She could see the gasometers in the distance and the crisscross metalwork of the railway bridge. Typically, a few yards from their house, Freda decided she wanted to walk. Then she wanted to show Alice her new shoes. Mary had cleaning to do, but by now she was so hot and tired that all she wanted was to sit down and have a cup of tea. Wondering if Alice would help her solve the Hetty mystery, she knocked on her door.

'Auntie Alice, look at my new shoes.' Freda did a little dance on the doorstep.

'How lovely.'

Although she'd tried to make her voice jolly, Alice had a slumped look about her and her eyes were red and puffy, as if she'd been crying. Something had happened, something bad.

'Alice, what's wrong?' Mary had a sinking feeling in her stomach.

'Oh, Mary.' Alice took her hands. She was trembling. 'I've had the most awful morning.'

'Is it Harry?' If something had happened to Harry, Thomas would be devastated.

'No, my love, not Harry.' She closed her eyes and shook her

head, as if trying to shake away some unwelcome image. 'Come inside. I don't want to talk about it here.'

Once they got into the scullery, Alice gave Freda two apples and sent her out into the garden to give one to Harold. Whatever she had to say, she obviously didn't want her to hear.

'It was Vera. I was about to clean the step this morning when I heard someone screaming in the street. Vera was standing in the middle of the road shouting, "Help me, help me." Of course, I went out, but at first I couldn't get any sense out of her. She just kept wailing, tearing at her hair and asking me to help her.'

'What was wrong with her?'

'It was her son, Timmy.'

Alice suddenly realised she hadn't even put the kettle on. She took it to the sink and turned on the tap, but then forgot what she was doing and washed her hands instead.

'What about him?'

Mary took the kettle from the draining board. It was already full, so she put it on the range.

'She said she went to wake him up this morning and found him dead. I thought she must be mistaken so I took her inside and went to check. Oh, Mary, it was horrible. His face was all . . . it was a kind of purplish black. I've never seen anything like it. She said he went to bed last night feeling a bit rough and just didn't wake up. He was only fourteen, her only child.'

'The poor, poor woman.'

'She said it must be flu, just like her husband. But did you ever hear of flu turning someone purple? Or killing them overnight?'

'No.'

Mary took the cups out of the cupboard, spooned the tea into the pot and put everything onto a tray. She'd watched Alice make tea enough times to know where everything was kept, and Alice clearly wasn't capable of making it herself at the moment.

'If it's flu, it's a very strange kind of flu. It scared me, Mary, really scared me. I got her mother – she lives just around the corner in Summers Street, and then I came indoors and scrubbed myself. I scrubbed so hard my hands were raw. I didn't touch the boy . . . I didn't even go right into the room, but I was so afraid that whatever it was – the germ – might be on my hands. Then I scrubbed everything in the house that I might have touched; the door handles, the gate, even things I knew I hadn't touched. I even changed my clothes. My God, Mary, it was just the most horrific thing.'

Alice had a small bottle of brandy at the back of her kitchen cabinet. She kept it for medicinal purposes and Christmas cakes. Mary poured a good measure and made Alice drink it. She screwed up her face at the taste, but the colour slowly returned to her cheeks.

Then Mary finished making the tea. Brandy and tea, the cure for everything. The children were still in the garden playing. Mary and Alice sat in the parlour, watched them through the window and talked about everything but the events of the morning. It all sounded so gruesome, and even Mary didn't want to think about it, so she did all she could to distract poor Alice.

'Did you know Katie has been writing to my brother Willy?'

'Our Katie, Harry's sister?'

'Yes. My sister Lib told me about it. I have no idea how she knows because Willy never writes to us and barely writes to Mum, but you know Lib, she should have been a detective. She finds out everything about everyone.'

'So, do you think . . . ?'

'They're secretly courting? Yes I do.' Mary poured out another cup of tea. 'Sorry, I couldn't find any cake. You really must give me the recipe for that carrot and beetroot one.'

'I wonder what Esther would make of that?'

'The cake?' It was a weak attempt at a joke.

'No, Katie and Willy.' Finally, Alice smiled again. A little tea and brandy, some gossip and a feeble joke had done the trick.

'I think it's more about what Elijah will make of it. Katie's the apple of his eye. I'm not sure he'll think my brother is good enough for her.'

'The Prince of Wales wouldn't be good enough as far as Elijah is concerned. Esther will talk him round, though. He's your brother after all, and you're her favourite daughter-in-law.'

'Don't be silly, she likes you just as well.'

'She does not! She's never forgiven me for the shotgun wedding. As if it was all my fault and Harry played no part in it. In her eyes, I'll always be a fallen woman who trapped her perfect son into marriage. It could be worse, though, I could be Martha.'

'It's not Martha's fault, though, not really. She'd marry Hariph in a heartbeat if she could. She told me that.'

'It's a sad state of affairs.'

'You'd think there'd be something she could do . . .'

Mary was cut short by a loud clap of thunder. She and Alice ran out into the garden to get Freda and Harold inside, just as the first fat spots of rain began to fall.

15 - Saturday 20 July 1918

When Thomas left the hut, he didn't look back once. He could scarcely remember the last time he'd worn civilian clothes, and they felt alien to him. There was a stink of mothballs about everything, and the fine worsted fabric seemed insubstantial after the rough wool of his uniform and the hospital blues. The dark grey jacket and trousers were a little crumpled from the bag Mary had carried them in, as was the white shirt, but any creases would soon fall out. The shirt was loose around the collar, and, without braces, the trousers might not have stayed up. He'd obviously lost weight since 1914, but that was hardly a surprise given the army diet and all the marching. Once he'd buttoned the waistcoat and put the jacket on, he did at least look more like his old self, even if he didn't feel it. They'd offered him a new suit, but to his mind, the alternative of fifty-two shillings and sixpence was more useful. He almost forgot about the Silver War Badge, but Nurse Macklin reminded him.

'Oh, Thomas, don't you look fine. Let me just help you pin this on, you don't want to be getting any white feathers.'

Impatiently, he watched the despotic sister fuss as she took inventory of the hospital blues and all the other items he had to return. She blustered and frowned and counted everything at least twice, disappointed to find nothing lost or damaged. He was glad to be rid of it all. Finally, after she'd ticked countless boxes and he'd signed enough forms to satisfy her, she gave him a wealth of pieces of paper, including a train ticket and a ration book. Then he was free to go. If the woman had managed a smile her face would probably have cracked. He'd be glad to see the back of her, too, but he was almost sad to say goodbye to the nurses. They really were angels.

He smiled when he found Mary, Eric and Freda on the veranda outside the hut. Freda, surrounded by a group of young nurses, danced to show off her new shoes, clapped her hands and sang, 'Mary, Mary, little fairy, cows in the garden go.'

A little away from them, Joe was kneeling beside Eric in the middle of a story about that first Christmas in the trenches.

'. . . So we climbed up out of the trench into No Man's Land, a bit slow and careful like, in case it was a trap, and they'd start shooting at us. They didn't, though. We all shook hands and swapped a few souvenirs.' He reached into his pocket and pulled out a brass button with a crown on it. Eric's eyes nearly popped out of his head. 'This came off a German soldier's tunic. I swapped him for one of mine, like a good luck charm it was.'

'Was my Pappy there?' Eric asked.

'Your Pappy was the first one over the top, my lad. He went to check it was safe for the rest of us.'

Mary saw him first. She took one look at him and her chin began to tremble. Was it because he looked terrible or because he looked good? She kissed him on the lips, linked her arm through his and said jauntily, 'Come on, Mr Brodrick, we have a train to catch.'

How strange to be called Mr after all this time. It underlined his departure from army life, even though he was technically on final leave so not quite officially free of all things military. He took Freda's little hand and, with Eric marching ahead, walked away from the hospital and the army and into the real world.

Joe walked with them to the train station, not the one where the wounded were unloaded, but the civilian station on the edge of the village. After all, Thomas was effectively now a civilian.

'Just to make sure you really go,' Joe said, as they ambled past all the little cottages. 'I wish I was coming on the train with you. I'm pretty sure they're going to send me back to the front. They say my bones are knitting and my shoulder feels much better now. I think it's finally healing. If I'm lucky, I might get another few weeks.'

'It doesn't seem fair to send you back when you've been wounded,' Mary said.

Did she believe a wounded man would be allowed to just go home, having paid his dues to king and country, even if he was healed and fit for action? If that had been the case, there'd be hardly anyone left at the front. Joe had been crocked twice before, though admittedly not seriously enough to get him sent back to England. If he was lucky this would be his last wound.

'I wish you were in charge of the army,' Joe chuckled. 'I'm going to try and swing it as long as I can and lay it on thick. You never know, if I can hold out a bit longer it might all be over before I get back. The French and the Yanks made short work of halting the Hun on the Marne this week. They knew exactly what Jerry was up to and drove him back straight off. This big push we've all been waiting for looks like it might be starting.'

It was all anyone had talked about in the hut. Rumour had it the Allies had known the enemy were about to push forward, right down to the exact place and date. Maybe they had spies in the German camp? No one knew for sure, but it sounded as if the Hun were on the back foot. Thomas hoped it was true, but you could never believe what the newspapers said. They were more interested in keeping morale up than actually reporting facts. They'd even made the Somme sound like a victory. From where he'd stood it had seemed anything but. Thomas shook the thoughts from his head. He would rather not think about the war at all. Memories crowded in enough as it was.

He bade a sad farewell to Joe outside the station, with lots of hand shaking and back patting. He wouldn't miss the army, the trenches or the incessant shelling in the slightest, but he did miss the men, and Joe was probably the last of them he'd see now until they came home. *If* they came home.

'You take care of yourself, mate,' he said to Joe. 'Keep out of it for as long as you can and, if you do end up back there, keep your bloody head down.'

'Well, I certainly won't be hanging any washing out, that's for sure,' Joe winked.

'Cheeky blighter.' Thomas pretended to punch him in the shoulder. 'I'll try to visit you when I can. Just make sure you write to let me know what's happening. I'll be mad as hell if I come all this way and find you've gone back over there. If that happens, I might have to come and track you down in France to give you a piece of my mind.'

Then, with one final wave, Thomas turned and took Mary, Eric and Freda through the door of the station.

*

A woman dressed in a black wool coat and a stationmaster's hat glanced at the ticket he'd been given amongst all the paperwork. Mary showed her return tickets and they walked onto the platform just as the train arrived. It must be their lucky day. It all happened so quickly. He was sitting on the train before he realised that the woman dressed up as a stationmaster actually *was* the stationmaster. He could hardly believe it. Had the world really changed so much since he'd been away that women were in charge of the railways?

16 - Sunday 21 July 1918

The deafening noise shook him awake. The ground beneath him vibrated like the skin of a drum. He sprang up, hit his head, then fumbled around in the dark for his helmet and rifle as debris fell from the roof of the makeshift dugout. They'd marched half the night, dug in as best they could in the mud and piled up soggy sandbags to build these funk holes in the rubble of Eagle Trench. Then they'd all but fallen asleep on their feet. Now, barely aware of where he was, the wall of noise added to the confusion. Howitzer and mortar shells burst continuously. The Hun were hitting them from all sides of the salient; salvo after salvo of heavy shells. He crawled from the funk hole. There was no time to think of anything but getting out before the whole lot caved in and became his grave.

Mist swirled around. The cacophony of sound and scent – damp earth, sharp, sweet cordite and rotting flesh – overloaded his senses. The dark shapes of men appeared and disappeared. Bright flashes of starburst shells illuminated frightened, disoriented faces, and the darkness that followed them seemed even darker. Mouths moved but the ferocious noise stole away their words. Was this the end? Would the war be lost here in some godforsaken part of Flanders, or wherever it was they actually were? Had all those men died for nothing?

*

'Tom . . . Tom . . . Thomas!' Someone shook his arm. The men faded away and were replaced by solid walls, a thinly curtained sash window and Mary's white face in the darkness. 'It's just thunder, come back to bed.'

Another flash and crash made him jump. The hairs on his arms stood to attention. He sat down on the side of the bed and put his head in his hands. He had no memory of getting up. Had he been sleepwalking? Mary put her arms around him. He sank into her warmth.

'Sorry, I was dreaming . . .'

How could he explain the horror? She could never understand, and he wouldn't want her to. The things he'd seen, and done. She shouldn't have to carry that burden.

He got back into bed and curled around her. After years of sleeping squashed into a dugout with unwashed men, it was peculiar to share a bed with his wife. Her soft hair tickled his face. He inhaled her scent, soap and flowers, and slowly relaxed. The storm still raged outside, further away now. Blue-white light permeated his closed eyelids and he heard a rumbling growl and then rain thrashing against the glass. It was just a storm, but every rumble and flash made his muscles tense again. He'd been sure being at home would stop the dreams. Perhaps he was asking too much too soon, especially with the noise of the storm.

*

When the morning came, Mary said nothing about his nightmare, but he noticed her worried glances as he ate breakfast and got ready for church. The routine should have felt familiar, but it didn't. Everything was strange. The bread was chewy and almost black and there was no butter or dripping – just a thin scrape of margarine.

'What on earth is this?' He wrinkled his nose.

'It's war bread. They put potatoes in it to make the flour go further.'

'Isn't there any dripping? it might be edible if there were?'

'The meat ration wasn't enough to make dripping. It was lucky the butcher even had any meat.'

'Crikey, we got better food in the trenches.'

Eric asked incessant questions about the war and being shot. Freda, like a little stranger, chattered away in a language he barely understood, and Mary bustled about doing things she probably always did, things he had no part in. His Sunday suit felt as if it belonged to someone else. The house wasn't quite as he remembered it, either. The smell of coal, soap, lavender and a hint of vinegar seemed different, but he didn't know how. Nothing was where he thought it would be, but he couldn't tell if it was because he'd remembered wrong or because Mary had moved things while he was at war. Most of all he felt as if he was in the way. There was nothing for him to do, no orders to obey. All he'd wanted was to be home, but instead of floating on cloud nine, he felt faintly despondent and lost.

Then the woman from next door called round. He didn't know Hetty well. She'd moved in not long before he went off to France, though Mary had often mentioned her in her letters to him, so he felt he knew her. Quite frankly, he didn't much care for what he'd heard. In real life she was all hips and mouth, not much taller than Mary, with a chest as flat as a pancake.

'How lovely for Mary to have you home,' she smiled.

Her child stared up at him with his mouth open, as if he wasn't quite the full shilling. Thomas was dismayed to discover she and the child would be walking to church with them, along with Alice's next-door neighbour, Effie, her docker husband and their three young children. He'd imagined it would just be the four of them. If it had been Alice and her boys, he wouldn't have minded, but Mary said Alice didn't go to church anymore.

The walk might have been pleasant. The world had been

washed clean by the storm. The flowers were perky and vivid in the little gardens they passed. Without the awful humidity of the last few days, the heady scent of damp earth and roses hung in the air. He was proud to have Mary on his arm, to hold Freda's tiny hand and to have Eric marching in front, with his chin up and his shoulders back like a little soldier. The docker, Charlie, was a burly man a few years younger than him, with thick, dark brows and a harassed look. In another life they might have been friends, but they had nothing in common and Charlie was too busy trying to control his three young boys to talk. There looked to be barely a year between any of them, and they were quite a handful. Hetty wittered on the whole time while her child sullenly dragged his feet and constantly looked sideways at him.

'You know Norah Thorne has gone back to work as a typist in Winstanley's office. Her husband's hardly cold and she's acting as if she'd never married. It's disrespectful, that's what it is.'

Thomas had no idea who Hetty was talking about, but so far, he hadn't heard a good word about anyone.

'She's probably working because she needs the money,' Mary said.

'Well, she has money coming in from the army pension, which is more than I got, and I managed to wear respectable mourning clothes. If her skirt was much shorter, you'd be able to see the frills on the bottom of her knickers.' Hetty pursed her lips.

'I think these shorter skirts look nice, and they're much more practical,' Effie said. 'It's the twentieth century. Women in the factories are even wearing trousers, and why shouldn't they?'

'Well, I don't hold with it. Widows should wear respectable mourning clothes and women shouldn't dress like men – it isn't proper.' Hetty looked away sulkily.

'I suppose you don't think they should have the bloody vote, either?' Effie snapped.

'I think some of us have more pressing matters to worry about than voting,' Hetty snapped back. 'All this suffrage stuff is missing the point. It's not votes we need, it's equality and fairness. I mean, why should we have to stop work when we marry? Why should we get paid so much less?'

'Being able to vote means the men in charge will have to listen to us,' Effie said.

'But none of us is over thirty, so we can't vote anyway.' Hetty smirked as if she'd scored a point. 'And whether we can or can't, it's men making all the rules, rich men at that. Until that changes, they will get away with doing whatever they want, like they always have. The vote doesn't help women like me at all. It doesn't put money in my pocket or food on my table.'

'I'd like to know what does,' Effie muttered

None of it was remotely interesting. As far as Thomas could

tell, it was all a lot of gossip and complaining. By the time they reached the top of the road, he had concluded he didn't like Hetty or her child at all.

When the church came into view, his mind overlaid it with the ruined church at Albert. He saw the golden statue of the virgin leaning at an impossible angle from the top of the shell-raddled bell tower. He shook his head to clear the image. The virgin had fallen in the spring, but he hadn't seen it, so in his mind it still hung there, a monument to the stupidity of the war.

Thomas's neighbour and her bank manager son said good morning on the church steps. Zillah's face said she was pleased to see him and wanted to chat, but the son hustled her off quickly. With his curly black moustache and gold watch chain, he looked like a pompous arse. Mary said the motorcar parked on the corner was his. Looking at his fat gut, it might have done him good to walk to church, but he probably just wanted to show off.

Winstanley the solicitor, a large black crow of a man, Beeston the undertaker and McCormack the police inspector were also gathered on the steps with a group of other well-dressed men he didn't recognise. The banker, solicitor, policeman and undertaker were in their forties or fifties, but the other men were all far younger. As they passed, he caught the end of a joke.

'. . . a Gladstone collar, would you believe.'

This incomprehensible punch line was followed by a braying

laugh from the young fops. They paid him no attention, but he felt
the anger rising inside him. Why were these shallow young men not
at the front fighting for their country? How had they escaped the
horror and the death and stayed at home in their comfortable lives
and fancy mock military suits? He walked past with a curled lip and
clenched fists, stamping down the urge to punch the lot of them.
Hetty called them the 'local bourgeoisie' and muttered, 'not one of
them is any better than they should be.'

The interior of the church was all cold stone and dark
wrought iron. The sun hadn't yet made its way round to the stained-
glass window, and this added to the chill and gloom after the
brightness outside. Apart from the fops and a few local shopkeepers,
dockers and errand boys, who were all either too old or too young to
fight, the congregation was all women. And how drab they seemed,
dressed in dull blues, browns and blacks, with none of the gay
colours he remembered or the fripperies and the feathers. Their faces
seemed pale and pinched and their eyes stared at him suspiciously,
with a glint of something that could have been anger or disgust. They
thought he was a conchie, a coward. When their gaze travelled to his
right lapel and the war badge, the looks changed to pity. He wasn't
sure whether he'd rather be thought a coward or a cripple. Perhaps
the truth was he was a little of both.

17 - Monday 22 July 1918

For four long years, Mary had dreamed of having Thomas safely home, but it hadn't turned out as well as she'd expected. When she filled the copper boiler for the Monday wash, her head was a fog of tiredness and worry. What with Thomas being so restless in the night, tossing and turning, throwing out arms and legs and muttering unintelligibly, sleep had been hard to come by. On Saturday night, he'd even sprung out of bed, stood at the window and shouted wildly at some unseen enemy. He was asleep but with his eyes open, and he was obviously back in the middle of the war. She couldn't cope with that happening too often. It was a wonder he hadn't woken Freda. In the morning, he acted as if nothing had happened, and she hadn't mentioned it. If he didn't remember, it was probably best she didn't remind him. He must have seen some terrible things for them to haunt his dreams so vividly.

She'd thought going to church would do him good, but he'd been somewhere between petulant and angry the whole time. Hetty, with her incessant prattle and the way she wrangled with Effie, may have played a part, and it probably didn't help that people stared when they saw a strange man out of uniform. He wasn't much better at home, though. He was like a visitor, awkward with the children, and either quiet and gloomy or irritable and on the edge of anger. He wandered about listlessly, picked things up and put them down again, read a page or two of a book, or went out into the garden and came straight back in. He couldn't settle to anything. He grumbled about the food, as if it were Mary's fault everything was rationed. She did her best with what she could get. It was as if her joking, happy husband had disappeared and been replaced by a sullen, grumpy stranger. What if the Thomas she remembered never returned?

When the copper was lit and she went back into the parlour, she found Freda perched on Thomas's lap and Eric sat cross-legged on the floor at his feet. The three of them were giggling.

'Sing the song for Mummy,' Thomas said, and Freda sang.

'It's a long way to tickle fairy

It's a long way to go

Goodbye Pickle Lily, Goodbye furry bear . . .'

'She's priceless, isn't she,' he snorted. 'We had a chap in France who made up silly songs, but he's got nothing on her.'

This was a glimpse of the old Thomas. What a relief to know he was still in there somewhere. Then Hetty knocked on the door with her basket of washing and the giggles abruptly stopped. When Hetty took Eric to school, and Thomas realised she was coming back, he got annoyed. 'She helps you do your laundry? Why would she do that, doesn't she have her own to do?'

'We do it all together. Hetty's, Alice's, Zillah's and ours. It's much quicker that way.'

'Well, she gets on my nerves.'

He sat in the chair scowling like a five-year-old in a sulk.

*

Alice was delighted to see him. She came through the back door, dumped her washing and went straight to the parlour, her face lit up with excitement. She embraced him, as if to make sure he was really there and not a figment of her imagination.

'What a sight for sore eyes you are,' she said when she finally let him go. 'It's almost as good as seeing Harry walk through the door. I'd have popped round sooner, but I wanted to give you a chance to settle in. The last thing you need is a load of visitors.'

Then Harold ran in from the garden, sat beside Freda at Thomas's feet and, with the curiosity of a three-year-old, said, 'Are you my daddy's brother? Have you finished fighting now? Did you bring your gun home?'

Alice and Mary left them to it and went back to the scullery.

'He looks awfully drawn and thin.' Alice kept her voice low so he wouldn't overhear. 'Is he really well enough to be home from hospital?'

'They say his wound has healed well and now he just has to build his strength up. I'm more worried about his mind.'

'How do you mean, his mind?' Alice frowned. 'Not shell shock or anything?'

'No. At least I don't think so. He's just not himself, as if all the things he's seen are stuck in his head, even though he's hardly said a word about the war.'

'And you haven't asked?'

'Part of me would like to know so I could understand what he's been through and why he's changed so, but talking about it might just make him remember it even more.'

'You're probably right. Harry hasn't said much about what it's like on the ship, at least not anything of any consequence. They probably don't think we'd understand or don't want to burden us. After all, we don't tell them what it's like to carry a child and give birth. We talk to each other about those things because they'd never understand.'

When Hetty came back, Thomas was teaching Harold and Freda to sing *Pack up Your Troubles* and laughing when Freda sang, 'pick up the bubbles.' As soon as he saw Hetty, his smile faded. He watched with his chin resting on his fist and a scowl on his face as she took off her jacket and hat.

'Those Jones boys were climbing all over the logs again this morning,' she grumbled, as she tied her pinafore around her waist. 'When I shouted at them, the little blighters gave me a mouthful. The cheek of them. It's only a matter of time before one of them drowns.'

'I think I'll go for a walk.' Thomas snatched up his jacket angrily and looked around for his hat. 'Shall I take Freda and Harold with me, so we can *all* keep out of your way?'

It felt like an accusation. Admittedly, Hetty could be difficult to like at times, but if he gave her a chance . . .

'He seems a bit grumpy,' Hetty said when he'd gone.

'He just needs a little time to adjust.' Mary hoped she was right. She knew she had to make allowances, but right now she thought he was being childish.

'You'd be grumpy too if someone had shot you.' Alice shook her head in exasperation.

It turned out to be a blessing that Thomas had gone out. If he'd heard some of the things Hetty said as she wrung the clothes through the mangle he'd have been embarrassed and even more set against her.

'You look tired today, Mary.' Hetty folded a bed sheet into the basket.

'I am a little.' She carried on pounding the next batch of washing. 'Thomas has been very restless in his sleep, and I've been so used to sleeping alone. I think we're both finding it difficult to adjust.'

'I wager you are,' Hetty sniggered. 'I'm surprised you got any sleep at all, after all the time he's been away. A man has appetites. I should imagine he had a lot of making up to do. Sleep being the least part.'

'Something like that.'

Mary carried on pummelling the clothes, grateful for the steamy heat to hide her blushes. She didn't want to discuss that kind of thing with anyone, especially not Hetty. She'd dreamed of Thomas being back home and sharing her bed. Their tender reunion, the long, loving kisses and the gentle but urgent intimacy had been just as she'd imagined. Afterwards, though, as he held her in his arms, her head resting against his chest, she'd felt the sobs shuddering through his body. She'd never known him to cry and, though he'd tried to hide it, it frightened her. She remembered Hetty's comment about the French women with their painted faces and black teeth. Had their lovemaking disappointed him in some way, or did his wound cause him more pain than he admitted? She'd seen the livid, cross-shaped scar on his back, slightly puckered and sore looking, and been half sad, half horrified. He said he was much better, but clearly he wasn't completely healed in body or in mind, and she had no idea how to help him with either.

18 - Monday 22 July 1918

When he stormed out of the house, Thomas had no idea where to go or what to do with two three-year-old children he barely knew. He walked aimlessly along the road with one child on each hand. Anger and resentment bubbled inside him. What was the point of being at home if that bloody woman was there all the time, wittering on and taking advantage of Mary's kindness? She even had Mary doing her washing. What kind of woman couldn't manage her own laundry? Walking to church with her was bad enough, but it wasn't right that he should be chased out of his own home. If he didn't put a stop to it somehow, he might as well be married to Hetty and Mary. Exactly how he was going to get rid of her was a question he couldn't answer.

After a while, the rhythmic steps, the weak sun on his face and the warm little hands in his began to calm him down. They strolled past Eric's school and across the valley, then climbed slowly and left the river behind. He barely registered his surroundings and gave no thought to where he was going. Instead, he thought about the things Mary had told him about Hetty. Perhaps he could find out what secrets she was hiding and somehow use them to squeeze her out of their lives? They went steadily upwards, past houses much like theirs, across junction after junction with little shops or pubs on the corner. When the straight road ran out, he turned left. He could just as easily have turned right. It was merely a whim. The houses here were slightly grander and semi-detached, with bay windows upstairs and down. He'd quite like to live in such a house, but the fifty odd shillings from the army wouldn't buy one, although maybe moving was the way to get rid of Hetty. When they came to a wide, tree-lined road, he realised his aimless wandering had taken them to The Avenue. The common was right ahead. A taxicab came clip-clopping past. They crossed the road.

Was the army encampment still at the top of the common? Harold might have liked it, but if Thomas never saw another tent or hut for the rest of his life he'd be happy, so he headed towards the boating lake. There were a few women with perambulators about, but thankfully, he saw no soldiers. Beside the lake he found a shady tree and sat down. The water was beautifully clear and still, painted with the reflection of the sky and the overhanging foliage.

'Keep away from the edge,' he told Harold, as he ran along the path with his arms outstretched.

'I'm an aeroplane,' Harold shouted back.

A family of swans floated majestically on the centre of the lake, a pen and cob with five, grey-feathered cygnets. These were the kind of scenes he'd dreamed of in the trenches. He pulled the battered packet of Woodbines from his pocket, lit one and leaned his back against the tree. He exhaled a stream of smoke, closed his eyes and inhaled the musky, earthy scent. Birds sang and the leaves gently rustled in the breeze. Slowly, the last of his anger ebbed away.

'Do fairies live here?'

Freda broke into his thoughts. She pointed to a cleft in the bottom of one of the nearby tree trunks, which almost looked as if it might be a hidden doorway.

'Perhaps.'

'I like fairies.'

Pleasant as it was to sit beside the water, watch the swans and talk about fairies and aeroplanes, they couldn't stay there all day. His cigarette was finished. Freda and Harold ran back and forth along the path, pretending to fly and look for fairies. They were restless. Reluctantly, he called them back, took their hands and headed towards home. He wasn't sure what he was going to do when he got there.

They slowly retraced their footsteps, back across the common, past the fancy houses and down the hill towards home. The neat little dwellings didn't seem as real as the ruins he'd marched past for the last four years. He imagined all the filthy French children in tattered rags and the women with their weary faces and sad eyes. The sound as a cart rattled past made him jump. If there'd been a ditch, he might well have pulled Freda and Harold into it. It took a moment or two to realise it was just the milk cart, and a moment more to notice a woman at the reins. He remembered the female stationmaster at Netley. If women had taken all the men's jobs, what were his chances of finding work at the end of his final leave?

Although he didn't know much about the alchemy of laundry,

he was sure Hetty would still be in his scullery. He didn't want to see her, and the nearer he got to his front door, the more the black mood gathered. When they turned by the timber pond he saw Zillah ahead, walking very slowly and leaning heavily on her stick.

'What a pleasant surprise,' she said when they drew level with her. 'Although you look as if you've dropped a penny and found a farthing.'

'I'm trying to keep out of the way while Mary, Alice and Hetty do the laundry,' he said.

'They won't be finished yet. Why don't you come and join me for a cup of tea?'

He followed her into her parlour. She left him while she went to make a pot of tea and find some cake. He'd never been in her house before. It was a mirror image of his own, but he was surprised by the lavishness packed so tightly into every inch; the soft, comfortable chairs and the highly polished side tables covered with hundreds of ornaments and curios. He walked around the room looking at the framed photographs on every available surface. Some were very old and faded, showing groups of people captured for posterity, perhaps Zillah's parents or even her grandparents. Most were of William at various ages; as a baby wrapped in a lace shawl, as a skinny young lad in a sailor suit, and as a young man with a serious face in a tailed suit and bow tie. The French windows were open and, while he'd been looking at the photographs, Harold had run out into the garden. Freda had gone straight to a large dolls' house in the corner of the room and was playing with the little wooden dolls.

Zillah came back, poured the tea and transferred cake onto plates.

'I love to have the children around me.' She nodded towards Freda. 'There was a time when I thought I might have grandchildren of my own, but it wasn't to be.'

'William doesn't have any children, then?'

Gossip aside, all Thomas knew about the man was that he was a bank manager and drove a motorcar.

'Sadly not. Rebecca, his wife, caught polio the summer after they married. A terrible illness. She was lucky to survive, but it left her paralysed. She was such a vibrant young thing too. It was a tragedy.'

'I'm so sorry. That must be difficult to cope with.'

He felt guilty for taking a dislike to the man based on the way he dressed and a few rumours about him keeping a mistress. If he did, perhaps it was understandable. Although he hadn't done it himself, lots of the men in France used the red lights when they had the chance. He didn't really blame them for trying to blot out reality, however briefly. They didn't consider it cheating on their wives or sweethearts, but saw it as more of a bodily function, like eating and sleeping. Maybe William felt the same, or was he trapped in a marriage he couldn't get out of, like Martha? Either way, who was he to judge the man?

'He employs a nurse to care for her, but it really is no kind of life. Sometimes, I think it might have been better if she hadn't survived, but I suppose the good Lord has a plan for all of us, even if it can sometimes seem like a very cruel one. We all have our crosses to bear. I would think you'd know more about that than most, after what you've been through. How are you feeling now? Are your wounds healing well?'

'Plenty have it a lot worse than me. I can't complain because getting shot got me home, and the rest of them are still out there.'

A vision of his friends still stuck in the filth and mayhem flashed into his head.

'You must have witnessed some terrible things in the war,' she said, as if she'd seen the vision too.

'It's best forgotten.'

He had no intention of discussing what he'd seen and done with Zillah.

'I'm sure that's easier said than done. Men like you will probably find homecoming harder than they'd expected.' She looked at him as if she could see all the confusion and dismay inside him. It was unnerving. 'Much has changed since you left, Thomas, and it's going to take some getting used to, both for you and for Mary. It hasn't been easy for her, either.'

'She seems to be doing very well without me. I feel like a hindrance. Then Hetty's there every time I turn around.'

He couldn't keep the distain out of his voice when he said her name.

'Yes,' Zillah chuckled, almost choking on her cake. 'Hetty is an acquired taste, but she means well. Despite her many faults, she's been a great help to Mary.'

'It looks to me like Mary's the one doing the helping. She was always a great one for taking in waifs and strays.'

'Hetty's been good company for Mary. She's taken her mind off worrying about you all the time.'

Zillah finished the last mouthful of cake and wiped at the corner of her mouth with a napkin.

'I can see having her moaning on with barely a breath would make it difficult to think, let alone worry, but to me it looks as if Hetty's taking advantage. She's got Mary doing her washing and looking after that son of hers all the time. He seems a bit . . . peculiar, as if he's . . .' He didn't want to say feeble minded, but he couldn't think of a kinder term.

'Awkward, fearful, shy? It's no surprise, the poor little mite. William was much the same at that age. He was small for his age, too, and the other children picked on him, not just for his size, but because he had no father. My husband Hubert was a soldier, an officer. He died when William was just a baby. Unlike George, though, we had money to soften the blow and he knew that Hubert was a brave man. He could take some pride in that. Poor George has no father, no money and nothing much to be proud of. Hetty's certainly doing everything she can to give him a chance in life. Don't judge her too harshly, Thomas.'

'That may be easier said than done,' he smiled, as he drained his teacup, 'but I promise I'll try my best.'

19 - Tuesday 23 July 1918

When Thomas got out of bed, Mary was already up, dressed and preparing breakfast. She looked worn out, a shadow of the happy, smiling wife he'd left behind in 1914. Whatever Zillah said, he laid the blame firmly at Hetty's door. Mary seemed to be doing half her work as well as her own. When he came back from the privy, she had a cup of tea and a bowl of porridge waiting for him on the kitchen table, and there was bread and scrape for Eric and Freda, but she hadn't set a place for herself.

'You need to eat too,' he said.

'There'll be time for that once I've got Eric off to school.' She was already halfway to the back door. 'I need to get the coal in and fill the range before I go.'

'But you've barely sat down since I got home.'

It was true. She'd done nothing but bustle about cooking, cleaning and tending the garden. Even when she sat down in the evening, she was busy sewing, mending or knitting. 'Why do you need to get the coal in now? Can't it wait?'

'It won't come through the door by itself,' she snapped. 'And if I don't get the coal in the range now, it won't be hot enough to do the ironing when I get back.'

It was most unlike Mary to be waspish with him. He didn't believe he deserved it. He'd only been trying to help.

While he ate his porridge, he watched her lug in the scuttle of coal and put the two flat irons on top of the range to warm. He wished there was something he could do to help, but he wasn't up to hefting coal about yet, and he wouldn't know where to start with the ironing. He felt helpless. Perhaps there was something he *could* do to help, though. He could take Eric to school to save her the job, and he could look after Freda while she worked. He had a lot of ground to make up with the children, and now was his chance.

Mary seemed pleased enough when he suggested the idea, and Eric was so excited he barely finished his breakfast, and he was dressed and ready to go in a flash. This suited Thomas. If they left early, they could avoid Hetty and her child. Whatever Zillah said, he felt no sympathy for the woman, and he certainly didn't want to spend time with her if he didn't have to. The morning air was chilly. Thomas was glad he'd wrapped a muffler around Eric's neck before they left and sorry he'd forgotten to wrap one around his own.

'Shall we wait for George and Gordon?' Eric asked when they came to the bridge.

The streets were still empty and, much as he'd hoped to avoid Hetty, he could see Eric was disappointed that none of his friends were around to see him with his pappy.

'If you like.'

'Did Granny or Gramps walk you to school?'

'No, son, Gramps was at work at the blanket factory and Granny had her spinning and weaving to do, along with all the housework. I used to go alone. At least until Uncle Hariph was old enough to start school.'

'Gordon walks on his own, but Mummy worries about the railway line. She thinks I won't use the bridge. Did you have to cross the railway when you were a boy?'

'There were no railways near our house, but sometimes I cadged a lift up the hill on the milkman's cart, or, better still, the baker's. If I was very lucky, the baker's man might give me a bun.'

'You were a baker's man before you went to war, weren't you?'

'I was.'

'Were you allowed to eat all the buns and cakes you wanted?'

'No, son, the baker's wife counted them very carefully and I had to account for them all. If I wanted to eat one, I had to pay for it just like everyone else.'

'Oh, I thought I might like to be a baker's man when I grow up, but perhaps I shan't if you're not allowed to eat the buns.'

'So, what else do you think you might like to be?'

'I don't know.' Eric wrinkled his nose, as he tried to decide. 'Perhaps I could fly an aeroplane or maybe look after birds, like the men who train the carrier pigeons. I think I should like that because I like birds. Did you see the carrier pigeons in the trenches, Pappy?'

'We sometimes did, son, and very brave birds they were too.'

There was still no sign of any other children. Thomas grasped for something to keep Eric's interest. There was a story about a pigeon. He wasn't sure if it was true, but Eric didn't need to know that. 'One bird at Passchendaele was especially brave. It was on the Menin Road. The infantry had captured a huge German dugout, along with scores of German prisoners. The only problem was, our own artillery was firing on us because they believed we were Germans, and the Germans were firing on us because they knew we weren't. We had to get a message back to headquarters, so they'd know to stop shooting, and that was where the carrier pigeon came in.'

'Did you release him, Pappy? What was his name?' Eric's eyes were like saucers.

'No, I didn't release him, and I'm afraid I didn't know his name.'

He didn't know because he hadn't been on the Menin Road at all. His abiding memory of Passchendaele was of struggling to pull poor Dougie out of the mud, but that wasn't a story he'd ever want to tell Eric, or anyone else for that matter. Instead, he told his son how the pigeons went by numbers, just like the soldiers, and how they had special handlers who carried them around in wicker baskets. Then he explained how the messages were folded up and put in tiny cylinders attached to the pigeon's legs.

'It was about nine miles or so to the headquarters, and it should have taken this pigeon less than five and twenty minutes. In the end, it took him almost a whole day to get back to his loft because a German sniper shot him, and he was badly wounded.'

'Just like you were wounded, Pappy?'

'Oh, much worse than I was wounded, son. He'd had his little leg shot away and was in a terrible state, but he kept right on flying because he knew he had to get his message through. They found him on the floor of the loft, or so they say, close to death, but still carrying his message. That message saved many men.'

By this time, several other children had arrived, including Thomas's nephew, Gordon, and he found he had an audience hanging on his every word.

'Are you Eric's Pa?' one of the older boys asked.

'I am.'

'Were you in the trenches?'

'I was.'

'And you got shot, like Eric says?'

'I did.'

Then Hetty arrived and all the children ran over the bridge. Eric was in the middle of a knot of lads. Right at the back of the group was Hetty's son, George. He was one of the smallest children there, and he was completely alone. He dragged his feet and looked down at them miserably. It was piteous to see the lad like that. It wasn't his fault he had Hetty for a mother, or that his father had died. Perhaps Zillah was right, and he should try harder to be kind to the boy, even if he couldn't manage to feel kindly towards his mother. Now there was no way to escape walking back with her. Thank goodness it was such a short walk. She gabbled on the whole time about queues for food and the big pile of ironing waiting for her at home.

'There's always so much of it, and standing for so long makes my back ache. I do suffer so with my back. If men had to put up with ironing, I'm sure one of them would have invented a machine to do it by now, or fabric that doesn't crease . . .' she went on and on.

He tried his best to tune her out. What did he care about her and her silly problems?

They'd passed the timber pond, where a few straggling schoolboys skimmed stones and dared each other to walk out on the floating logs, when he saw Miss Newman cycling down the opposite side of the road towards them, her Dalmatian dog running along behind. Thomas tipped his hat. She waved back at them but didn't stop to talk. He knew her from his old baker's round. She usually said hello when their paths crossed, although now her wave was probably for Hetty rather than him. Her job was to visit the Titanic widows all over the town. There must be quite a few around here, although he didn't know where. Most of them kept themselves to themselves. Some of the widows saw Miss Newman as a kindly friend, others believed she was a Mansion House spy plotting to stop their money. He braced himself for Hetty to offer some opinion, probably not a kind one, but she'd gone suddenly silent. He turned to her. She was red in the face and looked as if she'd been caught out in something. Whatever it was, it involved Miss Newman. Next time he bumped into her, Thomas would have to see if he could find out more.

20 - Wednesday 24 July 1918

Understandably, the little Wednesday knitting club had been disbanded, but there was still work to do. The lavender Mary and Alice had harvested had dried well, despite the changeable weather. Now it was ready to be put into bags. It was one of the more pleasant chores they usually shared. Smiling, sensible Alice was enough to cheer anyone up, so Mary suggested Thomas might like to come along too. He'd always got on well with Alice. Besides, it would get them both out of the house.

'Lavender bags? I hardly think I'd be any use with those.'

He had the look of a child who'd been told to come inside for dinner.

'I wasn't expecting you to help fill the bags. I just thought you'd like to spend some time with Alice. She hardly had a chance to talk to you on Monday. She's been terribly worried about you.'

Alice wasn't the only one. Thomas tried hard to be helpful, and he put on a cheerful face, especially with the children, but Mary saw his suppressed anger and the dark looks. His mind was on the war and his friends still out there fighting. If he'd only talk to her about it, she might be able to help, or at least understand, but the few tentative questions she'd asked had been met with short, sharp replies. Before the war he'd had work to keep him busy, but he wasn't well enough yet to look for a job, and it was clear that most of the time he didn't know what to do with himself. He walked Eric to school and took Freda with him when he went out, but it hardly filled his days.

'I thought I might go and see Joe.'

'You can visit Joe any time.'

Mary tried hard not to sound like his mother. He'd barely left the hospital, so why was he so eager to go back? He must have noticed her irritation because he agreed to go with her to Alice's. His face said he'd rather not, though. Perhaps he felt guilty about Harry, still out at sea while he was safely at home.

*

Alice flounced around him, took his hand and led him into the parlour, plumped the cushions on the old chintz armchair and even pulled up a footstool for his feet. Thomas looked embarrassed by all the fuss. The dining table was already set out with all the makings of the lavender bags. A big bowl of dried flower heads sat in the centre and filled the room with their fragrance. The two women got to work, sewing oddments of sheets too old to be turned and dresses too worn to repair into bags to stuff with the dried flowers. They had a pot of tea and a trench cake Alice had made from the government recipe. It had the slightly Christmassy taste of spices and fruit but wasn't quite as nice as the carrot and beetroot cake. Thomas fell on it eagerly enough but stayed firmly planted in the armchair with Freda on his lap and Harold at his feet. To keep them amused, he told them a funny tale about a stubborn mule loaded with food supplies and how all the hungry soldiers had had to push and pull to coax him to move. Then the mule had changed his mind and run off at top speed, with all the men chasing after him. Once the tale was over, the children got bored and ran out into the garden to play.

Alice poured more tea and tried to make conversation with Thomas. 'What do you think about the Russian Tsar being shot by the Bolsheviks? Will it make any difference to the war?'

'He was a tyrant, or so they say,' Thomas shrugged, 'and the Bolsheviks have already signed a treaty with Germany.'

'Do you think the Germans might use it as an excuse to rip the treaty up? After all, his wife was German.'

'From what I hear, they have enough on their hands on the Western Front, and the Russians are too busy fighting amongst themselves like the traitors they are.'

His answers were so curt she soon gave up and left him alone.

'How's Vera now?' Mary carefully spooned lavender into the bag she'd just finished. 'Have you seen her?'

'She's come down with the flu, too, or so her mother says. She went to stay with her and she's recovering slowly, but she's refused to go back to the house, or even go outside. I don't blame her. I can't bear to think about that morning, seeing the poor lad like that.'

Alice put down the bag she was sewing and suppressed a shudder. 'He was such a cheery thing. He'd just started work at the docks and had his whole life ahead of him. I can't imagine how she must feel. We all worry about our men being at war, but she thought hers were safe working at the docks. To have her husband die of something as trivial as flu, and then her son so quickly afterwards . . .'

'Are they sure it was really flu?' Mary wrinkled her nose. 'It was so quick. It almost sounds like some kind of poisoning, or maybe a gas escape. You said the poor child's face was purple, perhaps he suffocated?'

'One of the chaps at the hospital died like that.' Thomas made them jump. They'd forgotten he was there. 'Most of them played it down and tried to hush it up, but one of the nurses told me it was flu, and by all accounts they've had quite a few cases.'

'Why do they want to hush it up?' Alice asked.

'I think they're afraid it'll cause panic and disrupt the war effort. They can't afford to lose public support. Look what happened in Russia.'

'That wouldn't happen here, though, surely?' Alice frowned. 'British people wouldn't riot and revolt.'

'They might. Half the French infantry mutinied after the Aisne. Anyway, it sounds as if there's another big push coming, and they don't want soldiers to be worrying about getting sick, or their families at home getting sick. How would they ever recruit new ones to replace the dead?'

'But would flu kill someone that quickly?' Mary still couldn't believe it. 'Vera's husband went to bed feeling a little off colour and was dead before morning. Her son was the same.'

'The chap in the bed next to me went exactly like that. Geoffrey, his name was. The day before, he was chatting away nineteen to the dozen, and he was perfectly healthy when he went to sleep. In the morning, he had a temperature, so they took him off to the isolation ward and he was dead by the afternoon. A lot of the men were talking about it. There were similar stories about other hospitals, and even a school in Scotland. The nurse I talked to said it was Spanish flu, the same as we had in the trenches in the spring. Remember, Mary?'

'I remember you writing to tell me you'd had the flu, but you said it wasn't bad at all, just a few days' rest in the hospital.'

'Well, this nurse thinks it's the same thing, only much worse. She was quite worried about it. She said she was glad she didn't have to work in the isolation ward. If this chap worked at the docks, he might have caught it there. After all, the sick and wounded come in on ships.'

'Arthur's job was taking the wounded men off the ships,' Alice said. 'He couldn't join up because he lost an eye when he was a boy, but he was proud to be helping the war effort. Perhaps that's how he caught it.'

'If it spreads about anything like the way it did in the trenches, we're all going to have to watch out.' Thomas put down his teacup with a frown. 'Although it's unlikely to be too bad for most people, unless they're old or sick.'

'But how can we avoid it?' Mary didn't like the sound of this flu at all, especially not the idea of people dropping dead before they really knew they were ill.

'I don't know.' Thomas shook his head sadly. 'I suppose it's just like any other flu, all we can really do is hope we don't catch it. In the trenches, we all kept our heads down and hoped the next shell didn't have our name on it, and I suppose this is much the same, only there's less chance of catching the flu than there is of getting killed in a trench.'

It was the most he'd ever said about the war, and the image of him sat in a dirty hole in the ground hoping he didn't get blown up was powerful. This flu sounded disturbing, but Thomas was right, worrying wasn't going to help. The trouble was, worrying was the one thing Mary was really good at, and she wasn't sure she knew how to stop.

21 - Thursday 25 July 1918

When Thomas got back from the railway bridge, he found Mary and Freda in the kitchen. Freda was standing on a stool, wearing the little apron Mary had made for her. She had a miniature rolling pin in her hand and a small ball of dough in front of her. Her face was a picture of concentration as she tried to imitate her mother rolling out the pastry for a pie. She had flour all round her mouth and on her apron. Thomas had watched his mother teach his little sister Katie exactly this way. He smiled and imagined Freda in years to come, grown up and teaching her daughter to cook. With a fond look he left them to it and went down to the old shed at the bottom of the garden. It looked as if no one had been in there since 1914. They probably hadn't. The place was full of cobwebs. It smelled of mould and damp, but his toolbox was still under the bench, covered by a layer of dust. He sat on the old three-legged stool, cleaned it off and spent a while sharpening tools, scrubbing off rust and oiling things.

As a young lad, he'd enjoyed making things from scraps of wood, at first just simple boats to sail on the river with Hariph and Harry, then more complicated contraptions, such as soapbox carts and convoluted mazes for their marbles. Watching Freda play with Zillah's fancy dolls' house had reminded him of the simple one he'd made for Katie. Mary said he needed something to do, so he'd come up with the idea of making a dolls' house for Freda, maybe more of a fairy house, to go with her obsession with fairies. It was better than the embroidery and basket weaving they'd tried to foist on him at the hospital. What was the world coming to? They'd given women the right to vote and now they were at the reigns of milk floats and in charge of the railway stations. Did they expect men to sit at home and do the women's work now?

There were a few odd bits of wood in the corner of the shed, but he'd need to get more before he made a start on building anything. There used to be several little boatbuilding yards on the waterfront behind the gasworks. If they were still there, he might be able to cadge some scraps of wood from one of them, in exchange for a few pennies. He headed towards the river with a spring in his step, pleased to finally have something useful to occupy him. He strolled along, poking his head around corners where boats looked as if they might be being built or repaired. There were vessels in all stages of construction and decay, but if anyone was actually working in any of the yards they were nowhere to be seen. Perhaps Thorneycroft's, the naval works on the other side of the river, had taken on all the shipwrights, or maybe they'd all joined up?

Off the main road there was a small yacht repair wharf overlooked by dilapidated terraced houses. A few upturned boats suggested someone might be doing some work. He didn't hold out much hope, but he had nothing better to do so he went to investigate. He crunched across the muddy shingle and found a slipway, stacks of timber and several decaying boats, but other than a handful of seagulls squabbling there was no one about. Disappointed, he turned back towards the road. That was when he saw Hetty coming out of one of the tumbledown waterside houses. What was she up to? He leaned against a rotten old boat and watched. Earlier, by the railway bridge, he thought he'd had a lucky escape when she said she had 'a bit of business to attend to'. It meant he didn't have to put up with her on the walk home. What business could she have here, though? His curiosity was well and truly piqued. Mary was worried Hetty was getting into some kind of trouble, maybe with the black market. She was in the right place for it in this run-down area, with houses that regularly flooded and people who barely scraped a living.

The walls of the house looked damp, and the door opened straight onto the street. A young, Romany-looking woman stood in the doorway with a child on her hip. The youngster, a dark-haired girl of maybe two, was pale and scrawny. She looked as if she could do with being better fed, but then so did most of the people around this way. What possible business could Hetty have with this careworn and harassed woman, or was it merely a social call of some kind? The idea of Hetty having friends in these parts didn't ring true somehow. There was something fishy about the scene.

Hetty and the woman stood and talked for a while. They looked as if they were having an argument. Thomas strained his ears but caught none of it. A chilly breeze from the water carried the smell of rotting seaweed. He turned up the collar of his jacket, so intent on watching the women he almost jumped out of his skin when he heard, 'Wotcha up to, mush?'

When he turned, a young man in a pair of patched and worn trousers, a thick knitted jumper and a flat cap was limping towards him across the shingle. He stopped in front of Thomas with his legs apart and his arms folded. It was an intimidating stance. He was a swarthy chap, maybe in his mid-twenties, but weather beaten.

'Nothing, what are you up to?'

He wasn't afraid of one unarmed man.

'Mending boats.' The man nodded towards one of the upturned vessels. He must have been hidden behind it all the time. Then his eyes rested on the shiny, silver war badge. His arms relaxed and his face broke into a smile. 'You've not been back for long by the look of it. In France was you, or Belgium?'

'Both, but I was in France when I was shot. It was about a month ago. What about you?'

The man had no war badge, but the limp and his bearing suggested he'd seen action somewhere.

'Arras, last Easter. Got in the way of a shell and lost all me toes on this foot.' He pointed to his left leg.

A vivid memory flashed through Thomas's mind; the crunch of snow under his feet, tiny flakes swirling through smoke and the eyes of three Hun as he fired his rifle. So, this man had been in the

Easter snow at Arras too.

'Blown clean off like the work of a guillotine they was. I'm no good to the army now, 'cause I can't march nowhere and marching seems to be their favourite thing of all, other than sending us poor bloody infantry scrabbling over the top to be slaughtered. I'm still good for mending boats, though. Where'd you get hit?'

'Near Amiens. I was hit by a sniper and lost a lung, so I'm no good to them now, either.' Thomas shrugged, as if it could have been worse.

'So, wotcha doing round here, then?' The question was friendly this time.

'I came to see if I could get some scrap wood from one of the boat builders, to make something for my daughter. Though so far, you're the only person I've seen all morning.'

Thomas pulled his Woodbines out of his pocket and offered the packet to the man.

'Don't mind if I do.' He took a cigarette, struck a match, and held it out for Thomas to light his. 'The name's Bert by the way.'

'Thomas.' He put out his hand and Bert shook it.

'I thought you was up to no good.' He nodded towards the house across the road. 'It looked like you was watching my sister, Rose.'

Neither of the women were anywhere to be seen now. Thomas took a long drag on his cigarette to give him time to think. 'If you mean the woman standing at the door just now, I was, sort of. She reminded me of the wife of one of the chaps in my section. I was trying to decide if it was her and whether to pay her a visit, but then I thought I was probably wrong.'

'She ain't no soldier's wife,' Bert said.

'Good job I didn't pay her a visit then. She'd have thought I was mad, talking about her soldier husband.'

'Specially as she ain't got no husband.' He gave something between a snort and a bitter laugh. 'She got a bellyful and was left high and dry.'

'That's rough.' Thomas took another drag on his cigarette. 'Something similar happened to my sister-in-law.'

'There's a lot of it about, especially where the smarmy shite who knocked her up is concerned.' Bert ground his cigarette out under his good foot angrily. 'He gave her money and the name of a doctor to sort it. When she wouldn't, he washed his hands. When I came back and found out, I was all for squeezing the life out of the bugger. Rose wouldn't have it, though. She said he weren't worth swinging for. So, for now, I'm biding me time trying to work out how to make him pay his dues. He can afford to pay plenty, too.' He rubbed his thumb across his first two fingers. 'Anyhow, enough of that, you was needing some scrap wood you said?'

*

It turned out that Bert's cousin Frank owned the boat repair yard and was more than happy to help out another wounded Tommy. When he went home, Thomas was loaded down with wood but still none the wiser about what Hetty had been up to. He spent the afternoon hidden away in the shed. He found the act of measuring, sawing and fixing the pieces of the house together therapeutic. He hardly thought about the war, his wounds or the distance between him and Mary at all, but he did think about Hetty and Rose. They seemed unlikely friends and even less likely business partners. He quite liked Bert, though, so maybe he'd pay him another visit soon and see what else he could find out.

22 - Friday 26 July 1918

The fairy house had begun to take shape, although at the moment it looked more like a large birdhouse. It needed something like driftwood or seashells to give it the magical look Thomas had in mind. Seashells were thin on the ground along the shore here, but they were plentiful on the other side of the River Itchen at Weston. A stroll by the sea with Mary would be like old times, an echo of their walks along Southsea seafront when they were courting. Perhaps it was what they needed to get back on track. It was less than a mile to the floating bridge and about another mile to the shore. The weather was nice. It would almost be like a holiday.

When they got to the floating bridge slipway, Freda wanted to run down the slimy slope towards the incoming ferry. Mary was afraid she'd slip or get caught up in the giant chains, so she picked her up. They walked against the tide of people and carts plodding up the slope. The carts were driven by women or old men. Almost all the foot passengers were women, too, with weary faces and shopping baskets on their arms. This was not the world as he remembered it, the world he'd been fighting for all those years. He saw their curious glances and the way their faces changed when they noticed the war badge on his lapel. He didn't like the looks of accusation, but he liked the looks of pity even less. Then he thought of all the men who wouldn't be coming back and felt ashamed. For the entire journey, all five minutes or so, Freda pointed at boats and seagulls and waved madly at the people on the opposite ferry as they passed by. How lovely it must be to find such joy in little things.

The stares from the women lined up outside the shops made him uncomfortable, but soon enough they had left them all behind. They passed the shipyard and the Rolling Mills, where Mary said women made all the shells for the war. Was there anything the women weren't doing now? Then the sea was in sight. In the shade, it was quite chilly for late July, but when the sun shone through the scattered clouds the warmth of summer was pleasant. The foreshore was a mass of flowering grasses entwined with bindweed flowers, like little white trumpets swaying in the sea breeze. Mary stopped when she spotted wild garlic amongst them and crushed the leaves between her fingers, so the sharp tang rose into the salty air.

A magpie was perched amongst a mass of seagulls on the seaweed thatch of the weathered wooden fisherman's hut. It followed them with its beady eyes as they passed.

'My grandpa would have found that roof intriguing,' Mary said.

The magpie gave a rasping call and swooped down to pluck some sparkling bauble from the shingle. It reminded Thomas of the bird he'd seen escape the sniper's bullet on the Somme. 'He was a thatcher most of his life, wasn't he?' he asked.

Out at sea, a boat bobbed on the water. The white sails billowed in the breeze. Its hull was painted bright yellow. The colour reflected on the tips of the waves and made it appear to sit in a flickering puddle of sun. Freda pulled her hands free and ran joyously along the shingle. Mary sat on a hummock of spiky grass, shaded her eyes with her hand and watched her, while Thomas began to look around for driftwood, interesting pebbles and shells. When he looked back at Mary, her narrow- brimmed hat was slightly crooked and some of her hair had come loose and blown across her face. She looked so beautiful it made him catch his breath.

Amongst all the clumps of grass and shingle he spotted a curved piece of driftwood, just right for the fairy house. It was well-weathered and as light as cork. He took it to Mary, dropped it into her basket and then went back to the tide line to look for pretty shells and stones. Further along the bay, a white heron walked up and down the water margin. Its odd jerky walk made him think of an Egyptian hieroglyph come to life. Freda's laughter rose above the sound of the lapping waves. Slowly he picked up a handful of shells; pinkish-white cockles, Turks caps shining green, lilac or turquoise – depending on which way he turned them – the pink-tinged spiral of some kind of large snail half worn away by the tide, and a greenish stone, almost heart-shaped and covered with barnacles. He shoved them all into his jacket pockets. The little yellow sailboat had turned and was now level with him. Freda ran into his arms just as he spotted a hag stone.

'This is a magic stone.' He held it up to her eye. 'Look through the hole and see if any fairies are hiding.'

She squinted through the stone for a while, then pouted. 'No fairies.'

'Shall we take it home to look for fairies there?'

'Yes,' she said, laughing and clapping her hands.

Now he had enough shells, so he went back to the foreshore and sat beside Mary. With a smile he straightened her hat and put his arm around her shoulder. She turned, smiled back and then kissed him on the cheek. They sat like that for a long time, not talking, just enjoying the feel of the weak sun on their faces, the salty spray from the incoming tide and Freda running in circles on the shingle. This was what he'd dreamed of for so long. None of the other stuff really mattered.

'I suppose we should go back—' Mary finally broke the spell '—before she wears herself out completely and we have to carry her all the way.'

So, they retraced their steps to the floating bridge. Freda was less excited by the return journey and not long after they reached the shore, she began to run out of energy. Like a clockwork toy slowly running down, her steps became slower and her feet began to drag. Then she started to cry. She was such a happy child, and this was the first time Thomas had seen her shed any tears. It wrenched at his heart, so he picked her up. She wound her legs around his waist, put her arms around his neck and hid her wet face in his shoulder.

'She's worn herself out with all that running around.' He

smiled and shifted her weight slightly to stop the shells in his pocket digging in, and to ease the ache in his scarred back.

She began to sob again.

Mary frowned and put her hand on Freda's forehead. 'She feels a little feverish. I hope she's not coming down with anything.'

23 - Friday 26 July 1918

Mary watched Thomas pace up and down the parlour with Freda in his arms. His face was a picture of misery and fear. Freda was deathly pale and limp, her eyes half open and glazed.

'Perhaps it's just from all the excitement, or a touch of sunstroke.' She put her hand against Freda's forehead again. She was burning hot and, now she was closer, Mary could see her teeth chattering. Sunstroke was clutching at straws. It hadn't been nearly hot enough. She tried hard not to think of Vera's son but couldn't keep the image out of her mind. 'Why don't you go and get a cold flannel, while I put her in her cot.'

She took Freda's limp body from Thomas's arms and carried her towards the stairs. By the time he came to the bedroom with the flannel, she'd undressed her and laid her in the cot. When Mary placed the flannel over Freda's forehead she whimpered and tried to push it away.

'There, there.' She gently stroked the wet hair back from Freda's face. 'Close your eyes and go to sleep. Mummy's here, and Pappy, too.'

'If it's not too much sun maybe it's some childhood ailment that will soon pass.' Thomas leaned over the cot. 'Katie used to get fevers all the time when she was small. They said it was her tonsils.'

'Maybe.' From his eyes, she could see Thomas didn't believe it any more than she did. 'I think I have some aspirin tablets in the cupboard. There was something about them in the newspaper a few weeks back, so I bought some just in case. I could try to dissolve one in water for her to sip.'

'Sips of water might do her good. They kept making me drink water in the hospital when I had . . . when I was ill in spring. I'll open the window, too, and let some fresh air in. They swear by that in the hospital. It clears away the miasmas that cause illness.'

She found the brown glass bottle of aspirin tablets in the cupboard and, with some difficulty, managed to crush one into a glass of water. When she went back to the bedroom, Thomas was knelt on the floor beside the cot gently humming *It's a Long Way to Tipperary*. There were tears in his eyes. They frightened Mary almost as much as the sight of Freda's limp little body. Her skin was so pale it was almost translucent, save for an angry red circle on each cheek. Mary had a sudden vision of the night she'd dreamed of the War Office letter. The moonlight through the window had made Freda look like a ghost child, with blue-white skin and silver hair. Although it was daylight now and the curtains rose and fell as the wind gusted through the open window, Freda looked almost as ethereal as she had that night.

They took it in turns to kneel beside the cot or take the flannel to the scullery and run it under the cold tap. Mary tried to get Freda to sip some of the aspirin water from time to time, but more of it ended up running down her chin than going into her mouth. She watched helplessly as her child's breathing became faster and more laboured. Her face was so pale now it was almost blue. A faint, sickly smell emanated from her hot little body; something musty, like grass on the compost heap. Was this the miasma? She tried to push the window higher to get more air into the room. It might not make any difference but anything, no matter how silly it might seem, was worth a try.

24 - Friday 26 July 1918

Thomas opened his eyes. The light had begun to fade. His head was scrunched up at a funny angle, he had a crick in his neck and his legs and right arm had gone to sleep. Slowly he straightened up, rolled his shoulders and wiggled his toes, trying to get some blood to flow and make the pins and needles go away. It took him a moment to work out he was on the floor beside Freda's cot. Mary was beside him, asleep herself, with her legs folded under her and her forehead resting on the edge of the mattress at Freda's feet. The windows were still open and the room was icy cold. He looked into the cot, half afraid of what he might see. Freda was on her back with one arm raised above her head and the other across her chest. Her eyes were closed and the flannel they'd used to cool her fever was still draped across her forehead. It looked like she was peacefully sleeping. He wanted to reach out and touch her, but she was so still he was afraid he'd find her cold. He'd rather believe she was asleep a little longer.

When Hetty knocked on the door earlier, he'd been surprised to see her. They'd been so intent on Freda, the sips of water and the cool flannels to break the fever, that neither of them had given the time a single thought, or realised Eric would need meeting from school.

When he told her Freda was sick, she'd said, 'Don't worry, I'll look after Eric. The last thing you need to think about is amusing him. If need be, I'll keep him overnight. It won't be the first time, so he won't be concerned. He stayed with me when Freda was born.' She'd reached out and patted his arm reassuringly. 'Try not to worry too much. Children soon bounce back. Believe me, I know. At one time or another, George has had nearly every ailment known to man, apart from the plague. He's a sickly little blighter but he's usually right as rain by morning and whining for his breakfast. I'm sure Freda will be too.'

Hetty was the last person he'd expected to offer help or comfort. Her kindness brought a lump to his throat. Perhaps he'd misjudged her, just like he'd misjudged William.

He sat on the floor and looked at his daughter for a long time, but still he didn't dare to touch her. She was such a beautiful child. Her porcelain skin and little rosebud mouth made his heart ache. He'd missed so much of her life. To lose her now would be the ultimate cruelty. A tear escaped from his eye and rolled slowly down his cheek. All afternoon, both he and Mary had been careful not to mention the Spanish flu, but he'd thought about nothing else, and he could see in her face that Mary had too. All the signs were there; the sudden fever, the red spots on her little cheeks, just like poor old Geoffrey when they'd carried him out of the hut. He should never have let Mary come to see him at the hospital, not when he knew there was flu about. He wasn't sure he believed in God anymore, but he closed his eyes and prayed she was alive, and, if she wasn't, that God would spare Mary and little Eric. If he lost them too, there would be no point going on.

25 - Saturday 27 July 1918

Mary opened her eyes. Her head ached. The picture rail swayed and tilted at odd angles, as if she were on a boat. It made her feel sick, so she closed her eyes again. An icy draft ruffled her hair. She was cold. Her teeth began to chatter. She turned her head slightly and opened her eyes again. The window was wide open, and the curtains billowed into the room. She raised her arm to pull the covers up. Steam rose from her skin and she looked in wonder at her pale hand. It was so large it took up the whole room. As she stared at it, it seemed to grow smaller and smaller, moving away from her on a long, thin arm. How had her arms got so long? She tried to sit up, but her head was too heavy. Her long, snake-like arm fell and she could feel the quilted counterpane beneath her tiny little fingers. They'd opened the window because Freda had a fever. Why was she in bed when Freda needed her?

Thomas's voice came to her down a long tunnel. She couldn't make out what he was saying. Was it something about getting rid of miasmas? Hadn't they opened the windows to release them? There'd been a musty, rotten smell, but it was gone now. Perhaps the miasmas had gone too? Thomas's voice got louder and louder until it sounded as if it was coming from inside her head.

'I think she's a little cooler now.'

Slowly she turned her head towards the door. She'd expected

him to be standing right beside her, but there was no one there and the door was closed. The door panels warped and waved, as if she were seeing them through rippled water. She closed her eyes again.

Her mouth was dry. She ran her tongue over her lips. They were cracked and sore. With supreme effort, she managed to lift her head just enough to see the cot in the corner. It seemed miles away. She blinked a few times and tried to focus her eyes. The cot was empty except for the rag doll, Tilly. Her heart pounded in her ears. Where was Freda? She closed her eyes and Alice's voice came to her.

'His face was a kind of purplish-black . . . he went to bed and just didn't wake up.'

She remembered Freda's face; so pale it appeared blue, and her lips dark purple, as if she'd been eating blackberries. She closed her eyes. Her head fell back onto the pillow and the room swirled around her. She was so hot she must be on fire.

Then she heard Freda singing. 'Mary, Mary little fairy. Cows in the garden go. With silver bells and cockerel smells.'

26 - Tuesday 30 July 1918

As they slowly lowered the coffin into the grave, Thomas could hardly bear to look at it. Instead, he turned his gaze to the fine mist of glistening droplets that had settled on the arm of his black mourning suit. The overcast sky and the hint of drizzle in the air echoed his mood. The reverend's long-winded mumbling was interminable, but he didn't want it to end. The thought of leaving her in the cold, damp graveyard all alone was more than he could bear.

When the reverend said, 'We commit her body to the ground, earth to earth, ashes to ashes, dust to dust,' he shut his eyes against the sight of the earth sprinkled on top of her, but he couldn't shut out the sound.

Alice took his right hand and squeezed it. He squeezed back and glanced at her gratefully. Against the black of her dress and hat, her flaming hair looked brighter than ever. She dabbed at her red-rimmed eyes with a black-bordered handkerchief. Beside her, Hetty also mopped tears and stared forlornly towards the coffin. The pang of guilt for the things he'd thought and said about her was a physical pain. It made him wince. She'd done more than anyone to help him over the last few days. She'd looked after Eric while he and Mary desperately tried to get Freda's temperature down. When Mary took ill too, she was the one who went to fetch Alice. He wasn't sure what he'd have done without the pair of them. Ever practical, Alice had been worried about the spread of infection. She'd taken Eric and her boys off on the train to Witney to stay with their grandparents and sent telegrams to all the family, sparing him the job of breaking the dreadful news. All the while Hetty had bustled about. She'd brought him meals and made sure he ate them. He'd even grown used to her constant chatter, or, at least, learned to tune it out.

A half-suppressed sob came from his left. He turned to give Martha a watery smile. Her black dress and hat were understated, but the froth of raven curls fighting to escape from the long plait, her alabaster skin and the thickest, darkest lashes he'd ever seen made a stunning combination. She was such an exotic creature, with eyes so dark it was difficult to tell pupil from iris. It was easy to see why Hariph had fallen for her so quickly. Who wouldn't fall in love with her? He envied the women their tears. His throat hurt from holding his own back and his jaw ached from clenching it so tightly, but if he started to cry he might never be able to stop.

When it was finally over, Martha took his arm and led him to the waiting carriage. Alice and Hetty followed behind. On a different day, he'd have stopped to fuss over the horses – beautiful, black creatures all got up with plumes of ostrich feathers – or chatted to the driver who'd waited so patiently with nothing but a top hat and cape to keep the rain off. Now he barely registered them. He helped the ladies into the carriage then climbed in himself and silently took his place beside Alice. Even the stark contrast between lumpy old Hetty and exotic Martha opposite provoked barely a thought.

'At least she had a proper send off,' Hetty said. 'Zillah is a wonder arranging all this at such short notice. She said it was like losing one of her own. You know she paid for everything; the carriages, the coffin, even the food.'

Thomas cringed. He'd tried to protest but she would have none of it. It was only vanity on his part, though. What did it matter what any of them thought of him?

'It was very kind of her,' Martha said.

'Yes,' Hetty nodded. 'She even let me use her telephone to call the doctor. Her son insisted on having it installed. It seemed like a white elephant of a thing to me, sitting there in her parlour gathering dust with wires everywhere to trip over. Who'd have known it could be so useful?'

Useful? The old quack they'd contacted had marched in smoking a stinking pipe. He'd dropped his leather bag on the floor, briefly peered over his spectacles at them, stroked his handlebar moustache and said, 'She may pull through, only time will tell.'

He was more concerned with pocketing his fee and getting away as soon as possible in order to keep himself safe.

'It was so sudden. Just like Vera's husband and son,' Alice said sadly. 'She lost them both and then took sick herself. She pulled through, but now she has no one.'

'The poor thing,' Martha said. 'It sounds like something from a Greek tragedy.'

The conversation washed over Thomas. Far from being the weaker sex, these women were stronger than he would ever be. While he'd been helpless against the devastation unfolding around him, unable to do anything but try to control his emotions and appear strong, they'd been quietly taking care of all the details. As soon as Alice got back from Witney, she went through the house with carbolic soap and a mop like a dose of salts, as if she could wash the sickness away. Hetty covered mirrors, stopped clocks and festooned the front door with a beribboned yew wreath. Whether any of these superstitions did any good he couldn't tell, but at least she was doing something. Then there was Martha. She'd wafted in on a cloud of scent on Saturday evening and proved herself practical as well as pretty. She dealt with the sad task of washing and dressing Freda's tiny body and adorned the little white coffin with so many flowers the front parlour was like a florist shop. Once that was done, she shooed Thomas out of the sickroom and set about making all kinds of stinking poultices. The place smelt of a combination of flowers, camphor and eucalyptus, but without her, he might have lost Mary too.

When they got back to the house, Zillah was there waiting. She'd refused to intrude on their grief by coming to the service, but had taken charge of George and laid out a veritable feast in the front parlour for their return. Not that Thomas felt like eating. Mary was still too ill to get out of bed, never mind leave the house for the funeral. He lowered himself into the chair beside the hearth, drained by all the emotion of the day, and silently watched the women.

27 - Friday 2 August 1918

Why couldn't they all just leave her alone? They meant well and she was grateful for all they'd done, but all the prattle and fuss made her head ache. Nothing any of them did could ever make her feel better, but she didn't have the energy to stop them.

'You really should eat something,' Alice said when she waved away the tray of food she'd offered. 'You have Eric to think of, and Thomas, of course.'

'You need to keep warm now the fever has passed,' Hetty said as she plumped her pillows and draped a shawl over her shoulders.

'Put a drop of this brandy in her tea,' Martha suggested. 'If nothing else, it might bring some colour to her cheeks.'

She stared miserably at the empty cot in the corner and then closed her eyes. If she shut everything else out, she could still see Freda sleeping peacefully there with her old rag doll in her arms. Her fever had broken now but she wished it hadn't. In her delirium, she'd been sure Freda was in the bed beside her. She'd heard her sing and felt her stroke her forehead like a little nurse. When the fever broke so did the dream, and she had no choice but to face the truth. Freda was gone and nothing would bring her back. Even Thomas, with his eyes full of concern, couldn't take her pain away.

The world was strangely colourless. It wasn't just the mourning clothes, even the flowers they'd put on the chest beside the bed looked washed out and insipid. The food they brought her had no taste and the flowers had no scent. When she closed her eyes and conjured up the image of Freda, it was so vivid that it felt more real than this monotone world. The colours may have faded but sounds were strangely amplified. When the milk cart clattered past in the street it sounded like it was inside her head, and even though her door was shut, she could clearly hear the voices downstairs. All she wanted was to block out their stupid chatter and to retire to the dream world.

'Who's looking after Terrence, Kathleen and Leonard?' Alice asked Martha.

'My ma, although I have a notion they'll be looking after her more than she is them.'

'I thought she was an invalid?'

'My ma's had one foot in the grave since Pa died. Leastways, that's what she'd have us all think. Her acting's better than mine by a long way. Half her ailments are made up or in her head. Anyway, I've spent most of my life trying to keep her other foot in the land of the living.'

'That explains why you've been such a good nurse to Mary.'

'Well, I've had plenty of practice. If it wasn't for the children,

I might have joined the Red Cross instead of gallivanting about on the stage.'

She must have fallen asleep, because the next moment they were in the middle of a conversation about the war.

'They're retreating from the Marne, pushed back by the French and Americans,' Alice said. 'Do you think this is the beginning of the end, Thomas?'

'Maybe, who can tell.'

He didn't sound concerned either way.

'Perhaps it will all be over soon. I'd like to think so. I'd like Harry back home safe and well.'

'It's a good sign, but I wouldn't hold my breath. The Hun won't give in easily. We've pushed them back before.'

Mary wished she could close her ears as well as her eyes. She didn't want to hear about the war. She didn't even want to think about it. None of it mattered now.

28 - Monday 5 August 1918

In the morning, Martha had got Mary out of bed to sit in the parlour, but she was still far from well. She sat in the armchair opposite Thomas with a blanket over her knees and an empty look in her eyes. Her skin was like tissue paper, stretched tight over her bones. She didn't talk and barely ate, and when Thomas tried to initiate a conversation, she looked at him as if he were a stranger. It was as if his Mary had gone, leaving just a shell. It scared him and he didn't know what to do about it.

'Just let her be,' Martha said when she came in with yet another cup of tea that neither of them wanted. 'It takes a while for a mind to adjust to such a horrible loss. Give her some time.'

He wanted to remind her that Freda was his daughter, too, and that because of the war he'd barely got a chance to know her, but she meant well so he just nodded.

Last night he'd had a dream that wouldn't quite leave him, no matter how hard he tried to push it from his mind. It was just after Percy got wounded. Nobby and Davie had carried him off on a stretcher, with Lofty trailing behind to get his scratches cleaned up. He and Joe went back to searching the bodies that Percy, Lofty and the others had brought back from No Man's Land. They worked in silence. He was worried about Percy. The leg had looked bad; the chances were he'd lose it, and it seemed a cruel twist of fate for

someone so young and so suited to army life. He could have gone far
– he had the ambition and the courage for it. At least he was better
off than the chap in front of him. He'd looked down at the rotting
pile of bone and rags, but Freda's limp little body had replaced the
soldier.

If he'd had something to do, he might have been able to
chase the image from his mind, but the women wouldn't let him lift a
finger. It was August Bank Holiday, so he didn't even have an excuse
to walk to the shops. Not that he'd been out once since the funeral.
There was nothing for it but to sit in a silence broken only by
snatches of conversation drifting from the scullery, where Hetty,
Alice and Martha were doing the laundry.

'Lib would have come if she could but Mary's brother's sick.
Her mother can't be expected to look after Lib's children as well as
him.' Alice's voice was raised, she was obviously riled.

Hetty must have been moaning that Mary's sister Lib hadn't
come to help out. It didn't sound as if she was going to let it go.
'Your youngest is just a baby, though, isn't he, Martha? And your
mother is sick?'

'Leonard has just turned one, Kathleen's two and Terrence
will be six in November. Ma likes to make out she's sick, but she
isn't, and she's used to looking after them while I'm working.
Besides, my sisters and brothers are nearby, and they could all do
with helping out for a change.'

'At least you have family. I've got no one apart from George. If anything happened to me, he'd end up in the workhouse, poor little blighter.'

Thomas didn't catch what Hetty said next, but there was something about children being sent up chimneys and sold as slaves. Then she started going on about her health. 'I had a terrible time carrying him. He was lying awkwardly, the midwife said. He's been an awkward bugger ever since, too. Anyway, he played havoc with my poor back and my ankles swelled up like balloons. Twelve hours I was in labour . . .'

His opinion of Hetty might have taken an upturn, but her voice and her whining still grated. The last thing he wanted was to sit and listen to her going into graphic detail about giving birth. There were some things a man shouldn't have to endure. Mary's eyes were closed. She'd fallen asleep. He picked up his jacket and cigarettes and marched through the steamy scullery, past Alice, Martha and Hetty, and into the garden. He stomped towards the shed, tapped a Woodbine out of the packet and then put his hand in his jacket pocket to search for matches. His fingers found all the shells he'd collected for Freda's fairy house. The memory of her laughter as she ran around on the shingle in the sun was like a slap in the face. A huge wave of loss and grief broke over him. His legs almost buckled, and he had to lean on the shed, gasping for breath, as if he'd been shot again.

The shed was the only place he could be alone. When he

opened the door, the first thing he saw was the half-finished fairy house on the wooden bench beside his tools. The sight of it broke his heart. He collapsed onto the old, three-legged stool, swiped away the sawdust and curly wood shavings, put his head down on the bench and wept. All the pent-up emotions of the last four years poured out of him. When he heard Hetty and Martha's voices, he knew they must have finished the laundry and come into the garden to peg out the clothes. Now he was trapped in the shed. If he went outside, they'd see he'd been crying. Despite everything, he had too much pride for that. Soldiers don't cry. The little window was dirty and covered in cobwebs. He couldn't see them, and they couldn't see him, but he could hear their voices. As far as he could tell, the conversation was about Hetty's husband, George. At least it wasn't childbirth.

' . . . And I had a bad feeling about that ship right from the start. As soon as they started saying it was unsinkable, I said, "that's tempting fate, that is." George paid me no mind, though. He'd been on all the big ships and said they were as safe as houses, and that I was being silly. Of course, I was right. Little good it did me, though. My poor old George was a stoker. He had no chance at all. They never even found his body. All they were interested in were the passengers, the rich people.'

'There was a time when I thought my husband had gone down with the Titanic,' Martha said. 'He left in the spring of 1912. He said he was going to make his fortune in America, become a big star on the silver screen and send for me when he'd made it. Ma saw it differently. I was expecting Terrence and she said he didn't want to be saddled with a child. Maybe she saw the truth. He didn't write, not a word. Then I started to think about the Titanic sinking. He might've sailed on her. The timing was exactly right, and it explained why he hadn't written. I spent a long time trying to get information about the passengers, but his name wasn't on the list. Of course, he was an actor, and he may not have been using his real name, so I could never be sure he wasn't on the ship.'

Thomas had no idea Martha thought her husband was on the Titanic. He'd always believed the man was a scoundrel who'd upped and left his pregnant wife. Perhaps he'd been wrong, just like he'd been wrong about William Wells and Hetty.

'So, Thomas's brother is your second husband, then?' Hetty asked.

'Oh, we're not married,' Martha said matter-of-factly. 'We can't wed because I've no way of proving what happened to Bill.'

There was a long silence. Thomas wished Martha would be less open about it, especially with someone like Hetty, who loved to gossip. Not everyone would understand.

'And you're not worried about people finding out?'

'Not at all, I don't care a fig what people think. I wouldn't have lasted five minutes on the stage if I did, especially singing and dancing in the music halls.'

'Aren't people scandalised?'

'Small-minded ones, maybe, but what do I care about them? They're not the kind of people I want as friends.'

'But what about your reputation? Wouldn't it be better just to pretend you're married?'

'I am married. That's the bloody problem. I have been since I was seventeen. Bill was twenty-one, the most handsome man you'd ever laid eyes on. He had a shock of brown hair that flopped over his forehead, and the darkest, deepest eyes. As Shakespeare said, though, "All that glisters is not gold." The Bard is seldom wrong.'

'I meant pretend you're married to Thomas's brother. Wouldn't that make life easier for everyone?'

'You mean lie? I'd rather be an honest sinner than a virtuous liar. There's enough of them about. You'd be surprised how many respectable people are just liars, miscounting the months between the marriage bed and the childbed, passing themselves off as widows, or their children off as siblings. I can usually spot them a mile away. No, I'd rather tell the truth and be damned.'

It was strangely silent after that. Thomas couldn't make out whether they'd just stopped talking or had finished pegging out the washing and gone inside.

29 - Wednesday 7 August 1918

The funny little cottage, with its steeply angled roof, smelt of damp and decay, but it was better than death and sweat. Trickles of dusty mortar fell on them now and then, when a shell landed particularly close, but there were three beds with straw stuffed mattresses and a roof over their heads, albeit a rusty corrugated iron one. It was more than enough to keep them happy. There was even a garden of sorts, containing weedy vegetables, emaciated chickens and the scrawniest cow any of them had ever seen. The strange, bent and wizened old crone who owned the place looked suspiciously like a witch. She had wispy grey hair, whiskers on her chin and not a tooth in her head. She barely spoke any English, but she seemed happy enough to offer them beds.

'Only witchcraft could get milk out of that skinny old heifer of hers.' Wally looked at his mug of chocolat chaud suspiciously and then took a sip, 'but it tastes better than anything I've had since 1914.'

'She's probably cast a spell on you,' Joe laughed. 'I swear I saw her making magic signs behind your back earlier. That cow could be the last soldier who was billeted here. Maybe she fancies magicking herself up a pig. If Wally's disappeared in the morning and she offers us bacon for breakfast, we'll know I'm right.'

'Well, witch or not, it's better than a barn or a tent,' Thomas said.

They were eating crusty bread and a watery stew that may or may not have had one of the chickens in it, when a particularly loud explosion shook a chunk of plaster loose from the cracked and patched-up ceiling. It fell in a shower of white dust and hit Wally on the head.

'That was a bit close for comfort.' He brushed the powdery plaster out of his hair and rubbed his head. 'Still, it's thickened this stew a bit.'

Joe and Thomas were still laughing when Madame rushed in waving her hands about wildly. She gabbled something unintelligible about 'les enfants blesses,' and grabbed at their arms. It was obvious someone had been hurt and she wanted them to come and help.

A shell had hit another decrepit cottage a little further along the winding dirt road. It was now a pile of rubble, apart from one ragged segment of wall topped by wooden rafters sticking up like the bones of a whale. Villagers and other billeted soldiers had already begun to dig in the wreckage with their bare hands. Thomas, Wally and Joe were soon alongside them. The ground was a mass of stone, broken bricks and pieces of splintered wood. Scraps of fabric fluttered in the breeze. They dug until their hands bled, threw bricks behind them and clawed away the dust and debris in their desperate search for survivors. More shells burst nearby.

Just as Thomas uncovered a tiny red shoe, someone shouted,

'Get back, that wall is going to come down soon.'

At first, he thought it belonged to a doll, but then he saw a dusty little leg. He and Joe ignored the danger and dug frantically, without a thought for the wall that teetered precariously above them. In moments, they'd uncovered enough of the child, a girl of maybe two or three, to pull her from the wreckage. Thomas cradled her in his arms and tenderly wiped the chalky dust from her mouth and eyes. She was still warm and, apart from all the dirt, looked like a little rag doll. They'd been too late to save her.

*

He woke with a start, gasping for air. He'd hoped he'd seen the last of these dreams, but this one brought back the raw emotion he'd experienced that day in the ruined French village. Now, in the dark bedroom, with Mary asleep beside him, he felt the same mixture of sadness, helplessness and the hot anger that had made them all want to take revenge. It was one thing for soldiers to shell, shoot and bayonet each other, they'd all signed up for it, but shelling women and children was unforgivable. There was something more to this dream, though. When he'd looked into the face of the poor dead girl, it was Freda he saw.

He couldn't shake off the anger. He couldn't even talk about it. Only someone who'd been there would understand. He thought about going to see Joe, or even Bert at the boatyard, but he didn't want to stray too far from Mary. She'd been ill for a week now and she was still so frail he was afraid he might yet lose her. Staying close was about all he could do. All day, she sat wrapped in her shawl in the chair, either staring into space or sleeping. He couldn't tell how much of it was grief and how much was the illness, and he didn't know what to do about either. Alice, Martha and Hetty did all the practical things. They took it in turns to sit with her, clean, cook and generally run the house. Zillah popped in now and then with books and little treats. Alice's neighbour Effie left food on the doorstep, but she was too afraid to come inside the plague house. Thomas couldn't blame her. He was eternally grateful for all they did, but most of the time he felt surplus to requirements. This morning, he was so restless and filled with anger he couldn't sit still.

Martha gently brushed and plaited Mary's hair and quietly sang *The Boy I Love Is Up in The Gallery*. Her voice was sweet and true, and he swore he detected a hint of a smile on Mary's lips, but that may have been wishful thinking.

Martha looked up as he went past for the third time. 'You're fidgety this morning. Do something useful and gather up a few cushions and put them on that old bench in the garden. It'd do Mary good to sit outside for a while.'

He was glad to have something practical to do. While on his way through the scullery with an armful of cushions, he passed Alice.

She was grating carrots and beetroot. Her fingers were crimson from the juice.

'I hope you don't mind, I dug these up from the vegetable garden.' She looked up and smiled. 'I'm making a cake to try to tempt her. She's had nothing but a few sips of chicken soup all week, and she said she enjoyed my carrot and beetroot cake.'

'Anything's worth a try,' he said.

The sight of her with Mary's apron tied around her waist reminded him of Freda perched on the stool with her little rolling pin. It might have been a lifetime ago.

Mary sat on the cushions he'd laid out but still said nothing. Although the day was warm, Martha spread a blanket over Mary's knees then sat beside her. Thomas cast his eyes across the vegetable garden. It was dotted with sunny yellow dandelion flowers. Pulling them from the ground would use up some of his energy and make him feel useful. He slowly worked his way down the garden with a small spade and fork, attacking each weed as if his life depended on it, cutting them down viciously and throwing the dead bodies into the old wicker trug. As he worked, he half listened to Martha telling Mary a story about the time Harry Houdini came to Plymouth. She was a wonderful storyteller, and he was soon caught up in the tale. He could almost see the great showman standing on the edge of the local bridge in nothing but a pair of knickers and restrained by handcuffs, chains and locks.

'He drew in a few deep breaths and then dived into the creek like it was the most ordinary thing to do. As he disappeared beneath the water, the crowd around Stonehouse Bridge fell completely silent. We were all holding our breath, too.'

Martha drew in a deep breath and paused for what felt like an eternity. Thomas stopped his work and looked at Mary. There might have been a flicker of interest in her eyes, but he couldn't be sure. When Martha finally exhaled and carried on with her tale, he realised he'd been holding his breath, too.

'And then his head broke the water and the crowd roared. He swam to the shore then climbed straight into a cab, still dripping wet, and went back to the theatre. I swear he must have only been under that water for a minute or so, but it felt like an hour. It was almost better than the show he put on later at the theatre, although it was over far sooner, of course. It was nearly ten years ago, but I remember it as if it were yesterday.'

The sun was high in the sky. Martha went inside to fetch some drinks. Thomas moved into the shade and sat cross-legged on the ground beside Mary. The mouth-watering aroma of Alice's baking wafted through the back door and the murmur of Zillah's voice drifted through her French windows. She must be talking to George, although he couldn't make out what she was saying. Since Mary had been sick, she'd been looking after him while Hetty went to work. Martha came back with a tray of tea and some slices of Alice's cake still warm from the oven. Thomas helped himself to a slice. The three of them sat in silence for a while, too busy with eating and drinking to talk. Mary sipped her tea, but she ignored the cake.

'I don't know why you're so upset, William.' Zillah's raised voice drifted from her parlour.

'For heaven's sake, Mother, I can't believe you let that dreadful woman palm her brat off on you again.' William's voice was loud, clear and angry.

Thomas looked at Martha and she arched one dark eyebrow in response.

'I *offered* to help out,' Zillah said. 'It's no hardship at all. I like having the children around.'

'But I came to take you out for a drive. I thought we might take afternoon tea.'

'We can still go. I'm sure George would be fine sitting on my lap in the motorcar. He'd probably enjoy it.'

'I won't have that filthy urchin in my vehicle. You shouldn't even allow him in your house, never mind touching your things. You only have to look at his mother to see he's probably riddled with disease.'

'George is a lovely, quiet little thing, no trouble at all. In fact, he reminds me of you at that age.'

Thomas raised his eyebrows. A man like William would find

that hard to swallow. Had Zillah said it just to bring him down a peg or two? Martha bit her bottom lip. She was trying not to laugh. Even Mary frowned and looked towards Zillah's garden.

'How can you compare that half-witted ragamuffin child to me, your only son?' William was shouting now, so angry he could hardly get the words out. 'I've never heard anything like it in my life. If I didn't know better, I'd think you were losing your faculties—'

'William!' Zillah snapped. 'Must I remind you that this is my house, and I am your mother? I'd thank you to show me a little respect and not to say such horrible things about Hetty or George. Is it any wonder I don't want to live with you?'

There was a loud bang, as if someone had slammed a door. It made Thomas jump. Then there was silence.

Mary, Martha and Thomas looked at each other. Finally, Martha spoke. 'He didn't take too kindly to that, did he?' she whispered.

'He's an insufferable snob,' Thomas whispered back.

'And a bully, too, by the sound of it,' Martha replied.

30 - Thursday 8 August 1918

The rain lashed against the parlour window. It sounded like handfuls of pebbles were being thrown against the glass. Although it was morning, it was so dark that Thomas had turned on the lights. Mary didn't care about the rain or the darkness. She didn't care about anything. The house was full of people coming and going, like shadowy ghosts drifting past. They made her weary with their chatter and fretting. Zillah brought an orange to tempt her. At least it smelled something like an orange, but it looked pale, almost grey – just like everything else. She hadn't seen an orange for so long, she wondered whether they'd always looked this way and she'd misremembered them. Alice, Martha and Hetty wafted in and out doing all the things she would normally do. She saw them come and go with no real interest. Then there was Thomas, always watching her with sad, worried eyes.

She let her eyelids drop and relaxed as Martha brushed and plaited her hair. As she brushed, she sang, 'Daisy, Daisy, give me your answer, do . . .'

With her eyes closed, she could almost imagine she was a child again and it was Mum brushing her hair and singing to her, although Mum's voice was nowhere near as melodic as Martha's. She'd give anything to feel those arms around her, have them soothe away the pain and make everything better like they always had.

Nothing was going to make this better, though. Every dream and hope had been crushed and she was empty. Sleep was her only comfort. In her dreams, Freda was still there.

'At least it's good for the garden.'

Thomas sounded far away. Perhaps he was at the back door? Cool air whistled through the house, brushed her skin and raised goose bumps.

'It could be worse, we could be out in it.' Hetty's voice sounded closer. 'There's holes in the soles of my boots and the cardboard hardly keeps the water out. I suffer so much with my feet, especially in the damp. A body would be soaked right through in a moment out there now. Imagine that.'

'I don't have to imagine, I've lived through four winters of it.'

She could almost taste Thomas's bitterness.

'Sorry, I didn't think.'

Hetty never did think.

'It must have been unbearable.' Martha's voice was like honey poured from the jar, warm and golden. 'It's wretched being soaked to the skin. It reminds me of the day Hariph first rode his motorcycle to Plymouth.'

'He was always too impulsive for his own good.' Thomas sounded closer now, too.

'He still is.' Martha's laugh was like music playing inside Mary's head. 'He turned up at the stage door looking like a drowned rat. His hair was all plastered to his head and water was dripping off the ends and running down his face. Heaven knows what he thought was going to happen. Who in their right mind would travel two hundred miles to see someone they scarcely knew, never mind on a motorcycle in the rain?'

'You weren't even courting?' Hetty gasped.

'No,' Martha said. 'I recognised him, though. He was the love-struck boy who'd sat in the front row of the theatre every night for the week we were playing in Oxford. The one who hung around the stage door and kept asking me to go for a drink with him.'

The words conjured images inside Mary's head, like something at the picture house. In her mind, Hariph and Martha acted out the tale, but, unlike the faded grey of the real world, they were in bright, shimmering colour more vivid than anything she'd ever seen.

'And did you?' Hetty asked.

'Not once. I didn't want to encourage him. It couldn't go anywhere. All the same, there he was in Plymouth, dripping wet and looking at me with those blue eyes of his all full of hope and longing.'

'So, what did you do?'

'I turned him away. I felt dreadful, but it was best for him. He

179

wouldn't take no for an answer, though. He pushed his motorcycle along the street beside me and told me silly jokes all the way home. I told him I had a husband, even if I didn't know where he was, and a child. The last thing I needed was a man. I thought that'd be the end of it, but he said, "I don't mind children. I used to be one once, and any husband that would leave a woman like you alone, even for a day, doesn't deserve to keep her."

'He came back every night to walk me home from the theatre. He told me about his family and the job he'd found in Plymouth mending bicycles. One day, he brought a little motorcycle toy he'd made. "For your boy," he said. It was the size of my hand but so intricate. I think it was then that I realised he wasn't ever going to give up, and that perhaps I didn't want him to.'

The story was familiar. Mary had heard parts of it from Thomas and Alice, and even from Hariph, but never from Martha's own lips. She kept her eyes shut as Martha told them all how Hariph had won over little Terrence, who'd never known a father. It was a full year before their friendship turned to something more, at least on Martha's part. Hariph had been in love with her from the moment he saw her. He made no bones about it.

' . . . But I knew being with me would ruin his life. We couldn't marry and I was so much older than him. I half wished he'd find a nice girl; one with no past; one who could give him all the things I couldn't; one his mother would welcome. It would break my heart if he did, but it was his heart I was thinking of.'

'What a beautiful, romantic story.' The stifled tears were clear in Hetty's voice.

'No more than anyone's, I should think,' Martha said. 'Look at Thomas and Mary. Imagine falling in love with your sister's lodger and then living all those miles apart, but still somehow managing to court each other. Everyone has a story to tell, even you. I'll venture the story of how you met your George was just as romantic.'

Mary heard the cynicism in Martha's voice. Maybe Hetty did, too, because there was a long silence.

Finally, she said, 'Not really. We met at a dance. We courted. We got married. It was all very normal and boring until the Titanic sank.'

The words jarred, like a discordant note in a symphony. What was she trying to hide? She was always so concerned about what people thought of her, but no one was judging except Hetty herself.

31 - Friday 9 August 1918

'Effie's a bit of a bossy boots, isn't she.' Martha eyed the two uniformed men at the gates of Netley Hospital.

'You wouldn't think it to look at her,' Thomas replied.

Since Effie had decided it was safe to come into the house, she'd done nothing but issue orders. She should have been in the army. He followed Martha's gaze. The guards leaned nonchalantly against the metal gatepost, deep in conversation.

'Actually, I quite like it. She knows her mind and isn't afraid to say so. Besides, she's right, you *are* no good to Mary if you don't look after yourself, and if she hadn't bossed you, you'd still be sat at home worrying.'

'And you wouldn't have had the chance to see the famous hospital.'

'There is that.' She took his arm and they walked through the gate together.

The guards couldn't take their eyes off her. He might not have been there for all they noticed. She was going to cause quite a stir when the wounded soldiers saw her. Her dress was so short it barely covered her knees and the loose velvet jacket over it clung to her curves. She was a striking woman, with more than her share of confidence. Thomas could see her walking straight across No Man's Land and through the German line without a single shot being fired, just the sound of jaws hitting boots. With an army of women like her, they'd have won the war in September 1914.

They walked towards the huts arm in arm. This was his first outing with Martha and, in all probability, his last. She'd be off on a train in the morning. He had to concede that Effie was right to force him out of the house. Mary was getting stronger, and he did need to get outside and away from all the women. He needed to see Joe, too. Their letters back and forth weren't enough. He missed the camaraderie, the easy jokes and the memories shared with someone who understood. Martha coming along too had scuppered his plans. There'd been no gracious way to put her off, though, and she'd turned out to be a far better companion than he'd ever have imagined. She was witty, outspoken, full of interesting tales and extremely observant.

'Don't worry, I know you need time to chat with your pal,' she said as they approached the huts. 'I've no intention of clinging like a limpet. I want to see the hospital and I'm sure there'll be someone happy to show me around.'

There were plenty of willing tour guides. The men clamoured to take her arm. She ended up walking towards the main hospital surrounded by hospital blues. It was all Thomas could do to stop Joe joining them.

'Your brother is one lucky man.' He watched her over his shoulder as they walked back towards the gate. 'She wouldn't have a sister by any chance?'

'You wouldn't last five minutes. She'd eat you for breakfast and not even bother to spit out your bones.'

'Is she one of those suffrage types, then, demanding the right to be like a man? I'm not sure I could live with a woman trying to boss me in my own home.'

'Nothing like that. I don't think she's worried about votes and the like. She's a "catch more flies with honey" type, and I get the feeling she'd sit in a trench and swear and joke with the best of them, without taking the slightest offence.'

*

They made it to the Prince Consort just as the doors opened. Thomas couldn't remember the last time he'd been in a pub. The lounge bar was empty apart from the shirt-sleeved barman. The sunlight coming through the sash windows at the front didn't penetrate far, but the place was clean, if a little dingy. It had the usual pub aroma of stale smoke and beer, with maybe a hint of beeswax from the highly polished tables. Thomas found it hard to imagine Prince Albert in such humble surroundings, but Joe appeared comfortable enough.

'These new pub hours are stupid,' Joe said as they took their pints of beer to a table. 'They weren't so concerned with daytime drinking when they gave us our rum ration before they sent us over the top.'

They mulled over Joe's slow recovery. The bones in his arm had set wrong thanks to the hasty work of the medics at the field hospital. Joe was philosophical. At least it kept him out of the trenches for a while longer, and he still had an arm, even if it didn't work properly yet.

'The way it's going it might be all over before I'm fit to go back.' He leaned back in his chair and rested his foot on his knee. 'We had the blighters on the run for sure yesterday. They say the Hun were hiding in shell holes and begging to surrender. Word is they're fed up with the war and are glad to be taken. Thirty thousand of them there were! Not sure if our lot were involved, but it was around Amiens, so I wouldn't be surprised.'

'Thirty thousand in one day?' Thomas wiped the beer froth off his lip and put his glass down. 'Are you sure?'

'That's what the papers say.' Joe took a gulp of his own beer, put his glass on the table and scratched beneath the sling on his arm. 'This damned thing is powerful itchy. It's almost as bad as the bloody lice on the front line.'

'They're one thing I'm happy to see the back of,' Thomas laughed. 'Just thinking about the little blighters makes me itch.'

'I know it sounds bonkers but I'm half sad to have missed the push. They say they've almost got them back as far as the Hindenburg Line. At this rate, they'll be walking into Berlin by the end of the week, and we'll have more German prisoners than they have fighting men.'

'Wally will be taking all the credit, no doubt. He'll be writing sonnets about his own bravery.'

'And saying if they'd put him in charge years ago, we'd have won the war in 1915.'

'I wonder how many of them are left?' Thomas stopped smiling and frowned sadly into his glass. 'There's just me, you and Wally of the ones who went out in '14.'

'If Wally has survived the push.' Joe rubbed the back of his neck, as if the sling irritated him.

'Well, you'd better make sure they don't send you back then. I don't want to be the only one who remembers singing on the train, puking on the boat and grumbling it'd be all over before we got there.'

'Or Ruby the rat, the stench of Ronnie's guts in that French cottage, Percy in tears because he got a Blighty wound and wouldn't be coming back, constantly yelling at Lofty to keep his head down.'

'Even when the bugger was kneeling, his head was almost over the parapet,' Thomas chuckled.

When Martha finally joined them, Thomas was draining his second pint and the barman had just rung the bell for last orders. Joe had a wistful look that said he didn't want them to leave. He offered to buy 'a quick one for the road', but they had a train to catch and, after a few minutes chat on the street outside the pub, they went their separate ways. The afternoon sun was in Thomas and Martha's eyes as they headed up the hill towards the station. Martha was full of all she'd seen, the size of the hospital building, the stoicism of the wounded men and the beauty of the views across Southampton Water.

*

They got off the train at St Denys and were half-way across Horseshoe Bridge when Thomas spotted Miss Newman pedalling furiously towards them with the hem of her coat flapping behind her. Her Dalmatian bounded up to them wagging its tail, and Martha stopped to pet it.

'Hello, Thomas, I knew it was you I saw the other week.' Miss Newman got off her bicycle with a smile, 'and is this your wife?'

'I'm Martha, his sister-in-law.' Martha held out her hand and

Miss Newman shook it.

'Pleased to meet you,' she said, then looked sadly at the war badge on Thomas's lapel. 'I see you've been wounded. Nothing too serious, I hope?'

'Enough to keep me out of the war for good, but I'll live.'

'It must have been your wife I saw you with the other week, then?'

This caught Thomas off guard. How could she have recognised him after all these years, but not Hetty? It made no sense at all. With her wide hips and flat chest, Hetty was quite distinctive, and Miss Newman must know her well after visiting her for more than six years. He *had* been walking nearest the kerb, maybe she just hadn't seen her properly.

'That was my neighbour, Hetty Harris. I thought it was her you were waving at, actually.'

'Hetty Harris?' Miss Newman frowned and screwed up her face, as if she were trying to place the name. She was a formidable looking woman, a few years older than Thomas, but her hair, scraped back into a bun under her wide-brimmed hat, was still dark. 'I don't recall a Hetty Harris. Should I know her?'

'She's one of your Titanic widows. Never stops talking and has a little lad called George, after her husband.'

'Are you sure her husband was lost on the Titanic and not some other ship?' She shook her head. 'I only visit the Titanic families and I don't know any Hetty Harris or a George Harris. There was Edward Harris in Portswood, Amos Harris in Shirley and Charlie and Cliff Harris in Chapel, but none of them had wives called Hetty.'

'Perhaps I got it wrong.' Thomas shrugged it off and tried to disguise his shock. He'd known Hetty had something to hide, but he'd never imagined it was this. If she wasn't a Titanic widow, what was she?

They exchanged a few more pleasantries and then parted company. Miss Newman cycled off towards St Denys with her dog trotting beside her, and he and Martha walked towards home. At first, neither of them spoke. Thomas was trying to digest this new information. He'd known all along there was something fishy about Hetty. Even Mary had suspected she had some kind of secret. He'd expected black market dealings, or a contravention of the Mansion House rules, but he'd never once questioned her story about losing her husband on the Titanic.

'Do you think she could be mistaken?' he said as they passed Eric's school. 'Perhaps Hetty is just a pet name?'

'She knows her clients very well, rattling off all those names without even thinking.' Martha shook her head emphatically. 'Something about her Titanic story didn't ring true from the start. I wouldn't be a very good actress if I couldn't spot someone else playing a part, and I was sure right away that she was.'

'But why?'

'Because she doesn't want people to know the truth, whatever that is.' She bit her lip, as if she were trying to work it out. 'I'd say there are two possibilities. Either she's a widow, but she doesn't want anyone to know who her husband was, or she isn't a widow at all.'

'So, she could have a husband hidden away somewhere?'

'She could. Maybe one she doesn't want knowing where she is, or maybe she never had a husband in the first place.'

32 - Friday 9 August 1918

Mary was trying to read another of Zillah's H.G. Wells books, *The Sleeper Awakes*. There was an irony in the title. She felt like a sleepwalker, trapped in a twilight world. She tried to read, but after a few minutes the words began to run together on the page. This made the plot a struggle to follow. Her eyes were not quite right. Although the world did have some colour back in it, nothing looked quite as she remembered. It was all flat and dull somehow, like a theatre set. Just holding the book was an effort, never mind reading it. She let it fall open on her lap and watched Effie and Alice shell peas at the dining table. They must have picked them from the garden.

Alice popped a pod with her thumbnail and gently pushed the peas into the bowl between her and Effie. 'I'll probably go to the station with Martha tomorrow, although her train is earlier than mine. I've missed my boys so much I can't wait to get to Witney to see them.'

'It was good of Harry's mother to take them. I'm always glad when my mother agrees to take my boys, but they're such a handful she doesn't do it often enough.' Effie picked up another pod. 'It's nice not to have bloody Samuel hanging off my tit for once, although I suppose it does stop me falling for another one. My Charlie doesn't know when to stop. Still, I suppose you'll both be pleased to have yours home.'

Mary was desperate to see Eric. Keeping him safe from the influenza, or whatever it was they'd had, was for the best, and she hadn't been well enough to look after him, but she missed him dreadfully. With him away it felt as if she'd lost both her children.

When Thomas and Martha got back, Alice was taking the bowl of peas out to the scullery and Effie was folding the discarded pods into the muslin cloth they'd used to keep the table clean. As soon as they walked into the parlour, Mary knew something was wrong. They brought a strange chill with them. Thomas crossed the room and kissed her cheek. She smelt the beer on his breath and saw the look he flashed at Martha, secretive, almost guilty, followed by the slight shake of Martha's head in response. Something had happened. Perhaps Thomas's friend Joe had been sent back to the front or had caught the influenza and died.

Then Effie asked, 'How's your friend?'

'His arm's set all wrong, but it means they're not sending him back yet, so that's good news,' Thomas said.

Alice had made a pot of tea. Cups and saucers rattled on the tray as she put it on the dining table. The sound jarred.

Effie dashed out to the scullery and came back with the cake .
Zillah had brought this morning. 'Mary, will you have a little slice of cake?' she asked.

'No thank you.' Her voice still sounded hoarse and weak,

even to her own ears.

The tea was poured, and the cake sliced. There was a lot of general chitchat about the hospital, the pub and Joe, but beneath it flowed an undercurrent of concealment, like a sinister black stream. Mary could almost see it rippling, filled with evil things, or was it all in her imagination? Had the illness affected her mind, or did being outside of it all allow her to see things she'd otherwise have missed?

'What's going on with you two?' Effie said. 'You're hiding something, I can tell.'

Martha opened her mouth to say something, but Thomas frowned and put his hand on her arm. They really were hiding something. Effie would not be deceived. She poked and prodded until, at last, Martha gave in. 'We accidentally discovered something about Hetty,' she said.

'I don't think it's any of our business, though,' Thomas added.

Mary wondered why Thomas was rushing to Hetty's defence. There was no love lost between them.

Effie raised her eyebrows. 'Let us be the judge of that.'

With some reluctance, Martha told the tale of meeting the Mansion House visitor on the way back from the station. For some reason Mary couldn't quite fathom, Hetty's name had been mentioned but Miss Newman had denied all knowledge of her.

Effie grasped it at once. 'Do you mean to say her husband wasn't killed on the Titanic?'

'We don't know that for certain,' Thomas said. 'She could be mistaken, or there could be another explanation, perhaps a change of name?'

'Balderdash!' Effie slapped her hand down on the table so hard the teacups jangled. It made Mary jump. 'I always knew there was something wrong about her.'

Alice looked concerned. 'Aren't we jumping to conclusions? If she told a lie about her husband, she may have had good reason. He might have done something terrible, something she's ashamed of. He could be a criminal of some kind, or a German even. It would hardly be her fault and it would be understandable for her to want to protect her son from something like that.'

'Or she may be hiding from him,' Martha said. 'Or she may never have had a husband in the first place.'

'Do you think she really might have been a doxy, like Vera said, and got caught out?' Effie suggested.

Martha shook her head slowly, as if she were seriously considering the question. 'No. She doesn't strike me as the type at all, and besides, whores don't generally care enough to lie about what they do.'

'Maybe it was a love affair that ended badly,' Alice suggested.

'Perhaps her heart was broken, and she was left to face the consequences. She wouldn't be the first woman to have been left in the lurch.' She raised her eyebrows at Martha as she said it.

'One way or another, it looks like she's used the Titanic story to hide some disgrace,' Martha said. 'It's far more common than you'd think. Not everyone is as shameless as me.'

'Or as strong.' Alice gave her a weak smile.

Mary's head spun with all their theories. She despised all the speculation, especially Effie calling Hetty a whore. Anger was rising in her, bubbling up from the pit of her stomach. Finally, it burst out of her mouth. 'Just shut up, all of you.' She rose from her chair beside the hearth. Her teacup fell to the floor and shattered. Everyone in the room stared at her. 'If Hetty *has* told a lie about her husband, and none of you really know that for sure, it isn't up to us to speculate. Does it really matter if he died on the Titanic or not, or even if he doesn't exist? Who are you to judge? Not one of you is bloody perfect, and it's none of your bloody business.'

As she spoke, she began to feel the effect of standing so suddenly. The room began to spin. She staggered forwards, her legs trembling like jelly and blood ringing in her ears. Thomas jumped up. His chair fell backwards and crashed to the floor as he sprang to catch her before she fell. Then, when he turned her back towards the chair, she saw Hetty standing in the doorway with her hands over her mouth and a look of total horror on her face.

33 - Friday 9 August 1918

Thomas didn't think he'd ever heard Mary swear before, or shout like that. Gently, he lowered her into the chair and picked up the blanket from the floor. All the time he had one eye on Hetty, who was frozen at the parlour door. How much of the conversation had she heard? Her face said it was more than enough. Alice took the blanket from his hands, shook it out and tucked it around Mary's knees, before kneeling to pick up the broken pieces of crockery. Effie and Martha stared at Hetty, shame written all over their faces. Apart from Alice, no one moved a muscle. Then Hetty suddenly came back to life. Like a scalded cat, she turned and ran towards the back door. She was sobbing. Thomas was torn between caring for Mary and comforting Hetty. Alice was with Mary, though, and he was responsible for Hetty's distress. He was the one who'd opened Pandora's box, even if he hadn't meant to. Whatever she'd done, however much she irritated him, she didn't deserve to hear them sit in judgement on her. He ran after her.

By the time he got outside, she was already disappearing through her own back door, her faded navy-blue skirt flapping behind her. He caught up with her just in time for the door to slam in his face. He could see her shape through the six panes of frosted glass and then he heard the key turn. Effie and Martha were right behind him, but when they saw the door shut, they stopped short, uncertain about what to do next. Martha's shoulders slumped and she bowed her head.

Then Effie began to hammer on the door. 'Hetty, open up.'

'Go away,' an anguished voice came back.

'Please Hetty. We . . . I . . . didn't mean to hurt you.'

'Go away!' It was more of a shout than a whimper now.

'Please talk to us,' Martha begged. 'How can we help if you shut us out?'

There was silence for a while. At least there were no words, but Thomas could hear things banging about behind the door. What was she doing? He, Martha and Effie looked nervously at each other.

'You don't think she'd do something stupid, do you?' Martha whispered.

Effie looked horrified and began to bang the door with her fists once again. 'Hetty, Hetty, open the bloody door.'

The door remained closed and the banging and clattering continued.

'Hetty, you really need to open the door,' Thomas said in his most reasonable tone. 'We're sorry and we're worried about you. If you don't let us in, I'm going to have to smash the glass and open the door myself.'

The noise stopped. A second later, the dark blue shape

moved close behind the glass and the key turned again, but the door didn't open. Martha bit her lip and Effie wrung her hands. Thomas reached out to turn the handle.

The room was a mess. Piles of unwashed dishes in the sink, clothing untidily folded on a chair and tin soldiers scattered on the flagstone floor. There was a fusty smell that spoke of neglect. In the middle of the mess, Hetty frantically pulled things out of cupboards and threw them into a large, wooden sugar crate on the kitchen table. Tears were streaming down her face.

Thomas gently took a saucepan out of her hand and put it on the table. 'What are you doing?'

'Well, I can hardly stay here *now*, can I?' she sobbed.

'So, you're just going to pack your things and run away, are you?' Martha stepped into the room. 'How's that going to solve anything? Where are you even going to go?'

'I don't bloody know, but I can't stay here.'

Her face was red, her eyes were wet, and her hair was coming down. It gave her a wild, desperate look.

'Wherever you go, you'll take your problems with you.' Martha crossed the room and took Hetty's hand. 'If you share them with us, we might be able to help.'

'No one can help me.' Hetty looked miserable and defeated.

'You don't know that.' Martha looked into her eyes. 'Even if we can't help, you'd be surprised at how liberating telling the truth is. Why don't you try it? It can't be any worse than what you're feeling now, can it?'

Hetty was silent for a long time. She blinked slowly, and a wealth of emotions passed across her tear-stained face: fear, anger, sorrow and, finally, something that looked like resignation.

Then she closed her eyes and quietly said, 'Alright.'

Martha still had hold of her hand. She gently led her out into the garden. Thomas and Effie moved aside to let them pass. George's laughter drifted across the gardens from Zillah's open French windows. Thomas was glad the boy was with Zillah and didn't have to witness any of this.

*

Alice was at the dining table glumly clearing up the tea things. Mary was slumped in the armchair with a look of wretchedness on her face. They both looked up as Martha, Hetty, Effie and Thomas came in. Martha pulled out a dining chair and Hetty collapsed onto it. She put her elbows on the table and her head in her hands. Thomas had never seen anyone look so defeated. Even the German prisoners they'd captured had some defiance underneath their fear and humiliation. Alice, Effie and Martha took seats at the table. Thomas stood behind Mary's chair and gently smoothed her hair.

Finally, when everyone had settled, Hetty raised her head and began to speak. 'So, now you know.' She slowly looked around the room. 'My George wasn't drowned on the Titanic at all. Fact is, there is no George. I never had a husband. I never even had a lover.' She paused, looked around the room again and blinked back tears. Of all the possibilities, this was the one Thomas least expected. Hetty raised her chin and continued. 'What I did have was a good job as a typist, a mother and father who were proud of me and a bright future ahead. My boss, though, he had other ideas.' She stopped again, drew in a deep breath and closed her eyes. 'He thought the girls he employed owed him something, and he meant to take it whether we wanted him to or not.

'Some of the girls left. Some of them just put up with his wandering hands because they needed a job. Some said it was only friendly flirting and it meant no harm. Me, I was fifteen, innocent and stupid. I didn't like being squeezed like a piece of fruit or his hot breath on my neck when I worked, but I tolerated it for the sake of my good job and my parents' pride. There were always other people about, so he couldn't ever . . .' She gulped and screwed up her face.

'Then he started asking me to stay late. A couple of girls had left, and we were behind with the work. What could I do, he was my boss? Of course, when we were alone, he took what he wanted even though I said no and pleaded with him. I even threatened to tell people what he was doing. "Who's going to believe you?" he said. And, when I found out about the bastard in my belly, he gave me money to get rid of it. He even told me where to go, but I couldn't bring myself to go through with it. He said he couldn't have a dirty whore working for him. After all, what would people say?

'My parents disowned me. I daren't tell them the truth. I used the money to pay for lodgings and found what work I could. Then George was born. The poor little mite, it wasn't his fault. I named him after a lad I used to be sweet on and told everyone my husband had died on the Titanic. I didn't want anyone calling my poor boy a bastard.'

34 - Monday 12 August 1918

Rain was falling again, as if all the water in the world had gathered in the black clouds overhead. The sloppy mud was up to their knees in places and shoring up the sides of the trench was like bailing the sea with a sieve. Was God trying to stop this madness by drowning the lot of them, just like poor old Dougie? Thomas sheltered in the soggy, mud-filled dugout and tried to clean his gun. The new lad poked his head round the tattered tarpaulin. He was shivering, whether from the cold or fear it was hard to tell. Shells shook the ground, flashes like lightning burst overhead. The boy was bewildered and scared, and who could blame him? He couldn't be more than sixteen and should have been at home with his mother, not here in this living hell.

They'd christened him Tiptoe because Wally saw him and said, 'He must have stood on tiptoe to get in. If he's five foot three, I'll eat my tin helmet.'

They'd done their best to keep an eye on him and distract him from the horrors. It was an impossible task. Beyond the crumbling walls of the trench was a world of putrid, rotting flesh. Dead men as far as the eye could see. Bodies in contorted poses just as they'd died, some facing the sky, others the mud. They were now half buried, swelled up with gas and blackish-blue.

'Sir, how soon do you think I could get leave?' he asked.

'You'll be lucky to get home this side of Christmas, lad.' Thomas replied.

'But I must, sir. I want to marry my Ena.'

'She'll just have to wait a while, son.'

'But she can't. She's going to have a baby, sir.'

'I see.'

It was hard to believe this trembling boy had fathered a child. Probably he'd had one mad fling before he left for the front.

'Well, I'm not sure if there's anything I can do, but I promise I'll try.'

'Sir, thank you, sir.'

Tiptoe grinned as if it were a done deal and retreated backwards like a pauper edging away from a king. Anyone would think Thomas was a general, not a mere corporal.

Seconds later there was a terrific explosion, and a shower of mud and metal blew through the tarpaulin. Thomas dashed outside to inspect the damage. The side of the trench was blown away and there was Tiptoe on his back in the muddy water. His right leg looked like something in a butcher's window. Everything below his mid-thigh was gone and blood was spurting from the stump. His eyes were wide, and his face was white under the dirt. While men swarmed to fill the hole in the trench with sandbags, Thomas wrapped a tourniquet above the wound, but the blood kept flowing. Tiptoe began to shake and shudder. He fumbled desperately in the pocket of his jacket. 'My Ena's photo,' he stammered.

Thomas put his bloody hand in the lad's pocket and pulled out the crumpled and soggy photograph. Tiptoe looked at it and smiled. Then the light went out in his eyes.

*

Thomas stared at the bedroom ceiling. It was beginning to get light, but instead of picture rails and light fittings he saw the spiky, ginger hair and eager, freckled face of poor Tiptoe. Waking or sleeping, the ghosts of the lost haunted him. Anything could summon them: a word, a smell, something he saw on the street. Tiptoe had been on his mind ever since he'd heard Hetty's story. What had become of his Ena? She must have had her baby by now. Did it look like Tiptoe? Had she abandoned it to some orphanage, or had she bought a cheap gold ring and told the world her soldier husband was dead? If she had, could he blame her? Thanks to this war, the world must be overflowing with fatherless children. If there was no compassion for them and their mothers, married or not, what kind of future had they all been fighting for?

The creak of the bedroom door broke into his thoughts. Eric

padded across the room and stood beside the bed in his striped pyjamas. He looked lost and afraid. Thomas put his finger to his lips and carefully got out of bed, so as not to disturb Mary. He took the boy's hand and led him down to the scullery. 'Let's see if we can work this range and make some breakfast for Mummy, shall we?'

Eric looked at him with big, worried eyes. 'Do you think Freda is in heaven?'

'I'm certain of it.'

It was a lie. If God or heaven did exist, then how was the madness in France and Belgium still going on? What kind of God would let young lads go to their deaths in such a terrible way, leave innocent children fatherless and take beautiful little girls like Freda?

'Can we visit her?'

'I'm afraid not.'

'Will Mummy go to heaven, too?'

'Mummy is much better now. She just needs to rest and get stronger.'

At least this was true. Mary was still weak, but she smiled and spoke more every day. Having Eric home had done her good.

Four years of cooking over Heath Robinson contraptions of mess tins and candles had not prepared him for using the range. His efforts to make breakfast produced nothing but a cup of tea and laughter from Eric, but his son's amusement was more welcome than anything he might have cooked. The boy was bewildered by all the changes in his life and frightened by the loss of his sister and his mother's illness.

Thankfully, Alice and Hetty arrived to rescue Thomas while Mary was still asleep and blissfully unaware of her husband's uselessness. Between them they got the copper boiling for the Monday wash and made breakfast, while Thomas read George and Eric a story from Eric's *Little Wizard Stories from Oz*. Hetty was still subdued. She'd refused point blank to discuss George's father at all, but Thomas had a theory. The more he thought about Hetty's story, the more little snippets of other things began to make sense. The way he saw it, a man like that had to be stopped before he ruined any more lives. Still, there'd been quite enough speculation as it was, so he kept his thoughts to himself, at least for now. After breakfast, he left Hetty and Alice to their laundry and Mary to watch the boys play. He wanted to visit Bert.

*

It was still early, but as he walked towards the wharf, the sun burned the back of Thomas's neck. If this weather kept up, the washing would dry in record time. A couple of swans basked on the green algae of the slipway. They watched him as he made his way across the mud to the upturned boats. The gentle breeze cooled him and carried the smell of salty seaweed. On the opposite bank there were trees, a few clusters of ships' masts and one or two houses huddled on a hill. He heard the distant rumble of a train. How different this was to the calm green river of his childhood. He thought about the water meadows dotted with sheep and the model boats he used to sail with his brothers. He was smiling at the memory when Bert limped across the road with a tool bag over his arm.

'Wotcha, mush.' Bert grinned and shook his hand as if he were an old friend. 'How'd the dolls' house work out?'

'It didn't.' This part of the conversation was inevitable, but Thomas wasn't looking forward to it. 'We lost our little girl to the Spanish flu a few days after I met you.'

'Bloody hell.' Bert shook his head sadly. 'Don't rightly know what to say.'

'Nothing you can say. It was so quick she was gone before we knew it.'

'Something like that happened here, too. Young Alf went the same way. He was just a nipper. Helping unload the boats one day, gone the next. It might have been the flu, but it strikes me that it's not really flu season yet.'

'We had a chap at the hospital with it and we also lost two neighbours. They say it's Spanish flu, but it's much worse than the flu we had in the trenches in spring.'

'I had a few days in the hospital with that meself. Perhaps it's come back on the hospital ships?'

'That's what I thought, too.'

Bert dropped his heavy bag onto the ground with a grateful sigh. 'Where you off to?' He knelt and began to rummage amongst the tools.

'Nowhere really, I just fancied a bit of fresh air. My wife's been sick, too, and I've been stuck in a house full of women. Actually, I was hoping I'd bump into you.'

'Oh yeah?' Bert's hands stilled. He looked up and raised a thick black eyebrow.

'It's about my neighbour, Hetty Harris.' He watched Bert's expression carefully as he said the name.

'Hetty, eh?' A half smile twisted his face. 'Striking woman, stubborn though. I suppose she told you about the sugar?'

'Sugar?' Was he talking about the black market?

Bert gave Thomas a slow wink. 'Well, I might be able to get a couple of bags if you're interested. No questions asked. Hetty's your neighbour, you say?'

'She is.' Bert obviously had a soft spot for her. Should he go on or should he just pretend he wanted to buy some black-market sugar? Hetty's secret wasn't his to reveal, but he couldn't find out more without giving her away. He crouched, then looked about to make sure no one was within earshot. 'I'm not after sugar. It's Hetty's son, George, or rather his real father, I'm interested in.'

Bert narrowed his eyes. 'She's told you, then? I'm surprised. She usually clings to her tale like glue.'

'I found out by accident. She told me what happened to her, but she won't say who did it. It sounded so much like your sister's story, I wondered . . . ? If I'm right, and what she says is true, he needs to be stopped.'

Bert curled his lip. 'Oh, it's true all right. That shite arse has been dipping his wick all over the show, and you're right, George is another of his bastards. There's at least one other, maybe more. As for stopping him – I'd like to kill him, but it'd be better to make him pay. Those women shouldn't be living in the gutter bringing up his bastards while he's . . . Hetty tried, but even she backed down in the end. He called her bluff. She didn't want anyone to know the truth any more than he did. Who'd have come off worse, eh? And who'd be believed, Hetty Harris or William Wells?'

35 - Wednesday 14 August 1918

In a funny way, Mary missed the old Wednesday knitting club, but it looked as if it had been abandoned for good now. Vera hadn't left her mother's house since her son died and Effie was keeping a low profile after all the things she'd said about Hetty. To keep them busy, Alice had found some old flour sacks to turn into rag rugs. She, Hetty and Mary gathered a pile of ruined sheets and old clothes and sat at Mary's dining table cutting the fabric into long strips. It was a mindless, gentle task and the various garments provoked memories.

'This was the dress I was wearing when Harry first asked me to walk along the river with him.' Alice sliced into a faded green dress sprigged with blue flowers.

'This was a sheet I cut down for George's crib.' Hetty looked fondly at a scrap of blue-and-white striped flannelette.

She was still subdued, although she occasionally forgot herself and started on a tale about her George and the Titanic, before remembering they all knew it was a lie. When it happened they pretended not to notice. Things had almost gone back to normal, or as normal as they were ever going to be after everything that had taken place. Thomas was off buying cigarettes and a newspaper, and George, Eric, Gordon and Harold were out in the street playing football with some of the other lads. The front door was open, and Mary could hear the occasional thwack of a ball against the wall or a shout as someone scored a goal. She was slightly concerned about her windows, but it was better than worrying about them playing on the logs.

Since Monday afternoon, Mary had carried around the knowledge that William Wells was George's father. She didn't know what to do with the information any more than Thomas did. He felt bad enough already for tearing Hetty's world apart. Neither of them wanted to drag it all up again, but if there really were lots of other women like Hetty and Rose, and he was still at it, there had to be something they could do. She didn't want to cause Hetty any more grief, but what she knew might be the key to stopping the man once and for all. There was never going to be a good time to bring it up, so it might as well be now.

'Thomas knows a chap, another wounded man, who lives down by the wharves off Milbank Street. He told Thomas a story about his sister. Rose is her name.' She watched Hetty's face carefully. She had the blue-and-white crib sheet in her hands, but she paused her scissors and closed her eyes. 'She worked as a typist in a bank and her boss took advantage of her, got her in the family way and then sacked her when she wouldn't go to some doctor to sort out the problem.

'Apparently, she wasn't the first and probably not the last, either. Thomas said it made him so angry he wished he still had his rifle. It also reminded him of something similar he'd heard.'

Mary looked pointedly at Hetty and raised her eyebrow. It was obvious Hetty knew exactly what she was saying. Her cheeks flamed and her hands, still clutching the scissors and the sheet, trembled. Alice frowned and stared at Hetty. There was a long silence broken only by the tick of the clock on the mantel. Nothing moved except the dust motes floating in the weak sunbeam slanted across the dining table.

'William Wells is George's father, isn't he?'

Hetty dropped the scissors and nodded miserably. She half rose, as if she were about to run again, but Alice reached across the table and grabbed her hand. Whether this was to stop her leaving or to comfort her wasn't clear.

'Oh, my lovely,' she said. 'And here you are living in his mother's house.'

'I didn't know she was his mother.' Hetty's voice was barely above a whisper. 'I just answered the advertisement in the paper. The rent was cheap, Zillah was kind and I wanted George to have a garden to play in. If I'd known, I'd never have . . .'

'How many women has he done this to?' Mary asked gently. 'He needs to be stopped.'

Hetty shook her head sadly. 'It won't work. I always suspected there might be others. I thought if I could find them and we all spoke out . . .' She shrugged. 'Anyway, at the end of June, I

finally caught up with one of the girls, Louise, who left not long after
I started working there. She has a little boy, Bobby, a year or so older
than George. She refused to speak out about William, but she told
me about Rose, and I managed to track her down. Her brother was
all for exposing William, but Rose didn't want people to know what
had happened to her, or who Violet's father was. None of us did.

'Then I found out William was trying to get Zillah to sell her
houses. It's not just because he's afraid I'll tell her about George.
Rose told me he's in cahoots with the local bourgeoisie. They want to
invest in some project to build fancy apartments in town, and I think
he needs her money to do it. Anyway, after that I confronted him. I
told him I knew what he was up to, and I knew about Louise and
Rose. I threatened that if he didn't start supporting his children, I'd
go to the police and tell the local bourgeoisie what he'd done to us.

'He gave me some money to shut me up. It wasn't nearly
enough but I shared it with Rose and Louise. I'm fairly sure there are
more women and babies, but I haven't been able to find out for
certain. He promised me regular money, but when I went back for it,
he accused me of blackmail. He did give me something, but he said it
was the last I'd get and if I didn't keep my mouth shut, he'd have me
put in prison and George in the workhouse. He said, "Who'd take
your word against mine?" And he was right, too. Who would?
Besides, none of us wanted people to know about our shame.'

'It's his shame, not yours,' Alice said.

Hetty gave her a grateful, watery smile.

36 - Sunday 18 August 1918

Ever since they'd discovered William Wells was George's father, Thomas had been coming up with ways to stop him molesting any more girls. He said if he didn't come up with a plan soon, he was worried Bert would do something stupid. Mary listened patiently, but all his ideas – going to the police, the bank owners, Mr Winstanley the solicitor, even the reverend – hit the same stumbling block: being believed. Unless they could persuade Hetty and Rose to speak out it was hopeless and, even if they did, it was their word against his.

Mary had been quietly mulling over a different aspect of the problem. If William was George's father, then Zillah was his grandmother. Hetty was adamant Zillah must not know. She didn't think Zillah would believe it and she was worried she'd evict her or, if she did believe it, try to take George from her. Zillah might not want to think the worst of her son, no mother would, but Mary was sure she wouldn't throw Hetty out or try to take George. She was very fond of the boy, but she was fond of Hetty too. Mary felt torn between Hetty's wishes and Zillah's right to know she had a grandson, even if it broke her heart. By the time she went to collect Zillah's laundry for the morning wash, she'd decided to do as Hetty wished and keep her mouth shut. It was Hetty's secret to keep or tell. They'd meddled enough.

When she looked through the French windows, she saw the

old lady slumped in her slightly scuffed and cracked leather armchair. She looked very pale and was staring at nothing. For a split second, Mary thought she might be dead, after all, she must be in her seventies or eighties, but she looked up as Mary entered the room and gave her a half-hearted smile. Her eyes were pink, as if she'd been crying.

'Are you all right?'

'Just a disagreement with William,' she said. 'There are a lot of those these days. He persists in his ridiculous idea that I should sell my houses and move in with him. When I said no again, he said he'd found out about the influenza in the street and that I'd called on you when you were sick. He was furious.'

'I'm so sorry. I feel responsible.'

'Nonsense. Wild horses wouldn't have kept me away. Anyway, William was only thinking about himself, as usual. He accused me of being selfish. He said I could easily have passed it onto him, and had I thought about what would happen to Rebecca if she caught it. I'm afraid I told him, "She's got less of a life than I have, so it might be a blessing in disguise." I shouldn't have said it, but he shouldn't have called me a stupid old woman. He said he was thinking of speaking to Winstanley, or having me committed to the asylum, as I'd obviously lost my mind and needed protecting from myself. I'm afraid I told him not to come back if he was going to continue with his nonsense. He stormed off and now I'm worried he'll take me at my word and I'll end my days alone. Maybe I should just give in and do what he wants.' A single tear rolled down her cheek.

'Don't be silly.' Mary crouched down in front of her and took her hand. How dare he threaten his mother like that, especially after what he'd done. 'You shouldn't let him bully you into doing something you don't want. I'm sure he'll be back, and anyway, you have us – Alice, Thomas, Eric, Hetty George and me. We all care about you.'

'It isn't the same as family, though, is it?'

'Isn't it?' If she were in Zillah's shoes, wouldn't she want to know the truth, or at least some of it, however hard it was to swallow? 'Perhaps you have real family much closer than you think.'

Zillah tilted her head and frowned. 'I don't understand what you're saying. William is the only family I have in the world.'

'Actually, he's not . . .'

Very gently, Mary told her the bones of the story. She left out the worst of it, the fact that William had tried to make Hetty get rid of her child and that Hetty wasn't the only young girl he'd misused in such a terrible way. She couldn't bear to break Zillah's heart completely. When she'd finished speaking, Zillah sat for a long time, frowning and biting her knuckles. Minutes passed. So long that Mary's legs began to ache from crouching.

Finally, Zillah rose stiffly from her chair and crossed the room. She picked up a photograph from one of the little side tables and looked at it long and hard. Mary watched her. Then Zillah nodded and gave the photograph to Mary. It was a picture of William. He was wearing a sailor suit and casually leaning on what looked very much like the table the photograph had stood on. He was about George's age and, now she knew to look for it, the similarity was unmistakable.

'He was such a sweet boy,' Zillah said forlornly. 'I suppose I spoiled him, let him have too much of his own way. What he's done to Hetty and to little George is unforgivable, though. That poor, poor girl.'

37 - Monday 19 August 1918

Even though it was almost two months since Thomas had seen a trench or heard a shell bursting, this gentle, peaceful world still didn't feel real. He woke every morning expecting the mud and the blood and was haunted by echoes of it in the strangest of places, provoked by a smell, a sound or a shadow in Mary's eyes. Sometimes he looked at her and saw the shell-shocked men on the front line. She was stronger now, but she was still so quiet. She pottered about doing housework but without any of the normal songs and smiles. There was disappointment in her eyes, as if her spirit were broken.

The horror of losing Freda and how very ill she'd been were part of it. Perhaps he was part of it, too. He always said or did the wrong thing. Look at all the trouble he'd stirred up over Hetty. Mary hadn't said anything about it, but he got the feeling she was angry with him all the same. He couldn't say he blamed her. The war had changed him. He wasn't the man she married, and he was at home all the time reminding her of that.

It was time to think about finding work. If he wasn't under her feet all day, they might get along better. His final leave was almost up, the money from the army was fast running out and the meagre pension they'd offered to compensate for his wounds wouldn't feed them. He had an idea Mr Lowman might give him his old job back, or at least point him in the direction of someone who needed a willing man. If not, he'd see if Bert knew of anything. He was good with his hands, maybe he could learn to mend boats.

Down by the timber pond, some lads were dancing around attempting to coax a scrawny black dog back to the shore. A couple of the boys elbowed each other in the ribs and tried to work up the courage to walk out on the floating logs to fetch it. Thomas was relieved to see Eric wasn't amongst them. Walking across the piles of timber seasoning in the river was something of a rite of passage around here, but almost every year a boy drowned or else nearly lost his life slipping between the logs. Eric had been warned of the danger, but warnings had never stopped him, Hariph or Harry from doing stupid things when they were lads.

He spotted Eric and George behind the boathouse, on the little piece of muddy shingle by the slipway. They were laughing and skimming stones. Eric's stones skipped gracefully across the water, while poor George's landed with a plop and sank at once. Thomas lit a cigarette and watched with pride as Eric picked out better, flatter stones for George and patiently showed him again and again how to make them dance. It was good to know his son was a kind boy.

He finished his cigarette and threw the stub onto the shingle. It landed with a hiss next to an old leather boot sticking out of the slimy green mud. In a flash he was back beside the Somme and fancied there was a foot still rotting inside it. The notion was so vivid he swore he could smell the putrefying flesh. Of course, it was just a boot lost in the mud by bait diggers or washed up from somewhere, and the smell was just the mud of low tide. The Itchen disgorged all kinds of things, almost nothing stayed submerged forever. He shook his head to rid himself of the image then turned towards the railway line.

The old boot reminded him of a conversation he'd had with Bert. He worried about it as he plodded up the hill towards the bakery. They'd been talking about William Wells and how they might stop him hurting any more women. Bert said he knew where he could get hold of an old service revolver. He had a vague plan to kidnap William and force him to write a confession at gunpoint.

'What if he refused, though?'

'Then I'd shoot the bugger and dump his body in the river.'

Thomas said killing him might be taking things a bit far. The price Bert would pay for being caught was likely to be high. The noose was always a possibility. There wasn't a copper or a judge in the land who'd see his actions as justified, or side with him against a powerful man like William.

'Well, then, I'd just cut his cock off,' Bert said. 'That'd stop the bastard from doing it again.'

Thankfully, it was all just talk. At least, he hoped it was.

*

Mr Lowman came out from the back of the shop with a tray of loaves balanced on his flat-topped baker's hat. He positively beamed when he saw Thomas at the counter chatting with Mrs Lowman.

'As I live and breathe. I was only talking about you this morning.' He put the bread tray down on the counter, wiped his hand on his apron and held it out to Thomas.

'All good, I hope.' Thomas shook the huge, warm hand.

'Of course. I was telling Dottie, that's one of the girls I've got driving the vans, how you used to get round in half the time she takes, and you had twice as many orders because we had cakes and pastries back then instead of just bread.'

Mrs Lowman began to take the warm loaves off the tray and arrange them in the cabinet behind the counter. 'She's Dottie by name and dotty by nature. If she's not getting lost, she's standing about gossiping, and she says she can't lift the breadbasket when it's full, so she's back and forth to the van.'

'So, are you home on leave, then?' Mr Lowman drew his arm across his flushed forehead. It was warm in the shop but probably much cooler than in the back room with the big ovens.

'Wounded—' Thomas pointed to the war badge '—shot in

the lung, so I'm back for good.'

'Oh, that's too bad.' Mrs Lowman reached over the counter and patted his arm.

'Not if he doesn't have to go back it's not, Edith. So, I suppose you'll be looking for work?'

'Herb, he's been shot, for heaven's sake.' Mrs Lowman wagged her finger at her husband. 'Just because you want rid of Dottie there's no need to be haranguing poor Thomas into working before he's ready.'

'Actually, that was why I came here.'

*

Thomas left the baker's shop with a bag of warm bread and a job to start at the beginning of September. All in all, he'd say it had been a successful morning. He strolled down the hill feeling far lighter and more carefree than he had when he'd plodded up it. Now, if he could just stop Bert doing anything stupid.

38 - Thursday 22 August 1918

The sweltering, sticky weather left Mary listless and tired. Her clothes stuck to her body, and she could feel perspiration trickling between her breasts. Even though all the doors and windows were open, there wasn't the slightest hint of a breeze, and the oppressive heat sucked the air out of the room. She tried to work on her rag rug, but the fabric draped over her knees made her hot and irritable. Everything annoyed her today. Even the clatter as Eric tipped his tin soldiers out onto the floor made her want to scream. She couldn't tell if this prickling annoyance with everything was because of the heat, her worry over Thomas's fitness to return to work, or her guilt about revealing Hetty's secret to Zillah. She hadn't said what she was going to do with the information, but she was bound to confront Hetty at some point and, when she did, Hetty would probably go on the warpath. It all put her on edge, as if a great hammer were hanging over her head waiting to fall. As the days passed, the anticipation got worse, but as she'd told no one about talking to Zillah, she had to keep her anxieties to herself.

When Thomas's friend Joe turned up on the doorstep, he was a welcome distraction. All her irritation and nervousness evaporated the instant she saw his cheeky grin and the bunch of chrysanthemums in his hand. He was dressed in hospital blues and his arm was still strapped up and pinned in a pristine white sling.

She took the flowers. 'What a lovely surprise.'

By the time she'd dashed about finding a vase and come back in with a tray of tea, Thomas and Joe were seated on opposite sides of the dining table having an animated conversation about the war.

'The French took eight thousand more prisoners at Noyon,' Joe said. 'After all the ones they took at the beginning of the month, too. Can you even believe it? Where are they going to put them all?'

'They've got to feed the buggers, too.' Thomas shook his head. 'From what I hear, they're half-starved and giving themselves up to get a good meal.'

'Good might be overstating it a bit,' Joe laughed. 'Can't say I miss iron rations or cold Maconochie stew eaten out of a dirty mess tin in the pouring rain, with a few lice thrown in for good measure.'

'Remember that little chap we captured in spring? Herman or something, wasn't that his name?'

'We hardly captured him. If I remember rightly, he just dropped into the trench and put his hands in the air. Then Wally pretended he'd captured him.'

'No wonder, though, is it? He said they'd scarcely been able to believe the equipment and food we had when they overran our trenches in March. They thought we were all living like kings. He said he'd resolved right then to get captured as soon as he could. If we were living like kings, how bad must it have been for them?'

Quietly, Mary put the tray down, but she didn't pour the tea. This was the most she'd ever heard Thomas say about the war, and she didn't want to disturb them. The subject held a morbid fascination. She badly wanted to understand what he'd been through and why he'd changed so much. She stood perfectly still, and, from the corner of her eye, she could see Eric doing the same. He sat with one tin soldier in his hand and listened intently.

'And that was just the stuff we'd left behind, too.' Joe shook his head as if in disbelief. 'Everything we could carry went with us when we retreated.'

'If the Hun had fed and equipped their men better it might have been a different story altogether. Herman said they just stopped marching when they reached Albert and started looting – anything they could find: wine, food, clothes, even ordinary stuff like paper and pencils. They'd had nothing for so long they just couldn't help themselves, and even though there was nothing to stop them, none of their officers could make them go forward. If it weren't for that, they might have reached Paris and . . .' Thomas stuck out his bottom lip.

'Now we're pushing them back at Arras and our boys are marching back over the old Somme battlefields again, or so Wally says.'

'You've heard from Wally, then?'

'Just the odd letter. His last one was more about our Spanish lady friend and how so many of the men were falling for her and losing their hearts. He's just hoping the Hun are as fond of her as our boys.'

'How is your arm getting on?' Mary poured the tea and put a cup in front of Joe. She knew the Spanish lady was a euphemism for the flu and she didn't want to hear about it. She didn't even want to think about it. It made her picture Freda, blue and cold. Tears pricked her eyes.

'Oh, not so bad,' he shrugged. 'They've broken it again in order to fix it properly, or so they say. We shall see. Whether it works or not, I have another six or seven weeks at least before they can send me back, maybe more. Who knows, it might all be over before then.'

'Do you think it will be?' Mary asked.

As Joe opened his mouth to reply, shrill screams came from somewhere beyond the front door.

'What's that? It sounds like a child.' Joe was on his feet, an alarmed look on his face.

It did sound like a child, a child in pain or fear. Had one of the children been hurt outside or fallen in the timber pond? Thomas jumped to his feet, too. Both men ran to the front door, with Mary in hot pursuit.

The screams came from Hetty's wide-open front door. Mary

leaned over the garden wall and peered into her hallway. A bulky, dark-haired man had Hetty pinned to the wall. He had his back to them so she couldn't see his face, but it was his hands her eyes were drawn to. They were clasped around Hetty's throat. Her face was almost purple, her eyes were bulging and her hands clawed desperately at his. A bag of shopping had spilled on the floor beside her. Some apples had rolled as far as the doorsill and a bag of flour had split open.

'You've poisoned her against me . . .' he spat.

'Leave my ma alone,' George screamed, as he pulled at the man's leg. It must have been him they'd heard.

'Get off me, you filthy little bastard.' He viciously kicked the child away.

Poor George skidded across the floor like a rag doll, right through the spilt flour. Then everything happened in slow motion. Thomas leapt over the low wall between the front gardens and sprang through Hetty's door. He locked his arm around the man's throat and forced his head back so hard Mary thought he might have snapped his neck. The man's grip was broken and Hetty slithered towards the floor. In what seemed like a single, fluid movement, Thomas somehow spun around then pinned the man to the wall with a forearm across his throat. Mary caught sight of his face and gasped. It was William Wells.

'You dirty bloody coward,' Thomas spat through gritted

teeth, not loosening the pressure for a moment. William, his face red and his eyes filled with sheer terror, stared at him. 'What do you even know about killing? You're so spineless you prey on defenceless women and children. Well, let me tell you, I've killed my share of men, real men, a million times more deserving of life than you. I know all about your filthy games, all the lives you've ruined, and if you ever, ever touch Hetty again or come near her . . . if I even suspect you might have touched another woman, I will come and find you. Then my eyes will be the last things you see on this earth. Do you understand me?'

William tried to nod but he was pinned too hard to the wall to move. Thomas released him and, with a look of total disgust, said, 'Get out of my sight. If I ever see you again, I promise you'll regret it, and I'll make sure the world knows exactly what you are.'

William rubbed at his throat, picked up his hat from the floor and scurried out of the front door without a word.

Aghast, Mary leaned against her garden wall as he brushed past her. She couldn't even look at him. Thomas might have come home from the war full of anger, but he wasn't a violent man. She had never seen him so much as raise his hand to anyone, so this scene and his words had shocked her to the core. Of course, he'd been a soldier in a war, but she'd never really considered him killing anyone. She'd been so naive. Throughout it all, her eyes had been so fixed on William's face and Thomas's voice that she hadn't even looked at Hetty. She was in a heap on the floor, with Joe crouched beside her cradling her head and George kneeling at her feet crying and rocking back and forth. Her face was deathly white, and her eyes were closed. Had Thomas just let a murderer go? If Hetty was dead, it was all her fault for telling Zillah her secret.

She let out a huge sigh of relief when Hetty began to splutter and cough. Slowly, the colour returned to her cheeks. Her eyes were bloodshot, and she could see the dark red imprints of William's fingers on the skin of her neck. If they'd been slower, if all their doors and windows had been shut, or if George hadn't screamed, Hetty would be dead, Mary was sure of it.

Hetty struggled to sit up and tried to speak. 'I don't understand.' Her voice was hoarse and broken. 'Why did he do that? What did he mean?'

'I think you'd better come with me so I can explain.'

They all jumped and turned towards the gate. Zillah was leaning on the gatepost, breathing hard. Her wrinkled face was a picture of horror and grief. How long had she been there? How much had she seen and heard, and what did she mean to explain?

39 - Monday 2 September 1918

The return to work brought home just how much had changed since Thomas had last hitched a horse to a bread van back in the summer of 1914. The horse, Meg, was an old chestnut nag almost fit for the knacker's yard. She was grey about the face and had a mane streaked with white hairs. It made them a matching pair. He didn't ask what had become of poor Bunty, the black mare who used to pull his old baker's cart. It was probably better not to know. The best of the horses had been taken to the remount depots and shipped off to war. He'd rather not think of her rotting beside some French road full of bullet holes. She'd been such a good-tempered beast.

The other thing he didn't want to think about was Dottie, the young girl who'd lost her job so he could have his back. She might not have been the best delivery girl – Edith Lowman certainly didn't have anything good to say about her – but he felt bad all the same.

As they clip-clopped around the streets, with the sun just rising above the horizon and a sharpness to the chilly air that told of frost soon to come, he could almost imagine the last four years of war hadn't happened. Almost. It was still there in the back of his mind, popping up to ambush him at unexpected moments. It probably always would be. Not thinking about things was hard work, especially as the list of things not to think about kept growing. Since he came home, he'd added losing Freda, almost losing Mary and the burning rage when his arm was across William Wells's throat. He couldn't remember ever having been so angry, except perhaps once, in a small, ruined village in France. Only a supreme effort of will and the thought of Mary, Eric and the noose had kept him from snapping William's flabby neck. That monster had destroyed so many lives so casually, it was no less than he deserved. To think he'd once pitied him because of his disabled wife. Justified as his actions may have been, his violent reaction frightened him. Had the war turned him into a monster, too?

Meg was no Bunty. She was slow but she was docile and the rhythm of her hooves on the road was soothing. Shopkeepers bustled about setting out their wares to prepare for the day ahead. A greengrocer pulled down his awning and added a box of apples to the plums, cabbages and carrots on the tables outside his shop. A butcher stretched to hang skinny chickens in his window. The displays were far sparser than he remembered from before the war and the prices far higher. He settled into the tempo of the morning, checked his list now and then and reacquainted himself with familiar streets. He had a larger area to cover than before but fewer calls to make. Less bread was being made because of the shortages and vans were thin on the ground due to the lack of available men and horses. Most of the houses he had to call on now were in the more affluent parts of town, the villas with gravel drives, the mansions of Portland stone and the streets of large, detached houses. The women from the terraces and tenements around the waterside probably no longer had their bread delivered and, like Mary, walked to the shops with their baskets.

It was good to see some of his old regulars, although the constant need to tell the story of his Blighty wound quickly wore thin. There was sadness too. Many of the women he'd known told of lost husbands, sons and brothers. They were the ones dressed in black with drawn faces and solemn eyes. He'd witnessed the losses first-hand in Belgium and France, but to see it here in England brought home how far the consequences stretched. All those dead men rotting in No Man's Land or buried in makeshift cemeteries near the battlefields had families at home who loved them and would never stop missing them.

He'd changed so much that some of his old customers barely seemed to recognise him. Others, mainly in the humbler streets, were chatty and full of titbits of gossip. Hetty would have loved it. He learned of local squabbles resolved when men had died, and heard rumours of wives being unfaithful.

'That Flora Smith has been carrying on with the butcher while her husband's away, and all to get a bit of extra meat. How's she going to explain a baby born in 1917 to a husband whose last leave was at the end of 1915, eh? He might not be the brightest spark but even he can count to nine. There's one woman who won't be glad when the war ends.'

Thomas imagined her husband wouldn't be best pleased, either, if he made it home. Other than the war, food, or the lack of it, was the main topic of conversation. There were moans about the quality of the war bread and the ban on buns and cakes. Others told angry tales of profiteers, hoarders or black marketeers.

'Sally Robbins hid a sack of flour in her coal shed. She thought none of us knew but we did. Anyhow, it got overrun with little weevils and she had to throw it out. Serves her right too.'

'Fanny Mackay bought a sack of golden sugar from a man down the market. He said it was smuggled from the docks. She thought she could make a profit selling it off in smaller bags. When she got it home, it turned out to be builder's sand. Of course, she couldn't find him again to get her money back. She got what she deserved.'

Along The Avenue, lots of women were walking tiny dogs, small enough he could have picked each one up and popped it in his pocket. Where were all the big dogs? Was there some new rule about the size of hound you could walk on any particular day? It wouldn't have surprised him. If the Defence of the Realm Act could make whistling for a taxi illegal, or buying your mate a drink, why not what breed of dog you could walk and when? Perhaps tomorrow there'd be women walking Dobermans and Great Danes. Hopefully not. Big dogs generally seemed to see a man carrying a breadbasket as something to chase, and he wasn't fond of being chased.

When they got to the common, the horse decided to stop outside The Cowherds pub for no apparent reason. She refused to move on, despite all his cajoling. After a good five minutes of clicking and clucking, he had to get down from the cart and lead her for a while.

When he came to the gates of William Wells's big, double-fronted house, with its curved driveway and manicured lawn, his heart beat a little faster. He was sure the man wouldn't be there, but all the same he'd rather not have been knocking at his door. The maid answered, the same chubby young woman with mousey hair and little wire-rimmed spectacles as before the war. She was as snooty as ever but now he wondered if she was actually the nurse Zillah said looked after William's invalid wife.

'Two loaves today, please.' She wiped her hands on her white apron. 'And ask Mr Lowman if he could manage a lardy cake next time.'

'We're not doing cakes and buns for delivery at the moment.' He took out his ledger and wrote down the two loaves the woman had taken from the basket.

'Just tell him Mrs Wells asked. He'll do it for her,' she said with a tight smile. 'He always does special orders for Mrs Wells.'

Thomas made a note of it in his book. It irritated him that those with money could get things like lardy cake on a whim, while others, people like the families in the waterside houses, could barely scrape together enough to survive. He probably shouldn't begrudge a poor crippled woman such a small pleasure, but he begrudged her husband any pleasure at all. He wasn't convinced William would heed his warning. There had to be some way of stopping him for good that didn't involve all of them hanging.

40 - Wednesday 4 September 1918

'I almost wish Thomas could have come.' Hetty put the menu back on the table and leaned back. 'If it wasn't for him . . . well, I might not be alive, never mind sitting here trying to decide between sandwiches and cakes.'

Two weeks later and they were still talking about what had happened, chewing over all the details. Perhaps they always would be. The aftermath of William's attack had turned all their lives upside down, especially Hetty's. She was barely recognisable with her bobbed hair, simple, stylish grey dress and the little fur stole around her neck. It was as if the old Hetty *had* died that day and been replaced with this new, self-assured, well-groomed version. She seemed right at home in this swanky tearoom, with its bentwood chairs, marble-topped tables and Tiffany-style lampshades. The waitresses, with their black dresses, white aprons and little frilled hats like tiaras made Mary feel uncomfortable. Hetty was completely at ease, as if she'd been born to be waited on.

'If it hadn't been for me and my big mouth . . .' Mary tailed off. She wished she could forget about William's hands around Hetty's throat and Thomas talking about the men he'd killed. Like an itchy scab, they kept picking at it, though. 'I still feel guilty now. You told me not to tell her –'

'And I was wrong.' Hetty reached across the table and took

her hand. 'You needn't feel guilty at all. Think of all the good things that have come out of it, not just for me but for Zillah, too. She's gained a grandson and George has a proper family.'

She didn't mention the money. The old Hetty would have been focused on that.

'She didn't question it at all, you know.' Mary glanced at the menu without really taking it in. 'It was almost as if she had half an idea already.'

'Perhaps she had. George does look a lot like William did as a child. ' Hetty leaned forward and spoke in a hushed voice. 'Every time I dusted that photograph, I saw it and wondered how she didn't, although I hate to think of that man being any part of my boy. In fact, I don't like thinking about him at all. He'd rather have seen us both dead than have his mother acknowledge us. It was always about his reputation and what people would think of him.'

'Perhaps he should have thought about that in the beginning, then,' Mary whispered back.

'I think the final straw came when he went to Winstanley to try and have her declared incapable. He thought he'd be able to take control of her finances, but Winstanley told him she'd already signed the houses over to me and tied most of her money up in trust funds. The thought of losing all that money must have sent him mad. Of course, I didn't know about the houses, the will or the trust fund when he attacked me. I didn't even know Zillah knew about George.'

238

Hetty looked up as the waitress came over to take their order. 'Afternoon tea for three, please. Our friend is a little late but I'm sure she'll be here shortly.'

'Well, he was the master of his own downfall in the end, wasn't he?' Mary said once the waitress had gone. 'Look at the way they all turned their backs on him at church last week. They must all know at least some of it. If he'd just accepted it rather than . . .' And there it was again, the image of William with his hands around Hetty's throat.

'I'm not sure how he thought he was going to get away with it—' Hetty shook her head sadly '—but I suppose he might have if George hadn't shouted so loudly and Thomas and his friend hadn't come to the rescue. If Zillah hadn't come out to investigate all the noise and seen it with her own eyes, he still might have ended up with something. She's got pots of money, you know. Her husband left her a fortune when he died and she owns half the houses in our terrace, or at least she did before she signed them over to me. She saw him kick George, though, and heard what he said to him. I think that was the final straw for her. She's completely cut him off now. She's had papers drawn up and everything. If something happens to her, he'll get nothing, and if he tries to fight it, everyone will know exactly what he's done. I'll wager Winstanley has spread the word amongst the local bourgeoisie too. Now they know he's no use to them they don't want to know him.'

The waitress cut their conversation short when she appeared

with a large, three-tiered silver platter filled with tiny triangular sandwiches, dainty little bite-sized cakes and pastries. Mary had never seen such a spread and couldn't imagine how they would ever eat it all. She opened her mouth to say something, but Hetty, who was sitting in the chair facing the window, began to wave. Agnes Dunfold had arrived.

'Goodness me, I barely recognised you, Henrietta, and you must be Mary.' Agnes stuck out her hand and Mary shook it. She felt a fraud to be there at all, but Hetty had said she didn't want to face Agnes on her own. Now she was here, she didn't look in the least bit frightening. She was a plain, sturdily built woman with straggly grey hair, a careworn face and a tight, suspicious smile. She might once have had a spark of something about her, but if she had, it had long since been extinguished. She sat beside Hetty. The waitress appeared again with three little pots of tea, miniature milk jugs and delicate porcelain cups, plates and saucers on a tray. There was even a bowl filled with sugar lumps.

When she'd gone, Agnes got straight to the point. 'So, tell me, Henrietta, what exactly is all this about?' She waved her hand to indicate the spread laid out before them.

Mary poured the tea while Hetty told Agnes the bare facts about William's attack on her and the change in her fortunes.

'He wasn't always bad, you know,' Agnes said sadly when Hetty had finished her tale. 'When I first started at the bank, he was so kind and handsome that I couldn't help falling in love with him. I was just sorting and counting the notes in those days. Then he got the first typewriter and, being the only female on the staff, I was the obvious choice to operate it. I knew exactly what I was getting into, and I did it willingly, even though I knew all about his wife. To be honest, I felt a little sorry for her, and for him for being tied to her forever. It's such a tragic story.

'Then, when I found out I was having a baby . . . he'd have left her if he could, but it wouldn't have been right. He could never acknowledge it. He said, "The life of a child without a father isn't worth living. It would be better not to be born at all." So . . . well, you know what I did.' She looked down at the table and gulped a few times, as if she was swallowing tears. 'It broke my heart, and I think it may have broken his a little, too, because that was when he began to change. Perhaps we both did. We carried on as we were for a while. I half hoped there would be another baby. If there had been I'd have kept it, but the doctor . . . well, it didn't happen. Then he grew tired of me. I think it was the guilt over what we'd done. Anyway, he moved onto a younger, prettier typist, and then another – all young women I'd been put in charge of as a reward for staying silent.'

'And that is exactly why we need your help,' Hetty said. 'You know the names of all the others, the ones who kept their babies, like me.'

'But I don't see what use that is.' Agnes chose a sandwich from the platter and put it on her plate. 'I'm not going to speak out against him if that's what you want, and I doubt any of the others will. It would ruin their reputations, too, you must understand that.'

'That's not what I'm asking.' Hetty dropped a sugar lump into her tea and stirred it, then dropped in another for good measure. Sugar was a luxury too good to be wasted. 'I don't care about exposing him or making him pay for what he's done. I threatened him with that once before and it didn't work. Maybe if I could have persuaded Louise or Rose to join me, but neither would, no matter how hard I tried to convince them. What I now want to do is put it right as much as I can, and to do that I need their names, along with your assurance that you'll tell me if he ever touches another of the girls.'

'I don't think he'll dare do it again. I knew something had happened because he's really changed over the past couple of weeks. He's kept right away from the typing office, and he's been – I don't know how to explain it – quiet, scared, defeated. I've been worried about him. You have my word I'll tell you if he goes back to his old ways. I still can't see how you can put it right, though.' Agnes frowned.

'Actually, it was William's mother's idea. When she found out I wasn't the only one, she wanted to make amends. She had an idea that I could set up an office for people and businesses that need documents or manuscripts typed up. She has some contacts and she's going to finance it, so all the women will have safe, respectable jobs. It's going to take a little while to set up, but I won't be able to do it at all if I don't have their names. I know about Rose and Louise, but how many others are there, and who are they?'

'Not as many as you'd think.' Agnes sighed heavily. 'There were only four babies: yours, Louise's, Rose's and Minnie Delaney's. There were other girls, of course, but some were too clever to get caught and most of the ones who did got rid of the babies just as they were bid.'

41 - Sunday 22 September 1918

Thomas, Joe and Bert sat in the Junction Inn and watched the rain through the window. The pub was a step down from the Prince Consort. The arched windows and polished mahogany bar were attractive enough, but the dark wood of the tables was ringed with the imprint of a thousand wet glasses, the floor was slightly sticky underfoot and the air aromatic with stale tobacco and something else slightly unsavoury, possibly damp. Its main attraction was its proximity to St Denys Station. This made life easier for Joe, who had to be back at Netley Hospital before curfew, or risk a ticking off from the sister.

'All this rain reminds me of the Somme.' Joe lit a Woodbine. 'Remember how we huddled in the mud waiting for something to happen? Anything. Even going over the top seemed better than sitting there with the damp seeping up through our boots and the noise of our artillery whooshing over our heads.'

'If we'd known what was ahead, we'd likely not have been so eager.' Bert shook his head sadly. 'More men was lost than came back from my lot that first day, and even the ones that did crawl back to the trench was mostly injured.'

'I'll never forget watching the first wave being cut down before they'd even properly got to their feet. Those poor East Lancashires, it was like a scythe through grass.' Thomas shook out the match he'd used to light his own cigarette and dropped it into the rusty tin ashtray in the middle of the table. It looked as if it might once have been a bully beef tin. 'Until then I thought the Germans must all be dead. When our turn came it was as if we'd climbed into hell itself. God knows how any of us survived.'

'I still dream about it now,' Joe admitted.

'Me too,' Bert agreed.

'Do you think we'll ever forget?' Thomas took a swig of his beer. He enjoyed these get-togethers with Bert and Joe. It was oddly comforting to know he wasn't the only one who couldn't stop remembering. What he really wanted, though, was someone to tell him how to forget, or at least to assure him he would one day.

'How can we?' Joe licked the beer froth off his top lip. 'When you've stared into the fires of hell, it's etched permanently on your brain.'

They all stared miserably into their beer for a while, each contemplating a future plagued by nightmares and memories. At least that was what Thomas was thinking, and he had no reason to suppose the others were any different. He hoped it wasn't true. He needed to believe it would fade one day. The murmur of other conversations and the chink of glasses filled the silence.

'My cousin Frank has got a motorcycle.' Bert looked around to make sure no one was listening in. 'He's been following William

Wells to work out where he's most vulnerable. On Thursday night, he saw him going into the Masonic Lodge at the top of the forty steps. He left his motorcar right outside. I was thinking, I could hide inside it and wait for him to come out, maybe next Thursday, if I can get hold of the gun by then. I'll force him to drive off somewhere quieter –'

'They only meet once a month,' Joe said matter-of-factly.

Thomas stared at him. What did he know about Masonic lodges? Joe saw the look and gave a sheepish shrug. 'A chap I used to work with on the trams was a member.'

'Anyway, what if someone saw you get into the motorcar?' Thomas said. 'Or what if William shouted, and some of the other masons heard?'

Bert scratched his head awkwardly. 'Well, it ain't a perfect plan yet, but Frank is still following him.'

'And even if you did manage to make him drive off somewhere quiet, and you ended up shooting him, Agnes Dunfold wouldn't keep her mouth shut. Mary thinks she's still in love with him. Sooner or later, the police would work their way round to you, Bert, or at least to Hetty.'

They'd had these fanciful conversations a few times now. Most of the ideas Bert came up with were plain ridiculous, but this one sounded as if it might develop into a real plan. It might work if

Bert just frightened William with the gun and maybe made him write a confession, but Thomas didn't think Bert would stop at frightening him.

'I ain't seen much of Hetty of late.' Bert tried to look nonchalant but the colour high on his cheeks gave him away. 'I suppose she's busy with her typewriting.'

Thomas looked across the table at Joe and Joe winked back at him. They'd both concluded Bert was besotted with Hetty. It was part of the reason he was so set on getting back at William, but it might also be a good way to distract him from doing anything rash.

'All you can hear from her place is clack, clack, clack all day long, so she must be getting plenty of work,' Thomas said. 'I've hardly seen her myself.'

As soon as he'd stopped trying to get rid of her, she'd all but disappeared. How ironic.

'Rose is there for the most part and making good money, too. Last time I saw Hetty, she'd cut off her hair and got fancy new clothes. She looked like a proper lady,' Bert said wistfully.

'She's certainly moved up in the world,' Thomas agreed.

Poor Bert ground out his cigarette with a look of regret, as if someone had just stolen his favourite toy. He probably thought Hetty was too good for him now. Thomas somehow doubted it. He had an inkling she was lonely. He saw Joe bite his lip to stifle a witty remark and gave him a stern stare. Unrequited love was no joking matter.

They went back to talking about the progress of the war for a while.

'Wally wrote to tell me poor old Nobby copped it last week and Davie took some shrapnel in the leg,' Joe said. 'Apparently, the Americans chased Jerry out of Saint-Mihiel.'

'Bloody Yanks. If they hadn't sat on the fence for so long, it could have all been over in '16,' Bert said angrily. 'I'm surprised the buggers could fight at all, what with splinters up their arses. Think of all the lives that needn't have been lost.'

They chewed over the Allied successes, from France to Serbia, Turkey and the Middle East. Perhaps it really was coming to an end.

'It'd be nice to think it would all be over before I'm well enough to go back—' Joe nodded to his arm '—but I can't see it ending before New Year.'

'I'll wager February or March,' Bert said.

'June.' Thomas picked a date at random. He had as much trouble believing it would ever end as he did believing what he read in the papers.

When Joe went off to the privy, Thomas took the opportunity to speak to Bert about Hetty. 'You should tell her how you feel, you know.'

'She'd never look at the likes of me.' Bert rubbed his stubbly chin gloomily. 'What have I got to offer her except a bit of black-market stuff smuggled out of the docks? She don't need to depend on selling that now, though.'

'You might be surprised. I thought Mary was far too good for me, but women are strange creatures, they don't see things the way we do. Unless you try, how will you ever know?'

Even as he said it, Thomas had an idea his words were falling on deaf ears.

Bert shrugged and changed the subject. 'Did you hear about Olympic? She docked yesterday full of flu cases. They took 'em off to the isolation hospital. Over a hundred there were, and forty odd dead. They've been trying to hush it up, but Frank heard it from a docker who saw 'em all being carted off.'

'What's that? More flu?' Joe had come back and caught the tail end of the conversation. 'I heard Lloyd George almost died from it, although they're trying to make out it was just a cold. The story is he went to Manchester, got soaked in the rain and caught a bad chill. He was in bed in the town hall for ten days, but he's recovered now.'

'A cold my arse.' Bert took a sip of his pint. 'Ten days in bed don't sound like a cold to me.'

'For goodness' sake, don't mention it in front of Mary,'

Thomas said. 'She can't bear to hear about the flu. She thinks it's some kind of plague sent by God to punish us for the war.'

'Maybe it is,' Joe said.

42 - Saturday 28 September 1918

Lottie, the milk woman, waved as she passed. Thomas waved back. He was getting used to seeing women driving carts and omnibuses, just as he was getting used to the early starts and lumping the big wicker breadbasket from door to door again. It wasn't quite the world he'd left in 1914, but it was better than the Western Front. At least here he was in charge of his own destiny. He could stop when he wanted, pop into a shop to buy cigarettes, chat for a moment to Jim, the rag and bone man, and Fred, the coalman, or even pet Miss Newman's dog. It felt like tremendous freedom after army life. The biggest bonus was having no one shooting at him, although any loud and sudden noise, such as the backfiring of a motorcar, made him duck as if they were. The worst thing he had to worry about now was grumbles from the odd difficult customer about the war bread or the shortages. Luckily, they were few and far between.

A light drizzle was falling. Droplets sparkled on Meg's mane and made the reins slippery in his hands. He didn't mind the rain. He had the shelter of the overhanging van roof and a warm, dry house to go home to at the end of the day. Meg followed a tram past the stag gates. Thomas watched the view ahead getting steadily greener the nearer they got to the common. He chuckled to himself at the memory of the argument he'd witnessed earlier between Mrs Dash and Mrs Oliver. The spectacle of two well-to-do women in floral pinafores quarrelling loudly over ownership of the pile of manure

Meg had left smack bang between their two houses was comical. There was a brief moment when it looked as though they'd use their shovels as weapons, but in the end they both began to furiously scoop as much of the muck as they could into their buckets, cursing each other as they did so. It was all he could do not to laugh out loud. He was still smiling about it when Meg pulled up outside The Cowherds pub. She did the same thing every time they passed. One of the old baker's men must have liked a tipple there during their round. Somehow, he doubted it was his predecessor, Dottie. Outside the pub, a group of girls skipped with a long rope and sang.

'I had a little bird. Its name was Enza. I opened the window and in flew Enza.'

The smile left his face. After Geoffrey, the flurry of cases near his home, then Freda and Mary, he'd believed the epidemic was over. Now it looked like it was back searching for new victims. Over the last week or so, several of his customers told tales of people sick with flu. Maybe it had something to do with the men that came off Olympic at the docks.

It took a while, but reluctantly Meg moved on. At the Wells's house, he was surprised when a young lad with brown hair, thick glasses and legs like knobbly-kneed matchsticks answered the door. He looked to be two or three years older than Eric, perhaps more, as he was a skinny lad. The boy gawped at him myopically until the nurse – Thomas was now sure she was a nurse – came rushing along the hallway. 'Wilfred!' she shouted, 'how many times have I told you not to answer the door?'

The boy scurried away, with a helping hand on his backside. Still scowling, the nurse took the loaves without so much as a thank you. The boy must be her son, or maybe a much younger brother, and he was probably supposed to be seen and not heard. Perhaps he wasn't supposed to be there at all. It was none of Thomas's concern, though.

Soon enough, Meg was back in the stable and he was on the way home. He walked with his head down against the rain, brooding about the William Wells situation. All those pub conversations about killing or maiming him might have been pie in the sky, but Bert in particular was beginning to sound obsessed. The talk of guns and of Frank following William on his motorcycle worried him. Bert sounded deadly serious. He was convinced William was a threat to Hetty. Though talking about it in the pub and actually doing it were two entirely different things, weren't they? They'd all killed men, men who deserved to die far less than William Wells, but killing someone in battle was not the same as committing cold-blooded murder.

He passed a mass of scruffy lads crowded around the timber pond and strolled towards his house. He was looking forward to warming himself in front of the fire with a cup of tea. As he neared his terrace, he noticed Bert on Hetty's doorstep. He was all spruced up in his demob suit, wearing a bowler hat and carrying, of all things, a cane. The look he'd been aiming for was probably 'wealthy man about town', but he hadn't achieved it by a long shot. The suit was a touch too big, making him look more like Charlie Chaplain's tramp. Still, he'd obviously made an effort. Thomas held back and watched. Maybe Bert had finally decided to take his advice and declare his feelings to Hetty. The last thing he wanted was to put him off.

43 - Monday 30 September 1918

There was a rich, loamy scent of autumn in the air and a blast of chilly dampness when Mary opened the front door to send Eric off to school. Gordon and George were waiting at the gate. Hetty's typing and Thomas's return to work had finally put paid to the idea of walking the boys to the railway bridge, although she warned Eric every single morning not to cross the rails. He ran up the path and almost bumped into Hetty struggling towards the door with her basket of laundry. There was more of it these days, thanks to all the fancy clothes she'd bought, but now that she had no time to help, she paid Mary and Alice to do it for her, so they couldn't complain. Hetty's assistance had always been a token gesture and the money was more than welcome.

Mary was glad to get back to the warmth of the scullery, with the copper boiler bubbling away in the corner. Hetty dumped her wash basket on the kitchen table but made no move to leave.

'I'm at sixes and sevens with the clocks going back,' she said as she sank onto the rocking chair with a look halfway between a smile and a frown. 'Well, that and the gentleman caller I had on Saturday afternoon.'

'A gentleman?'

Mary began to sort the clothes in Hetty's basket into piles.

Thomas said he'd seen Bert on Hetty's doorstep. He seemed to think he was a good-hearted fellow, if a little rough around the edges. It might be nice for Hetty to have a man in her life. It would certainly be good for George.

'Well, not quite a gentleman.' Hetty looked down at her hands. 'Rose's brother, Bert.'

'Thomas has been spending a lot of time with him lately. He seems nice enough.'

'He is, I think.' Hetty's face went a little pink. 'He invited me to go for a drink with him.'

'And did you?'

'I said I'd think about it and let Rose know.'

'And?' Mary raised her eyebrows.

'I'm still thinking.'

'And have you reached any kind of conclusion?' Mary bit her lip to stop herself from laughing.

'I don't know what to do.' Hetty chewed at the side of her cheek. 'Just when I think I've got my life sorted out – the typing is going well, I've got enough money not to have to worry – and then this happens.'

'You make it sound like a bad thing. Don't you like him?'

'Oh, I like him well enough. He's no Douglas Fairbanks but he's a steady, hardworking kind of chap. Do I need a man complicating my life, though? I've got by well enough all this time. Besides, what would Zillah think? She might not like the idea at all, and then where would I be?'

'Zillah would likely be pleased for you. I'm sure she'd want you to have a little happiness and for George to have a father figure.'

Hetty looked horrified. 'It's only an invitation for a drink, not a marriage proposal.'

'Well, there'd be no harm in it then, would there?' Mary shook her head and took the last of the clothes from Hetty's basket.

'No harm in what?' Alice came through the back door with her own laundry. Her hair and skirt were wet. It must have started raining again.

'Nothing.' Hetty shot Mary a warning glare. 'I was just saying I was thinking of putting an advertisement in the newspaper to find Minnie Delaney. I've tried just about everything else.'

'Perhaps she doesn't want to be found.' Alice put her basket on the table and gave Mary an enquiring look. She knew Hetty was being evasive. 'She might have married and changed her name. Her husband might not know anything about her past, and she might want to keep it that way.'

'I was going to put "discretion assured," so she'd know I

wasn't about to tell everyone her business.' Hetty stood up, as if to go, then looked at the rain pounding on the window and seemed to think better of it. 'Talking of business, did you hear that Mr Winstanley has had to close his office because so many of his staff have come down with the flu?'

'There's been lots of it about again.' Alice began to put the coloured clothes into the tin bath. 'I'd think germs of any kind would spread easily in a big office.'

'Some of the girls have been taken to the isolation hospital. At least that's what Zillah told me. She said Norah Thorne has died. I can't say I liked her very much, but she wasn't even thirty. That's no age, is it? It's almost as if the youngest and fittest, the ones who'd normally be fine, are being hit the worst. All in all, it seems a very strange state of affairs. They say the hospital is getting overrun with cases.'

'Where's Harold?' Mary changed the subject. She didn't want to think about the flu.

'I left him playing with Bertie next door. They had all their soldiers set out on Effie's parlour floor, so I'd never have been able to drag him away anyway. Effie doesn't mind, she says one more makes no difference.' Alice looked anxiously at the scullery window. The rain was really coming down now. 'We're going to have to set the airers up by the look of it. Remember when Thomas told us about the men rowing down Millbank Street to the pub in boats? If this rain keeps falling, I'll wager they'll be doing that again soon.'

Mary began to stuff the white washing into the copper boiler. She couldn't stop thinking about the flu. She imagined she could smell the cloying, musty scent of sickness everywhere she went, as if it lurked in the shadows just waiting to take something else from her. The only place she was free of it was here, at home, and even then, the fear and the memories came upon her at odd moments. She missed Freda's chatter and her singing, the warm little arms around her neck and those big blue eyes smiling at her. When she went out, her heart jumped at every little blonde girl who passed by, and the sight of pretty ribbons in a shop window reminded her she had no one to buy them for. Sometimes she almost fancied Freda was there when she walked into a room. Was this what it was like for Thomas? He'd lost so much more than her. It wasn't only all the years of the children's lives he'd missed, but what he'd been through in those years. Did the things he'd seen and done haunt him as much as that one horrific day haunted her?

44 - Friday 4 October 1918

Thomas and Bert had already settled at a corner table in the Junction Inn and were patiently waiting for Joe's train to arrive. They'd even persuaded Edwin, the landlord, to sell them a pint on his behalf. As this was their fifth Friday evening in a row at the establishment, he'd begun to treat them as regulars. So far, they were his only customers, so there was little chance of anyone reporting him for breaking the rules.

'It's been near on a week and I still ain't heard nothing from Hetty.' Bert turned his glass around and around, but didn't pick it up. 'How much time does a woman need to make up her mind?'

Bert had told Thomas about his visit a couple of days after the event. Thomas had acted surprised. From what Mary said, things didn't sound hopeful for poor old Bert, and as he hated to be the bearer of bad news, he said nothing. He took a sip of his beer to give him thinking time and then said, 'It's hard to tell what goes on in women's minds. Perhaps you could try again, maybe suggest going somewhere with George. Heaven knows the lad could do with a man in his life, and if she sees you getting on well with him –'

'Maybe I could take them out on me boat?' Bert nodded to himself. 'The lad might like that.'

'It's worth a try, as long as you don't expect Hetty to row.'

'She's a gaff cutter, you cheeky beggar,' Bert snorted huffily. Seeing Thomas's blank face, he explained, 'That's a sailboat to you. She were one of the old Itchen Ferries. Got her for a song. Like a bloody sieve she were, but I fixed her up and she's a beauty now.'

A few minutes later, Joe arrived, minus his cast. He spotted them as soon as he came through the door and joined them with a sheepish grin.

'What's the verdict on the arm?' Thomas asked as soon as he'd sat down.

'Well—' Joe wrinkled his nose '—there's good news and there's bad.'

'They're not sending you back?'

It would be too bad now, when things looked as if they might be coming to an end.

'Not yet, the bone has set. It's better than it was but it's still not straight.' He rolled up his sleeve to reveal a white, dry-skinned arm, slightly crooked and wasted away. 'It's as weak as a baby's, too, because I haven't been able to use it for so long. The M.O. says it'll take a lot of work to build it up before I'm fit for action.'

'Bloody hell.' Bert stared at Joe's arm as if he'd never seen anything like it in his life. 'Show us the other one, else I'm going to believe they're both like that and you're just a sissy.'

Joe duly rolled up his other sleeve. This arm was brown, hairy and a completely normal size. When he put the two together the difference was even more pronounced.

'If they gave out medals for lead swinging, Private Wilson, you would have a chest full of them,' Thomas laughed.

As the light began to fade, the bar slowly began to fill up with working men in their fifties or older. They were wearing flat caps and baggy, threadbare jackets. Before long, the place was noisy and smoky. No one took much notice of Thomas, Bert and Joe. They'd purposely picked a table in the corner, knowing from previous experience the pub would get crowded as the evening wore on.

'I think I know how I can trap Wells.' Bert leaned forward and looked around to double-check for listening ears. 'You know Frank's been watching him. Well, it turns out he's got a dog. It's one of them silly little poodle things, looks like it's wearing a Russian hat.'

'A poodle? How does that help? Don't tell me you're going to capture it, train it to kill and then send it back?' Thomas laughed.

'No, but he parks his motorcar along Cemetery Road when he walks it on the common.' Bert waggled his eyebrows. 'It's very quiet along there at night, and I've got the gun now.'

Until he said that, it had sounded like yet more pie in the sky. Now it was deadly serious. Thomas shot a worried look at Joe, and the expression on Joe's face said he felt the same.

'It all comes back to the same thing, though, Bert.' Thomas tried to reason with him. 'If you shoot him, it'll be murder, and it'll likely come back to you, or to Hetty. One of you could swing for it.'

'Not if they think he shot himself.' Bert tapped his temple. 'If I hide in the car, shoot him right up close and then leave the gun there in his hand . . .'

'Won't they trace it back to you, though?' Joe said.

'They'll have a job,' Bert snorted. 'It's not as if I came by it legally, and I'd wipe it clean and wear gloves. If I put it in his hand, his will be the only prints on it, and didn't that Dunfold woman say he were acting odd and she were worried about him?'

'She also said he hadn't been near the typing office since Thomas almost strangled him, and he's got nothing to gain anymore from harming Hetty. I think you should just leave it, Bert,' Joe said. 'It's not worth risking the noose for him.'

'Maybe not.' Bert didn't look convinced. 'What if he keeps on doing it, though? Leopards don't change their spots.'

Thomas could see Bert wasn't going to be put off completely, so maybe it was time for damage limitation. 'If you're determined to frighten him, then threaten him with the gun by all means. Just don't load the bloody thing. That way you can't get yourself, or Hetty, in trouble.'

'You're probably right.' Bert rubbed at his chin regretfully.

Maybe he was finally giving up on his plan.

'Of course he is.' Joe smiled with relief. 'Especially when it looks as if the war really might be coming to an end. You don't want to be locked up for the party when that happens now, do you?'

They sat in silence for a long time after that. Bert looked gloomy and Joe and Thomas shot each other a series of worried glares and frowns. Joe, Thomas, and Wally, if he was still alive, were the last of the boys of '14, but Bert felt like one of them now and neither of them wanted to see him come to a bad end, especially not over a worm of a man like William Wells.

'I can't believe the Hindenburg Line is broken.' Thomas took a swig of beer.

'Our lads were involved in that, according to Wally,' Joe said. 'So, it must be true.'

'I suppose Wally was the first one through and without him it wouldn't have happened?' Thomas shook his head.

'All twenty miles of it, of course,' Joe chuckled.

'Just two days to push them out of Wipers, so they say.' Bert screwed up his mouth. 'Don't sound right to me.'

'If it's true about Bulgaria signing an armistice, the end really could be in sight,' Thomas said.

Joe bit his lip nervously. 'If that's true, it could still be months yet. I can't see it being over before Christmas. I'm pretty sure they'll have sent me back long before then.' He closed his eyes and took a deep breath. 'I've got to be honest, I'd rather not go, much as I'd like to see Jerry on the run.'

'It might not come to that.' Thomas hoped it wouldn't anyway. He drained his glass and wiped his mouth with the back of his hand. 'Another?'

Joe turned his wrist to check the time. For a brief moment, Thomas saw the luminous hands on his own watch glowing in the darkness. He flinched slightly, waiting for the thwack on his back.

'Why not?' Joe stood up. 'While I have the chance, I might as well get as much of this watered-down piss inside me as I can. It'll be rum rations and over the top again before I know it.'

45 - Monday 14 October 1918

Meg's breath came out in big clouds as they slowly clip-clopped past the Titanic Engineers' Memorial. Would they erect a memorial to the dead of this war one day? If they did, what kind of statue would they choose? What best reflected it? A giant rat with a human hand in its mouth sprang to mind, or maybe a dead horse, half-buried in mud, or the Grim Reaper with his scythe. Thomas's thoughts were running to the melancholy. It was that kind of morning. Heavy, menacing clouds had gathered above and sparkling white frost blanketed the ground. He'd dreamed of the war again last night. Now the images were stuck in his head and refused to budge.

He could still see the colours as the shells burst: black, white, pink and yellow, like a dreadful, deathly firework display. The noise had been louder than he had imagined possible. Every single gun in the German Army must have been firing on them. That any of them had survived could only have been a miracle. It had taken everything he had just to lie in the long grass, point his rifle and keep shooting, picking off anything that moved. When a target fell, he'd thought nothing of the man it had been. It was merely one less gun to shoot at him. He saw Joe, a few yards to his right with his rifle to his eye. To his left was Dougie in the same pose. Had they been as afraid as him? The terrific roar of the artillery and the rattle of the machine guns had beat so loudly in his head that even the pounding heat of the sun, the dryness of his mouth and the blisters on his feet barely registered. The din couldn't drive out the bitterness of being forced back, though. They'd passed through village after village with strange, unpronounceable names: Solesmes, Briastre, Le Coquelet and Le Cateau.

The dreams were less frequent now, but no less disturbing when they came. They set the tone for the day. The memory of roads full of villagers – old men with carts piled high, women with babies in their arms and dirt on their frightened faces – would stay with him forever. They were the same people who'd cheered them to victory just hours before. They must have retreated ten miles or more, filled with shame at letting those poor sods down.

Perhaps reading the news had brought it all back. If the newspapers were to be believed, a few days ago, the army had marched back to Cambrai and Le Cateau, taking eight thousand Hun prisoners along the way. Four long years and they were almost back to where they'd started. Most of the men in his dream were dead, and for what? The villages they'd retreated through were nothing but rubble now. Half of France had barely one stone left on top of another. Even the 'Golden Virgin' in Albert had fallen.

Meg stopped outside the next house, the first of the three-story terraces with mock Tudor gables and arched porches. Thomas had been so lost in his misery he hadn't even noticed passing the Stag Gates. He looked at his list, picked up the breadbasket and fixed a smile to his face. When he reached the door, he saw it had a black beribboned yew wreath tied to the knocker. It reminded him of the ones Hetty had put on their house at the end of July, and the little white coffin covered in flowers. He closed his eyes to shut the memory out and rapped on the door. No one answered. He was about to turn away when Mrs Lomas poked her head out of the porch next door.

'They're all at the isolation hospital with the flu,' she said. 'Maud caught it first and she was dead the next day. The others . . .' She shook her head and stuck out her bottom lip. It was the third flu house today.

He drove on towards the common. The trees were beginning to turn, and there was a definite blush of gold amongst the green. Little eddies of fallen leaves swirled into piles here and there. Meg swung to the right to avoid the tail end of a queue of coffin-filled carriages waiting in line on Cemetery Road. He counted five of them as he passed. The last ones were sticking out onto The Avenue. To make them wait like that there must be others further up. He'd thought the flu was all over, but, like all those long days waiting around in trenches, August had been nothing but a lull between battles. Just as the Hun crawled across No Man's Land in the dark, this fresh attack had crept up on them, and now they were in the midst of it again. Even the newspapers had started reporting on it. They said it was a more virulent type of flu than earlier in the year. Hadn't Donald said that back in July? Or was it Stanley? He couldn't quite recall. Either way, he couldn't see how it could be worse than what he'd seen in the summer.

As usual, Meg pulled up outside The Cowherds and refused to go on. He flicked the reins, but she just twitched her ears as if he were the one in the wrong and should be going inside. He sighed and got down from his seat. He wanted to get the round over with, but experience told him it was quicker to stop for a while rather than keep urging her forwards when she thought she knew better. He sat on the kerb and lit a cigarette. Across the road, a woman was walking a little dog. It reminded him of Bert and his outlandish plan to ambush William Wells. He wasn't talking about it anymore. Was his silence a sign that he'd given up on the idea, or that his plans were complete and there was no more to discuss? If he did do it, would he and Joe be accomplices? He stared miserably into the gutter.

Lottie saw him there, pulled her milk cart over and stopped in front of him. She jumped down from the cart with a frown. 'Are you all right, Thomas?'

'Just waiting for this blasted horse,' he said. 'She's got it in her head that we need to stop here every day, and the Four Horsemen of the Apocalypse couldn't make her move until she's ready. I swear she's part donkey.'

'That'll be old Cyril's fault. He always stopped at the pub for a drink,' she smiled. 'I thought you might have been sick or something.'

'Not me, but plenty are from what I see.'

'I know. I thought one of my customers had dropped dead

on me this morning. I turned to take the lid off the churn and when I turned back, Mrs Hollywell was spark out on the ground. I swear she was chatting to me a moment before. She looked like death, but her sisters picked her up and took her inside. They said there'd been flu in the house, so I suppose that's what it was. It seems to be everywhere at the moment. I've never seen anything like it. At this rate, I shall be asking for a longer ladle so I can stay further away from them.'

*

Driving back towards the bakery, Thomas wondered if the flu had finished with him yet. It had taken Freda and almost taken Mary, too. He and Mary were probably safe now – he'd never heard of anyone catching it twice – but what about Eric? Then there was Alice and her boys and Hetty, George and Zillah. Where would it end, and who would be left when it did?

46 - Wednesday 23 October 1918

When Bert had asked Thomas to meet him at the top of London Road at seven o'clock, he'd thought the worst. A sensible man would have said no, or just not turned up, but Bert was one of the boys of '14, even if he hadn't been on the train with them or in the same trenches and billets. He couldn't just abandon him. London Road was close enough to Cemetery Road to give him a good idea of what Bert was up to, but in the back of his mind he thought he might be able to talk him out of it, or stop him somehow. If he couldn't, he'd have to join him, whatever the consequences. He didn't usually go out on a Wednesday night, but he'd told Mary it was Bert's birthday. She seemed content with that explanation, and he hoped she'd never find out the truth.

It was a little after seven, the shops were all closed and the streets were empty. He paced up and down in the dark opposite the Ordnance Survey Office. A million thoughts were swirling round in his head, along with a feeling in the pit of his stomach that reminded him of waiting to go over the top. Then he saw Bert running down The Avenue, or at least the nearest a man with no toes on one foot can get to a run. He knew straight away it was too late. He was an alibi, not an accomplice. Either way, he was far more involved than he wanted to be.

Bert stopped in front of Thomas, out of breath and sweating with the effort, despite the chill of the evening. Beneath the smile of greeting was the haunted stare of someone fresh from the battlefield. Without a word they began to walk back towards town, as if this was just any other evening. They got as far as the corner of East Park, near the Titanic Engineers' Memorial, before Bert finally spoke. 'Well, that didn't go quite how I planned.' He rubbed his thumb nervously across his bottom lip. 'For a start, I thought that bloody dog was going to follow me.'

'So, what happened?'

There was only one dog he could be talking about and the only reason it would have tried to follow Bert was if William wasn't in a position to stop it.

'When I got to Cemetery Road the bloody dog was already running around in circles by William's car. He always parks it in the same place and it's dark and quiet there under all the trees, so I figured it were the best place. I meant to get there before he got back to it and hide in the back seat. Usually, he's regular as clockwork, so it struck me as a bit odd to see the dog there already. I can tell you, it gave me a bad feeling. I almost turned round and walked away, but there was no one about and I had the gun in me pocket.'

'Did you take the bullets out like I told you?'

'Course I didn't. What would have been the point of that?'

'Not going to the gallows for one.'

By this time, they'd reached the Park Inn. There were a few

people going in and out of the pub, so they were more or less whispering.

'That won't be happening, so don't you worry about it. Anyhow, I crept up to the car, with the bloody dog dancing around me all the time. I almost tripped over the bugger. I could see William just sitting there in the driver's seat, so I got the gun out of me pocket and had a good look around, just to make sure there was no one watching. Then I went up to the car door –'

'Did you –?'

Bert sucked in his breath, flicked his eyebrows and pushed open the pub door. 'Well, the bastard won't be dipping his wick where it's not wanted anymore.' He plastered a smile on his face and went inside. 'Bloody hell, I need a drink.'

47 - Thursday 24 October 1918

With a big bag of neck of lamb and some pearl barley in her basket, Mary walked towards home. A nice stew would be good for Thomas's hangover. He wasn't a drinker, but he'd been out celebrating Bert's birthday last night. She'd been in bed when he came in stinking like a brewery. This morning, he'd been holding his head and had barely said a word to her. It wasn't like him at all, but it wasn't as if he did it all the time so she couldn't complain. After all he'd been through, he deserved a bit of fun.

The low sun was bright but had no warmth. The first leaves were beginning to fall and something quite melancholy hung in the air, a musty hint of decay. It reminded her of time passing and this, in turn, made her think about Hetty. She still hadn't given Bert an answer, even though he'd now invited her to go out on his boat. When Thomas told her about it, she'd imagined one of the little wooden rowing boats moored up by the bridge. The idea of Hetty, George and Bert all in a little rowing boat on the river made her laugh. Apparently, though, it was some kind of sailboat. She still couldn't imagine Hetty going out in it, but she would be daft not to give poor Bert a chance. With so many eligible men lost in the war, and goodness only knew how many others still to be lost, she really couldn't afford to pass up a chance of happiness. Thomas said Bert was completely smitten with her and was moping around like a lost puppy because she wouldn't give him an answer. It was hard to understand why she was so reluctant. The way she blushed made it obvious she liked him.

When she turned the corner, the sight of Zillah down by the timber pond with Rose's daughter, Violet, caught her eye. Something about the scene looked wrong. Although it was milder than it had been recently, it wasn't warm by any means, and there were a few spots of drizzly rain in the air. Why was she standing there getting cold and damp? Curiosity and a little trill of alarm drew her down to the end of the road to investigate. Zillah was leant on her cane staring across the river. Violet was sat at her feet on the damp shingle, clutching one of the wooden dolls from the dolls' house. The look on Zillah's face could only be described as bereft. Had something happened to George, or Bobby? She didn't want to think about the flu but couldn't help herself.

She touched Zillah gently on the elbow. 'Is everything all right?'

'William is dead,' she said flatly.

'Oh, Zillah.' Mary stared at the jumble of floating logs. They looked like a giant game of jackstraws. So many thoughts and questions swirled around her head, but all that came out of her mouth was, 'When did it happen?'

'Yesterday night, up by the common, according to Rebecca. He was walking his dog.' Zillah didn't take her eyes from the river. Whether she actually saw it was another matter. It was as if she was talking to herself rather than to Mary. 'I know it sounds terrible, but I feel relieved. At least now he can't hurt anyone else. I'm sad, but only for the boy he used to be, not the man he became. He was such a gentle child. He was my whole world. When his father died, I did everything I could to make him happy, gave him everything he wanted.'

'It's what we do for our children.'

The water looked like beaten lead. In the distance, an omnibus and a carriage crossed the triple span of the bridge and darkened the spaces between the crisscross struts.

'Perhaps it is, but it doesn't mean we should. He was so small and vulnerable. It used to break my heart when he asked why he didn't have a father like all the other boys. I suppose I gave him too much trying to make it up to him. The other boys mistreated him, so I let him get away with things. I made him believe he could have anything he wanted without a thought for the cost. I couldn't give him a father or buy him friends, but if he wanted a toy, I bought it for him. When he wanted a nice house, I bought him one. I even pulled strings to get him the job he wanted. That was why he thought he could take what he wanted from Hetty and all the other women.' Now she turned, grasped Mary's arm and looked her in the eye. 'I turned him into a monster.'

'You can't blame yourself for what he's done.'

'Oh, but I do.' Zillah shook her head sadly. 'I didn't know

about the women, but I could see he'd become a cruel and selfish man. I covered up his mistakes and made excuses for him, especially after what happened to Rebecca. I watched him lie and cheat and use people and then discard them when they stopped being useful. He'd have done the same to me without a thought, I'm sure of it now. He asked Winstanley to help him have me certified insane, you know. I should have put a stop to it right at the start, made him see that other people's feelings and needs are important, too, and that he couldn't always have his own way.

'Perhaps things would have been different if Hubert hadn't inherited all that money and we'd stayed living here in our little house. But he'd wanted us to have a nicer house, and he'd wanted William to go to the best school and to have all the advantages that money could bring. Then Hubert was killed, and I suppose I tried to make it up to William by giving him more and more. Money doesn't bring happiness, though, any more than the things it can buy. That's why I came back here and why I've stayed here. Hubert and I had nothing when we started out, but it was the happiest time of my life.'

48 - Friday 25 October 1918

There was an air of celebration in the Junction Inn, at least on the table where Thomas, Bert and Joe were drinking. William Wells was dead. There was no need to worry about him abusing any other women, or trying to harm Hetty in some way to get revenge. Best of all, the shadow of the noose no longer plagued Thomas's thoughts.

'Personally, I'd have skedaddled as soon as I saw the dog was there.' Joe stubbed out his cigarette in the rusty old ashtray. 'Once a plan starts going off course it's rarely a good omen.'

'I almost did.' Bert sucked in his lips and shook his head. 'It put the wind up me, I can tell you. I'd been watching the bugger long enough to know his routine to the minute, so I could tell summat was up, but I was there with the gun in me pocket and no one about. Besides, I could see him in the driver's seat, and he hadn't moved, so I knew he hadn't seen me. I figured I could still sneak up on him.'

'You know you were a bloody idiot, don't you?' Joe said. 'What if someone had seen you standing there in the dark pointing a gun through the window of the car?'

'I'd been watching the place long enough to know hardly anyone goes up there after dark. Anyhow, it's not as if I actually shot him, is it? Even if someone did see me, all they'd have been able to say was that I was standing there with a gun in me hand looking at a dead man. Bloody frightened me half to death when I realised he was already dead. For a moment, I thought someone had beat me to it, maybe you or Thomas here.'

'Neither of us are that stupid,' Joe laughed. 'We've been trying to talk you out of it for weeks.'

'When I saw you running down The Avenue, I really thought you'd killed him.' Thomas didn't want to admit to Joe that he'd been prepared to help Bert kill William if it came to it.

'I almost wish I had, just so I could see him suffer. If I'd known he was going to get the flu I'd never have wasted me money on a gun and then just thrown the bloody thing in the river without even firing it once. Serves him right that he should die like that after using the idea of it to bully his mother all this time.' Bert's grumble was half hearted. Thomas was sure he hadn't relished the idea of murder, no matter how much he said he had. 'I wonder what happened to his little dog. It looked so lost going round and round like that.'

'Why would you care?' Joe chuckled. 'I didn't think you liked dogs, especially not ones that look as if they're wearing a Russian hat.'

'I don't, but it weren't the dog's fault, were it? I never intended for any harm to come to it. I even bought some dog biscuits to keep it quiet.'

'That's probably why it followed you, to get more biscuits,'

Thomas laughed.

'It followed me because it liked the look of me, I'd say, and why not, a handsome chap like me?'

'To a dog, perhaps,' Joe said, 'one with lots of hair in its eyes and a taste for dog biscuits.'

'It never even saw the biscuits. When I saw that Wells was all blue in the face and stone dead, I forgot all about them – another waste of bloody money.'

'Did you throw them in the river, too?' Thomas could hardly talk for laughing.

'Well, I didn't eat the bloody things, did I?' Bert snorted. 'I did think about giving them to Frank and telling him they were the new war biscuits, though.'

'You never.' Joe wiped away tears of laughter.

'Not yet.'

The evening was mild, more September than November, and their jackets were all draped on the backs of their chairs. Joe had his shirt sleeves rolled up. His damaged arm was browner and slightly less withered than it had been. At a glance, it almost looked normal. At this rate they'd be sending him back soon.

'Wally says they're driving them back slowly but steadily. There was a bit of a skirmish at first, but since they took Le Cateau, they've more or less had Jerry on the run.' Joe sounded cautiously optimistic.

'It's exactly what we meant to do back in '14.' Thomas could see himself lying on his stomach in the long grass with Joe on one side and Dougie on the other. He'd killed his first Hun that day, at least he supposed he had; they were just grey specks in the distance, not men who lived, breathed and had families at home. Now, he rather hoped he'd just wounded them, and they'd ended up in some German hospital. What did the Hun call a Blighty wound? Whatever it was he hoped that was all he'd inflicted.

'Four years, and all to be back where we started.' Bert shook his head sadly. 'Don't seem right, does it? All those poor sods dead.'

'Wally says they've left the smashed-up villages behind and are marching through fields with crops growing, woods with leaves on the trees and churches with spires,' Joe said. 'He passed through somewhere, perhaps a week ago, and they captured a whole load of prisoners, or more like they just surrendered, but you know how he likes to take credit for everything. Anyway, when he handed them over to the Military Police, they counted them all and gave him a receipt, as if he were delivering cattle to market.'

'Do you think it could really be coming to an end?' Thomas hardly dared to believe it. Even saying it felt like tempting fate.

'Well, Bulgaria is out, the Russians are out and the Austro-Hungarian Empire is falling apart.' Joe ticked each item off on his fingers. 'I'd say things are going our way, at least for now.'

'I heard the Kaiser was asking for talks with that American president, Wilson,' Bert said. 'He wants an armistice, too. It's telling that he don't want to speak with Lloyd George; he knows he won't put nothing past a Welshman. He probably thinks the Yank is a soft touch.'

'I'd like to believe that.' Joe rubbed his thumb slowly across his bottom lip. 'Wally believes it. He says they're all just hanging on, hoping their luck will hold out for another few weeks, maybe a month, and they won't cop it in the meantime. He thinks it'll all be over by Christmas. If the weather turns, though, and the Hun get a chance to dig in and regroup, it could be a different story come spring.'

'Well, we did say it'd all be over by Christmas back in '14, didn't we?' Thomas smiled. 'None of us said which Christmas, though.'

49 - Wednesday 30 October 1918

There was no getting away from the onion fumes. As soon as they had peeled one, Alice and Mary dropped it into the bowl of salty water in the middle of the kitchen table, but their eyes still watered all the same. It was a horrible chore, but they all loved pickled onions, so it had to be done. Besides, they'd be crying today with or without the onions.

'I still can't believe Effie is gone.' Alice wiped her tears with the back of her hand. 'Those poor little boys, especially Samuel, he's not even properly weaned. Thank goodness Harold fell out with them last month over those stupid soldiers. He said Bertie wouldn't share so he didn't like him anymore. I thought it would all blow over, but I'm glad it didn't.'

'Thank heavens none of Effie's children got it in the end,' Mary said. She felt shocked and vulnerable. Every time she closed her eyes, she saw Freda struggling to breathe. Would they ever be free of this plague? Her eyes were streaming, too, but still she peeled the onions and dropped them into the water, hardly aware she was doing it.

'Neither did her Charlie,' said Alice. 'Goodness knows where Effie caught it, or why they didn't for that matter.'

'Charlie works at the docks, like Vera's Arthur did. Thomas is convinced it comes back on the ships with the wounded.'

'He unloads cargo, though, not soldiers. Now he's been left with three little ones and no wife. He's taken them to stay with her mother in Swaythling, but I don't think she'll cope with them forever. Effie was always saying what a handful they were.'

'The poor little mites.' The idea that the flu might be lurking made Mary look around nervously, as if she might somehow catch sight of it skulking in the shadows like an evil vapour. Being able to see it would make it so easy to avoid.

'I worry about the boys.' Alice picked another onion out of the bag. Thankfully, there weren't many left now. 'At least it's not raining today, and they can play out in the fresh air. I don't much like the idea of sending Gordon back to school after half-term, though. It can't be healthy in those crowded classrooms. Half the children round here don't know what soap is for.'

'I'm not sure about sending Eric back, either.'

Mary would rather not think about any of it. She couldn't get away from it, though, any more than she could get away from the onion fumes, or her sadness at Effie's death. The flu was in all the newspapers now. In the summer they'd said it wasn't too bad and people had only died because they'd ignored the warning signs and tried to carry on as usual. She knew that was a lie. Now people were getting sick in their hundreds. Where was it going to end? The government health expert said people should avoid crowds, clean and disinfect things and open windows, as if that was going to do anything. Might it have made a difference if she'd known about that in the summer? Would Freda have caught it if they'd been more honest back then? Mary would have certainly thought twice about taking the children to the hospital to see Thomas, or to any of the other crowded places they'd visited. Now they were saying quinine could help, but they'd stopped selling it in the shops. What was the point of that? If she'd known to give Freda quinine, would she have survived? The idea made her angry. How many other people had died needlessly because they'd hushed it all up for the sake of the war?

She was saved from these unwelcome thoughts when Hetty came through the back door.

'Oh my.' She wrinkled her nose at the smell of onions and the sharp, acidic tang of the vinegar cooling in the pan. 'Pickling time. I can't say I miss that.'

'Aren't you supposed to be typing?' Alice put the last onion into the water with a grateful sigh and went to the sink to wash her hands.

'We're having the week off for half-term. Well, Rose and Louise are, I'm doing the urgent jobs.'

'So, you could have helped us with the onions after all?' Alice gave her a rueful smile as she dried her hands.

'She's far too high and mighty for peeling onions now.' Mary began to clear away all the onion skins.

'Actually, I've had a very busy week, and I come bearing gifts to cheer you up, so less of the cheek, please.' Hetty put a large paper bag in the space Mary had cleared on the kitchen table. 'It's lardy cake. Don't ask where I came by it, and I won't tell you any lies.'

Alice put the kettle on whilst Mary washed her hands. Once the tea was made they took it and the lardy cake into the parlour, away from the stink of the kitchen.

'So, what's been keeping you so busy, then?' Alice asked as she poured the tea.

'Well, yesterday morning I had William's funeral to go to.' She opened the bag of lardy cake and cut three gooey slices.

'You went?' Mary could hardly believe it. 'Why on earth would you do that?'

'We all went. Rose, Louise and me. Bert looked after all the children for us. He took them to the picture house.'

'I don't understand why any of you would want to go, though,' Alice said.

'We all wanted to be absolutely sure he really was dead. Besides, we couldn't let poor Zillah go on her own, not after everything she's done for us. She was his mother, after all, no matter what he'd done. It's a good job we did go, because the only other people there were his wife and her nurse.'

'Didn't any of the local bourgeoisie turn up?' Mary found it hard to believe they hadn't.

'Once they knew he wasn't going to get his hands on Zillah's money for their fancy schemes, they dropped him like a hot coal. It really was just his wife, her nurse and us. Even Agnes didn't go, and I thought she might have done.'

'I thought his wife was crippled,' Alice said.

'Rebecca was in a wheelchair, a big wicker thing like a giant perambulator. She was wrapped up in blankets and things, but she looks all hunched and wasted away, like an Egyptian mummy. As far as I could see, all she can move is her head and her hands. She spoke to Zillah briefly and thanked us for coming, but she had no idea who we were. I think she thought we were from the bank.'

'A good job, too,' Alice said between mouthfuls of lardy cake. 'This is delicious. I'd forgotten how good it is. We'd better save some for Thomas.'

'The nurse knew exactly who we were, though. She had a mouth like a bulldog's arse the whole time. To look at her you'd think we were spitting on his grave. Tempting as it was, we weren't. We were being very respectful, for Zillah's sake.'

'How did she know who you were, though?' Mary asked.

'That's what I was wondering,' Hetty said. 'Then, when it was all over, before she took Rebecca back to her carriage, she came to speak to me. She called me all sorts of things I won't repeat. It makes my ears red just thinking about them. You know how much I hate bad language. She was really angry that we were there. Really nasty she was, and all the time I was wondering how she knew who we were, because Rebecca obviously didn't. Then, finally, she said, "You can stop putting advertisements in the newspapers because I'm never going to answer them. I don't want anything to do with you, your poxy job or your money." It was Minnie Delaney.'

'And you didn't recognise her?' Alice said.

'She left the bank before I started. I had no idea what she looked like, but she certainly knew who I was.'

'But I thought you said she was Rebecca Wells's nurse?' Mary thought she must have missed something somewhere along the line.

'She is. As far as I can work out, she was the first of the typists to have a baby. Instead of sacking her, he gave her a job nursing his wife, probably to keep her quiet. It was a sight more than he did for the rest of us, but maybe he'd learned his lesson by then. He couldn't have us all nursing his wife, could he? She must be living the life of Riley in that big house. From what I saw, Rebecca Wells is very fond of her, as well as being dependent. Along with a pension from the bank and William's house, she has her own money, or so Zillah says. Her father set up a trust fund after she got sick. She's got no children, no one to leave it to. I'd say Minnie has her eye on inheriting the lot.'

'So, Mrs Wells doesn't know who she is?' Alice topped up her teacup.

'William's hardly bloody likely to have told her, is he?' Hetty scoffed.

'What about the child?' Mary licked her sticky fingers.

'I have no idea. According to Agnes, she kept the baby, but that's as much as I know. Maybe she gave it away or her parents took it on. Poor Rebecca hasn't the slightest clue who she is and, nasty as she was to me, I'm not about to enlighten her. Minnie has made the best of a bad situation, just like the rest of us. She deserves whatever she gets from it. Good luck to her, I say.'

50 - Monday 11 November 1918

The steam from the laundry fogged the scullery window and the air was warm and thick with the scent of soap. Harold sat quietly at the kitchen table drawing pictures of tanks and soldiers on a piece of brown paper left over from a parcel. Alice and Mary worked away, scrubbing and rinsing. Their hands were red and their hair damp. Nothing would dry today. The sky was a dark grey blanket, dropping miserable drizzle. The pile of wet clothes slowly building up in the baskets would have to be hung on the wooden airers Mary had already set out in the front parlour. At least it would be out of the way there while it slowly dried.

'Hetty told me they have machines to do the washing in America.' Alice looked up from the sheet she was running through the mangle. 'Can you imagine it? I think she has her eye on getting one.'

'If a man invented them, I can't see them getting things as clean as we do.' Mary poured another bucket of cold water onto the clothes she was rinsing. 'What do any of them know about laundry? It would be nice, though, if it worked. Think of all the time we'd save. We wouldn't know what to do with ourselves. I might even have time to read some of the books Zillah lends me.'

There was something other than rain in the air. It was almost an atmosphere of expectation. Peace talks were going on in France and it felt as if they were all holding their breath, waiting for the end. Would it come when they were up to their armpits in soapy water? Would it come at all, or was it just more false hope? Neither of them dared mention it in case putting it into words would court disaster.

When the church bells began to peal, they both stopped dead and looked at each other. Mary's hands stilled in the cold rinsing water and Alice stopped turning the mangle handle. There'd been no church bells since the war began. This could only be the armistice, an invasion or a zeppelin raid. Then the foghorns started, as if every ship in the docks was sounding its horn at once, just like a New Year's Eve before the war. Harold looked up from his drawing bewildered by all the noise. Alice bit her lip. Mary dried her hands. Then they all rushed to the front door to see what was happening, hardly daring to hope.

51 – Monday 11 November 1918

Thomas had walked up to the bakery in the dark and hitched Meg up by lamp light, but it wasn't much lighter now, even though the sun must be up there somewhere above the brooding clouds. Old Meg shone like a polished conker and her grizzled mane hung in sodden tangles. He wasn't thinking about the bitter cold, the drizzly rain, or even the next call on his round. His mind was on the dream he'd had last night. Thankfully, they plagued him less often now and, when they did come, they were more unsettling than distressing.

The bullets had whizzed past like swarms of angry wasps. From the corner of his eye, he'd seen men falling flat out, or dropping to their knees and lurching forward. Somehow, they'd got through their own wire and over the bodies of the poor East Lancashires, but they were still faced with the pitted shell holes of No Man's Land and the hail of machine gun fire. He'd shouted, 'Get down, lads.' Through the smoke he'd seen his men dropping to the muddy ground, but he couldn't tell if it was because they'd heard him or because they'd been hit. All around he heard moans, the sobbing gasps of lives ending and the high-pitched shriek of bullets overhead. When he looked to his right, he saw Ronnie wink and grin. To his left, young Percy caught his eye and tried to smile, as if fear wasn't gripping his heart.

Where was Percy now? Had he found a job? It probably

wouldn't have been easy with a shattered leg. At least he'd have a head start on all the others who'd likely be coming back soon. The talks going on somewhere in France and the implications they could have, good or bad, were also on his mind. Over the last week or so, there'd been so many rumours and stories going round. He couldn't tell what was true and what was wishful thinking, but something was coming, and coming soon. He wasn't sure he believed the tales of uprisings in Germany. He'd heard first-hand accounts of the French mutiny after the Second Battle of the Aisne in '17, so it was possible, but it seemed unlikely. The Germans were far more level-headed and obedient than the emotional and militant French. He'd read that the Kaiser had fled to Holland, but he didn't believe that for one minute. The Austro-Hungarian armistice was a fact, though, and it left Germany with no allies at all. He was certain the German government *were* discussing an armistice with Marshal Foch, but he had an idea the terms might be too hard for them to stomach. The French were never going to be as forgiving as the Americans, not after the way their country had been ravaged. As far as he could tell, any terms they offered would amount to an unconditional surrender, and he couldn't see the Kaiser, or his generals, allowing that.

Meg plodded through the Bargate arch, and he thought of all the men marching through the ancient stone gateway on their way to the docks back in 1914. How many of them would make the return journey? The van wheels rattled over the tramlines and a telegram boy whizzed past on his bicycle. That was probably bad news for someone. If the war really was going to end soon, the men who died now must be the unluckiest of all. He glanced at his watch. It was coming up to half past ten. Meg was moving faster now, eager to get to the clock tower to stop at the trough no doubt. She liked the smell of all the other horses, or that was his theory anyway. He'd probably light a cigarette and let her sniff around for a while. There was no rush, they'd made good time today. The big map of the world above the door of the *Echo* office was in sight. A young lad came dashing out holding his cap in his hand. What was he in such a tearing hurry for?

The boy shouted as he ran in front of Meg. 'They signed the armistice this morning. The war is over.' Then he carried on running towards the Bargate yelling out his message.

All around him, the shoppers and traders stood frozen in shock as they took in the news. Then people began to pour out of the shops and buildings cheering and shouting. He'd never seen anything like it.

He hardly dared to believe it was true, but he had no wish to join the celebrations. At a snail's pace, he drove through the growing crowd. People leaned out of windows and waved handkerchiefs. Someone started singing *Pack Up Your Troubles,* and, in seconds, others had joined in. On he went, past Palmerston Park, a glory of gold and amber he barely noticed, to the clock tower. Much to Meg's dismay, he didn't stop, or continue towards the common and her other favourite stopping place outside The Cowherds. Instead, he steered for home. This confused the poor horse. She swished her tail and put her ears back, but for once did as she was bid. She must have known something was afoot.

He urged her across the Six Dials junction and over the railway bridge towards the gasworks. The closer he got to home the more people he saw out on the streets. Some just stood on their doorsteps as if they were waiting for something to happen, others had little flags in their hands. A few cheered him as he went by, but why they should have thought a baker's van worth cheering, he couldn't fathom. As he turned onto his road the church bells began to ring and then all the ships started to sound their horns.

He wasn't sure how he felt. The war was over, as long as the Germans kept to the armistice, but what of all those men who'd died? Peace wouldn't bring them back. All the way home their faces had been going round and round in his head, like a parade of the dead. Ronnie, Dougie, Tiptoe, he'd watched them die, and all the nameless men littering the fields of France or buried in the makeshift cemeteries. Then there were all the broken men like Percy and the chaps at the hospital. Joe probably wouldn't have to go back, though, and Wally would be coming home, unless he'd been lost in the last few days. He wanted to feel happy, but he couldn't somehow.

People had emerged from their houses all along his street. Some had got their flags out, others looked confused, as if they'd come out to see what all the noise was about. Then he saw Mary and Alice on his doorstep in their aprons, young Harold's head poking out between their skirts. They had bewildered looks on their faces.

He dropped the reins, jumped down from the van and ran to them.

'They've signed the armistice.' He threw his arms around them both, relieved rather than joyous.

'My Harry will be coming home. I can hardly believe it.' Tears began to stream down Alice's face, four years of pent-up fear finally released.

Then Hetty's door opened and she, Louise and Rose emerged. 'Is it true? Is it really over?'

Moments later, Zillah poked her head out of her front door. She had a bottle of champagne in her hand and Violet clinging to her skirt. 'I've had this since 1910, waiting for the right occasion, but I think this is something to celebrate.' She fumbled for a few moments with the wire cradle, but with a little gentle twisting the cork popped, and a wisp of vapour rose from the neck of the bottle. 'Hetty, be a dear and fetch my champagne glasses from the dresser. They're the wide, shallow ones, like goblets.'

The neighbours danced and sang in the middle of the road. The rain still fell, a dull drizzle, but it didn't dampen their spirits. Poor Meg stood watching with a look on her face that said she'd never understand humans. Thomas would rather have gone inside. He didn't feel like drinking champagne or singing and dancing in the street, but he daren't leave the van and all the bread. Mrs Lowman would not be happy if all the neighbours helped themselves. Hetty came back with an armful of glasses and lined them up on the wall.

She'd just set the last glass down, and Zillah had started to pour the champagne, when Bert appeared on the corner of Union Road, running with the same awkward limping trot Thomas had seen on The Avenue the night William died. He ran straight up to Hetty, swept her off her feet, swung her around and then kissed her, smack on the lips. She squealed in protest then put her arms around his neck and kissed him back. Rose, still on the doorstep, with Violet now on her hip, clapped her hands gleefully.

'I think we should go into town.' Bert finally put Hetty down, but he kept his arm around her waist, as if he were afraid to let her go. 'There'll be the biggest party ever.'

'I've got my round to finish and the van to get back,' Thomas said.

'We've still got the washing half done,' added Mary. She looked at Alice. 'Or I have. You can go if you want. There's not much left to do.'

'I'd rather stay and help.' Alice had picked up Harold and couldn't seem to stop kissing him, much to his disgust.

Hetty looked between Bert, Louise and Rose, as if she couldn't decide what to do. 'I suppose the work can wait until tomorrow, but George is still at school.'

'I can look after George, Bobby and Violet,' Zillah said. 'And Eric, Harold and Gordon come to that. You young ones should go and enjoy yourselves. It isn't every day a war ends. First, though, we should make a toast.' She picked a glass up from the wall and raised it. 'To peace.'

52 - Tuesday 11 November 1919

Thomas pulled Meg up at the water trough on the corner of Watts Park and broke the ice so she could drink. He left her half a dozen apples and set off across the frosty grass towards the statue of Isaac Watts. Hopefully, the apples would keep her happy while he was gone. He glanced at his watch, the same one that had caused him so much trouble in the summer last year. It was five minutes to eleven. This seemed a fitting place to remember the dead, right where they were going to build the new cenotaph. It'd probably be ready by next November. The plans were for a kind of empty tomb, to signify all the men who were still lying undiscovered in the fields of France and Belgium. He couldn't quite imagine it, but it was better than the ideas he'd had, statues of the Grim Reaper and the like. A few flakes of powdery snow started to fall, a reminder of Arras, when he'd shot those three Germans. He still felt bad about that. Disgruntled about the snow, the seagull perching on Watts's head began to squawk.

It had been a funny kind of morning, what with Bert hammering on their door in a panic first thing. Mary was still asleep, and he was barely out of bed himself. Hetty's time had come, and poor old Bert was in a right state. Had he been like that when Eric was born? In a little over a month, he probably would be again, when it was Mary's turn. Since finding out she was expecting again, she'd been so much happier, more like her old self. They had names picked out; Esther if it was a girl, Ronald for a boy. He was half hoping for a girl, not to replace Freda, of course – that would be impossible – but to redress the balance somehow. Mary sent Bert off to fetch the midwife and then took George and Eric to Alice, so she could stay with Hetty.

When Thomas opened the front door to go to work, he could hear the screaming from Hetty's front bedroom. Harry left for work at the same time. He was as grey as a badger since coming back from the war. So was Hariph. Somehow it made him feel better about his own white hair.

Harry looked towards the noise in horror. 'Makes me glad I'm a man.'

'Mary had to force Bert out of the room. He wanted to stay and hold her hand.' Thomas shook his head at the idea. 'I think I'd rather go over the top again than have to be a part of that.'

'He'd be better off going to the pub and coming back when it's all over,' Harry laughed. 'That's what I did. It'd put me off for life if I had to hear Alice going through that, never mind watch.'

'I intend to be as far away as possible when Mary's time comes. I'm sure she'd rather I was, too. It's no place for a man.'

The snow was getting heavier. Now it covered the frosty grass. He glanced over at Meg, but she seemed happy enough munching apples. There were quite a few other people waiting about in the park, probably there for the same reason he was. A tram came slowly up the road and a coal cart clip-clopped past in the opposite direction. He looked at his watch again. It was almost eleven. The tram stopped and a couple of passengers got off; a tall man and a stout woman, also quite tall. Then the tram driver stepped down and walked across the park towards him. He recognised Joe at once, even in the black greatcoat and the shiny peaked cap. With a smile, Joe stopped beside him in the place where the cenotaph would one day be built. The two passengers stood a little way off. There was something familiar about both of them, but there was no time to think about it now, or to talk to Joe. The clock at the Above Bar junction began to chime. Apart from that there was complete silence. Even the seagull had stopped squawking.

He bowed his head and thought of the dead. Ronnie bleeding in his arms on the first day of the Somme, Dougie's eyes as he slipped beneath the mud at Passchendaele, Tiptoe smiling at the photo of his sweetheart in the rubble of the trench, the limp little girl in the wreckage of her house, and all the others who were never found and would never come back. He thought of the ones he'd seen fall from the corner of his eye, as he'd run across the battlefield, the ones hanging on the wire, the rotting corpses in No Man's Land and even those dead Germans in the trench. The memories were less raw now, the horror less vivid, and, in a strange way, he was glad of them. None of them should ever be forgotten. How many millions of men had died in the war? How many others had died of the flu? Maybe even more, but, to his mind, the war was to blame for them, too, including Freda. He'd worried it might come back this autumn, but, so far, there was no sign of it, thank goodness.

A peal of church bells and the sound of foghorns from the docks marked the end of the silence, just as they'd marked the end of the war. The snow was getting thicker. He'd have a job to finish his round at this rate. The tram passengers began to walk towards them as Joe said, 'I thought Bert would be here.'

'Hetty's time has come. I tried to get him to join me on my round to take his mind off it, but he was having none of it. If he had his way, he'd be right there in the room with her, but Mary threw him out. She's a force to be reckoned with these days. He's probably wearing out the floorboards about now.'

'Bert always was half madman, but I can't see why he'd want to see that.' Joe shook his head. 'Besides, I'm sure Hetty will tell him all about it afterwards, and in great detail.'

'No doubt she will. She'll probably bring it up regularly, just so he knows what he put her through. She's changed, but not that much. Talking of changing, isn't it about time you thought about settling down?'

'I'm having too much fun being single, mate.' Joe gave him a cheeky grin. 'There's a whole world of women out there. I'm spoilt for choice. Like when they sent me to Cologne last December. There were so many frauleins falling over themselves to be fraternised with. They're all, "Promenade with kamerad for schokolade?" It would have been rude to say no, even though the army didn't allow it.'

The tram passengers reached them, and Thomas was surprised to see the man was Lofty. He hadn't recognised him without all the mud and khaki.

'I thought it was you, Corporal Brodrick, and you too, Joe.' He shook both their hands vigorously.

'It's Thomas now, Lofty. We're not in the army anymore.'

'Well, then, it's Leonard if we're going to be like that,' Lofty grinned, 'or Lenny to my friends. This is my wife, Laura. We got married last month.'

She was a plump but pretty girl, with dark, almond-shaped eyes and an aquiline nose. Thomas couldn't get over the idea that he recognised her from somewhere. Was she a customer?

'Do we know each other?' he asked.

'No, but I think you know my brother, Percy,' she smiled.

So, that was it. He could see it now. They had the same eyes. 'And how's your brother doing?'

'Better than he was. His leg is healed now, although he still limps a little. He was very bad for a while, devastated he couldn't go back to fight. I told him he should count himself lucky he was safe, and that he hadn't lost the leg. He'd rather have stayed in the army, though. He's had a few jobs, but he doesn't seem able to settle to anything.'

They chatted for a while about Lenny's job at the docks, and about Wally, who somehow managed to come through everything unscathed and had signed on for another twelve years in the army as a sergeant. Then talk turned to Davie, who was working in a theatre somewhere, and all the others who hadn't made it home. Then Joe had to go back to his tram and Thomas had to finish his round.

The snow was so bad he could hardly see to drive. He'd spent so long plagued by memories of the war, and he'd wished so hard he could find a way to forget. Now he could see that remembering was more important than forgetting. All those men had answered the call to fight for king and country. They'd given everything they had for a better world, and, when it was all over, the ones who'd survived had been promised a land fit for heroes. What they'd actually got was two or three pointless medals, a head full of memories and a world they barely recognised. They called it the Great War and said it was a war to end wars. If it did, perhaps it would be worth it, but what a price they'd all paid. In a hundred years' time, when all the men who'd lived through it were gone, would anyone remember them? He hoped so, because if they didn't, then they might allow it to happen again. The words of one of the war poems kept going through his head as he and Meg ploughed their way through the ever-thickening snow.

They shall grow not old, as we that are left grow old:

Age shall not weary them, nor the years condemn.

At the going down of the sun and in the morning

We will remember them.

Acknowledgements

This book is a work of fiction, inspired by my grandparents, Thomas John and Mary Ann Haley. It is not their story but it owes a lot to them. I was about ten when I first saw the huge cross-shaped scar on my Pappy's back and learned how he got it. He acted as if being shot by a sniper while hanging out washing on the Western Front, was nothing much. He blamed the luminous hands on his watch and told me about being taken across France in a cattle truck. Sadly, I never knew Mary, but I got a sense of her from him.

This tale might have remained in my head had my long-suffering husband, Dave Keates, not given me membership to Ancestry.com as a gift. This uncovered other family members with intriguing stories and the beginnings of an idea began to germinate. Even then, facts were thin on the ground. I'd seen the scar and the sliver war badge and knew he'd been in the trenches but not where, or for how long. An educated guess told me he'd probably been taken to Netley Hospital, but the hospital records, like so many from the Great War, were lost. Without the help of Brenda Findlay from Netley Abbey Matters, I might never have known more. She found his name on a list of the wounded; at least we thought it was him.

Then, fate sent me a message from the other side of the world. Kevin Haley, a cousin I'd never met, contacted me through Ancestry. Thomas was his Pappy too. From Australia Kevin and

Lynne Haley, and Katrina Arnold shared their memories of Thomas and Mary. Kevin even had a photograph of Pappy in his uniform, taken in 1914. The cap badge and the stripes on his sleeves proved I had the right Thomas Haley. Now I had a date and, with help from the Royal Hampshire Regiment website, I was able to build up a picture of where he might have been and what battles he might have been involved in.

Richard Van Emden's wonderful books of first hand accounts from the Great War gave me an insight into what those poor infantrymen went through and what they thought about it. The memoirs of Kate Luard, a nurse on the Western Front, and websites such those of the Netley Military Cemetery and Netley Abbey Matters, told me about the evacuation and treatment of the wounded. The many groups and websites devoted to the history of Southampton, including SEE Southampton, Southampton Heritage Photos, Memories of Old Northam and Southampton and Hampshire Over the Years, brought Southampton at the end of the Great War alive, as did the Ordnance Survey archive of old maps and Kelly's Street Directories.

Information about the Spanish flu, particularly in England, was hard to come by. What little I knew came from Pappy's story of his daughter, Freda, playing in the morning and dead in the afternoon. Catherine Arnold's interesting book about the 1918 Pandemic was a great help, as was the National Library of Medicine. Then, when I was knee deep in research about Spanish flu, a new pandemic appeared and provided a greater understanding of what it must have been like to live through those dark days of disinformation, cover ups and conspiracies.

When I finally thought I had a book that might be worth publishing, Danielle Wrate, of Wrate's Editing Services, and proofreader Abby Sparks, gave me the advice and encouragement I needed to make it happen and Aleks Kruz and Hayley Yates, of Hangar47 (h47.uk), provided the technical expertise.

This book began as Thomas and Mary's story. From necessity I had to weave the weft of facts I'd uncovered through a warp of my imagination and add a sprinkling of fictitious extras to bring the story to life. As I began to write, the characters, both real and fictional, started to take on lives of their own. They became real people who spoke to me in my dreams. Often, they took the story in directions I hadn't planned but I went along with them, curious to see where they'd lead me. In the end, this is a fictional account of the last months of the Great War and the forgotten pandemic. It is also a tribute to all the women who suffered the uncertainty of waiting at home, all the victims of the Spanish flu and all the soldiers, whether they died in those foreign fields, or survived to relive them to the end of their days. They couldn't forget what they'd seen and done and we should never forget the sacrifices they made.

ABOUT THE AUTHOR

Marie Keates is a writer, blogger and walker, who can't resist the mystery of an unexplored trail and is mad about history. She lives in Southampton, and has spent much of her life working in the travel industry and writing copy on such diverse subjects as travel, canals, running and coffee. Her interest in Southampton's history has made her blog, www.iwalkalone.co.uk popular with local history groups, ex Sotonians and visitors to the city. Her debut novel, *Plagued*, was inspired by research into her family history and stories she heard at her grandfather's knee.

Printed in Great Britain
by Amazon